PRAISE FOR

The Problem with Murmur Lee

"*The Problem with Murmur Lee* is a brave and beautiful book. It might be called a mystery, but the questions it asks are not who killed or even how or why. The questions Fowler asks are the ones we all ask: What is the meaning of one human life? How do we cope with loss, sorrow, or with our deepest fears? Where she takes us is not to mourning but to celebration. I loved Murmur Lee and will never forget her."
—Dorothy Allison, author of *Bastard Out of Carolina*

"A powerful book full of mysticism and wisdom about life, the life ever after, and the wonder of it all." —*Southern Living*

"The verdict: Heartbreaking and hilarious. . . . If Fowler's characters are guilty of anything, they're guilty of living as close to the edge of heartbreak as they can. Fowler puts into everyday language the notes and chords of Welch and Hooker, along with Lucinda Williams and Edith Piaf. It's a moving, lyrical feast."
—*Atlanta Journal Constitution*

"Fowler portrays small-town Florida life in all its gritty energy— with lyricism, humor, and an obvious love for the people and place. This skillful piece of writing . . . will please Fowler's fans and entertain devotees of Alice Seabold's *The Lovely Bones* and Alice Hoffman's novels." —*Booklist*

"Fowler has created a touching story of death, family, love, and the power of friendship." —*Library Journal*

Also by Connie May Fowler

Broadway Books

NEW YORK

THE

Problem

WITH

Murmur Lee

A Novel

Connie May Fowler

Visit our website at www.broadwaybooks.com

First Broadway Books trade paperback edition published 2006.

Book design by Jennifer Ann Daddio

The Library of Congress has cataloged the hardcover as:
Fowler, Connie May.
The problem with Murmur Lee : a novel / by Connie May Fowler.—
1st ed.
p. cm.
I. Women—Crimes against—Fiction. 2. Dream interpretation—
Fiction. 3. Female friendship—Fiction. 4. Drowning victims—
Fiction. 5. Future life—Fiction. 6. Islands—Fiction.
7. Florida—Fiction. I. Title.

PS3556.O8265P76 2004
813'.54—dc22
2004055124
ISBN 0-7679-2145-3

1 3 5 7 9 10 8 6 4 2

FOR *Silas*

Acknowledgments

This novel was written in solitude but whispered into existence with the help of countless friends.

My agent, Joy Harris, and my editor, Deb Futter, are fierce warrior-angels, indeed. Their wit, intellect, and love guide, inspire, and sustain me.

Stephanie Abou and Alexia Paul at the Joy Harris Literary Agency are brilliant women for whom I possess boundless gratitude.

The Problem with Murmur Lee would have never been birthed without the patience and guidance of the dedicated, talented people at Doubleday. Thank you for believing. Anne Merrow, I owe you.

I am forever grateful to my dear sister, Deidre, and her husband, Phil, for their unflagging support. You saw me through the darkest days. Thank you.

Marcie Cramer and my Wednesday afternoon posse, your grace and wisdom inform every word of this novel.

Jerome Novey, you rock.

To my wonderful colleagues in the Rollins College Department of English and to Rita Bornstein, Roger Casey, and Lorrie Kyle, thank you for so freely sharing your talents and for the many opportunities you have given me and this book. Without your words of encouragement, the novel would still be stewing on a back burner. And to my students at Rollins, you inspire me. Indeed, you helped breathe magic into these pages.

Thank you to my friends—faculty, staff, and students—in the Spalding University MFA program. In you I discovered a community of writers whose generosity and brilliance gave me the confidence to push harder, to take greater chances, to believe with renewed fervor in the process.

And to my many friends who read pages, who offered advice, who listened to my fears and frustrations and dreams, who laughed with me, who broke bread with me, who never gave up on me, my gratitude and love transcend the devout simplicity inherent in the words *thank you*. Mitch and Melissa Alderman, Robyn Allers, Per Astrand, Barbara Carson, Ed Cohen, Dale Copans-Astrand, Mike Croley, Philip F. Deaver, Troy Ehlers, Annie Ferran, Kaye Gibbons, Jeni Hatter, Rhonda and Bob Heins, Paul Hiers, Silas House, Matthew Jaeger, Jill Jones, David Kahn, Lezlie Laws, Sam Leininger, Robin Lippincott, Cate McGowan, Kevin Miller, Sena Jeter Naslund, Sue and Socky O'Sullivan, Twila Papay, Kelly Parisi, Diana Raab, Gail Sinclair, Dimitri Smith, Cissie Spang, George Tucker, Mike and Zilpha Underwood, Laura van den Berg, Brad Watson, and Crystal Wilkinson: You are my heart.

The Problem with Murmur Lee

There is never a single approach

to something remembered.

—JOHN BERGER

A Letter from
Murmur Lee Harp
to Charleston Rowena Mudd

July 21, 2001

Dear Charlee,

Here is the swan feather I promised. Be forewarned:
This really works. An old celibate man in Jacksonville
Beach clued me in. He blames the feather for his
incessant faithfulness. By his own admission, he
cheated on his wife with all the consistency of a serial
killer until his wife threw the feather spell on him. He
spent the first decade of his marriage as a philanderer
and the last two as a model husband. In fact, he
buried her three years ago and remains true. It's sad,
really, that this works so well. I mean, the old guy is
never going to get laid again in his life.

Anyway, you have to sew the feather into his
pillowcase. You can't simply stick it in there. Do you
know how to sew anymore? You've been up there so

long, I suspect you've forgotten everything our
mothers tried to teach us. I can see how that is both
helpful and not. For instance, your mother, who was
truly a dear woman—you know I loved her—was
always insisting that you wear your hair short. That
was wrongheaded. You're a knockout when you let
those curls kiss your shoulders.

Also, when do I get to meet this Nigerian? Like I
said in this morning's E-mail, you CANNOT marry
until I have approved. I would give you the same
courtesy. Bring him down here and let me meet him
while the summer storms still rage. Don't let this get
past you. I know you. Once school kicks in, you'll be
too busy to even respond to E-mail. So book your
flights and I'll pick you up, and you two can have the
house all to yourselves.

We're having a bang-up summer, Charlee. Last
evening, Dr. Z was still running around Hastings in
his Roadmaster (I don't believe he has cleaned it out,
only added to the pile of crap, since you left here
however many years ago), treating the migrants, and I
took the liberty, as is my wont and his pleasure, to sit
on his dock and sip my beer and watch the end-of-
day glory unfold and settle. I was glad I did, because
last night's sunset turned out to be a rare breed of
awesome. The magnolia leaves quivered in the waning
light. The river glowed. The sky bloomed. The anvil
clouds towering in the west over the hammock
appeared to be lit from within. It was enough to
make my heart break and put itself back together out
of sheer joy: lilac, purple, orange, sage. This old
world, I'm telling you, pulsed with the sun's last

gasp—ba bap, ba bap, ba bap—and then both sea and sky took on a golden glaze.

Just when I was thinking life couldn't get any better, it did. A flock of terns rose from the river, spiraling up up up, a ribbon of black and white unfurling along a thermal. And then they disappeared. It was as if God had called them home.

What do you think of that? I'd really like to know. Also, if any of your professors would like to comment, I welcome their thoughts.

If the description of the sunset doesn't do it, then perhaps this will entice you home: The dragonflies are in peak form. And you know what they say . . . a bountiful season of dragonflies makes for a healthy uterus. Picture you and your beloved sitting on Z's dock—or my porch—quiet and beautiful and still—watching the dragons fly. Take right now, for instance. I'm on my back patio, writing this letter and am surrounded. They collide into one another—winged bumper cars—as they gorge on the mosquitoes, and with each collision, a faintly metallic whir strikes the air. I bet ants and cockroaches consider it to be a form of music, something akin to calypso.

So what do you think of my news about this guy I met? I mean, I'm a bit wary, yet ever so willing to throw every shred of caution to the wind.

My tendency toward behaving with abandon is fueled by my very real and reasonable desire for sex. I mean, it has been three months. I've done all sorts of spell casting. I even burned my pubes in a bird's nest. That should have brought me major boom-boom action. But no! I'm still walking about like a nun!

So for no other reason than carnal desire, I'm tempted to go forward with this. He's cute as hell. My pubes have grown back in. As good old Father Beaver used to say, "Perhaps this would make Jesus happy." I'll keep you posted. Love on the river should be very hot. I guess I ought to buy a new razor or get waxed. Or something.

I miss you, Charlee. Z misses you. Edith misses you. Lucinda misses you. The whole damn bunch of us do. So come visit before you get involved in all your books and God again. Besides, you know as well as I do, God isn't up there. She left Boston ages ago.

Love you lots,
Murmur

P.S. I forgot to tell you, that poor swan! And poor me! The spell doesn't work if you pick up a feather off the ground. You have to pluck it out of the poor bird's butt. You'd better be sure you really want this guy.

Murmur Lee Harp

*T*he pearl-faced moon dipped behind a cloud, darkening the night, as I sped upriver to meet my lover. We'd had many such river trysts. In fact, it was how we'd met five months prior: he on his way to check his crab traps and me anchored in the Matanzas, listening to Gillian Welch softly wail on my boom box. But tonight, it was the Iris Haven River, not the Matanzas, and it was New Year's Eve—a time that made me melancholy, because who among us could live up to the expectations born of fresh beginnings?

My skiff bounced along the swift chop, and as I brought her into the channel, I could see that Billy was already there. He owned a twenty-four-foot Wellcraft Fisherman, and if the tide had been low, he wouldn't have been in this river, as it ran shallow. But the New Year and broad, waning moon had given us a high tide, which made the river doable. I eased back on the throttle, my skin and hair wet with salt spray, not believing that I'd been with Billy for nearly half a year. As I churned doggedly on, closing the gap between us, I reminded myself that I deserved this happiness. My life was like most people's: a series of challenges made bearable by the sanctified gifts of friends and strangers. I wasn't going to sabotage things this time. I was going to love a man and allow him to love me back and simply accept that life could be this way. And if, on occasion, I needed to slip a pinch of cayenne into his coffee to keep him focused, or sweeten his table salt with a dusting of snipped egret feathers to make him want me more, well, I was up for that. Upon my approach, I heard John Lee Hooker on Billy's boom box: "One bourbon, one scotch, and one beer." What a fine way to bring in the New Year: with the blues.

I anchored off his leeward bow, and as I watched the line uncoil and disappear into the river, I yelled, "Hello!"

Billy poked his head out of the cabin, all smiles, his eyes polished by liquor. "Hey there." He stepped onto the deck and raised his Budweiser in greeting. Dressed in well-saddled jeans, a red cable-knit sweater, and a University of Florida baseball cap, he looked younger than his forty-five years. "What took you so long?" He shot me that gap-toothed Scots-Irish grin.

"I ran over to the hammock. Wanted to see if I could spot the owl we heard last night."

He didn't say anything. He just stared. I fiddled with my hair and felt myself blush. His gaze was direct and all about sex. Even though I was halfway through my third decade on this planet, I wobbled under the weight of his hazel eyes. I brought my slicker tighter about me. "Permission to come aboard, sir."

He held open his arms: a welcoming gesture. "Permission granted."

As he took my line in his big hands and pulled my skiff toward him, I felt light and happy, almost home.

*I*t was cold on the river, even though we were buffered from the easterly breeze by the dunes. Billy insisted I remove my slicker, because he "couldn't get to me through all that water-proofing." He wrapped me in an old gray sweater of his. It fit Billy snugly, but on me, it resembled a coat.

Overhead, clouds moved quickly and the moon's light wavered. We stayed on deck, both of us wanting to bring in the New Year in the wide, cold goodness of this river. Billy kissed the tip of my nose. Mr. Hooker howled, "Think twice before you go . . ."

"Happy New Year, baby." I touched Billy's face.

He rested his hands in my damp hair. "We're getting socked in," he said.

I followed his gaze. Fog billowed westward from the sea. Soon both the river and shore would be enveloped. "I love fog. Especially the way it tumbles in without warning." I wrapped my arms around him and spun a half turn—the perfect curl of a knot—resting the back of my head against his chest. "Fog is all about surprise, whereas rain is about, I don't know, enduring the moment."

He spun me back around—undoing the knot—leaned in, kissed me. He tasted like drawn butter and beer. "That makes no sense, you crazy woman, you."

"Yes, it does." I extricated myself and reached for my beer. I took a long swig and considered if I should try to convince him that rain is all about endurance, but he was on to something else.

"Listen to this." He popped out John Lee Hooker and fiddled with a plastic bag filled with CDs.

"No, Billy. Not again. I don't like this game. Listen, I'm

better on music than you. Get used to it. It's a"—I breathed in the wet air, searched for a suitable word—"gift."

He wasn't deterred. He hit the play button and looked at me smugly. He thought he had me stumped—it was written all over his wide face.

"Easy. Prokofiev. *Romeo and Juliet.*"

"Damn it!" He crushed his empty Budweiser with one hand, tossed it in a plastic bucket, opened the cooler, reached for another. "How do you know?"

"I saw the ballet on PBS." Actually, anyone with half a brain would know. That cubist, break-down-the-walls, big-as-a-bull physicality was *owned* by Prokofiev. I ran my hand lightly over my fog-frizzed hair. "I mean it, Billy, I really hate this game."

"Damn it all to hell." He pulled the CD bag up to his face and stared in. He was determined to prove to me that I didn't know as much about music as I thought I did. For a moment, I hated him.

"Just a couple of more, Murmur Lee." He slammed in a different CD, hit play, and smiled triumphantly.

"Raga. A form of classical Indian music." I spoke in a monotone. "But you've got the wrong season. That raga is to be played only in the summer. Listen to the F-sharp. It's called a Dipak, Billy." I admit, I pushed his buttons with this one, showing off just enough to make him wish he'd never started down this path. "But you've got the time of day right. Hear that tonality of the four-note scale, all of it way down deep? Definitely a nighttime melody."

His mouth pinched up—a sign that I tweaked his gall-bladder into producing a squirt or two of poison. He took off his cap, repositioned it, and then searched the CD bag like a dog clawing sand.

I emptied my beer and got a fresh one. If this goes on

much longer, I thought, I'm out of here. I popped the top and looked toward Zachary's dock, which, through the fog, appeared smudged. I could barely make out the plastic owl he'd nailed on the rail to keep away the seagulls and all their poop. Dumb idea. Right then, the voice of Egypt blossomed through the thick, liquored air.

"Umm Kulthum." I turned away from Billy, scooted past the cooler, and took three steps to the stern. "Nobody on the planet has a voice like hers. You know, she's like Piaf. And Orbison. Billie Holiday. Ella. Definitely Ella. Some might even say Sinatra. With chanteuses, it's not about tonal structure. It's all about the voice. And phrasing." He was not listening. He was already on to the next CD. I stared into the silk wall of mist, annoyed, thinking, I want to eat the fog; I want it to taste like melted vanilla ice cream.

He pressed the play button. As I zeroed in on the first fat chord, the wind hit us with something awful, something rotting, maybe an animal carcass soiling the evergreen promise of this New Year.

I started to say, Billy, baby, what's that smell? but I didn't get the chance. Everything—the river, the shore, the big dark sky—collapsed in a single bright flash. Right before I lost consciousness, I thought, Oh dear God, there is a lightning storm in my brain.

I do not remember plunging into the green river.

It was only after death consumed me that any sort of consciousness emerged. My first thought was, Have the stars all melted? Is that what rivers and seas truly are? The meltdown of heavenly bodies?

As the river flooded me, I longed for Billy. I wanted him to pull me into the air and back to life. Where was he?

I tried to close my mouth, but it would not move. Tiny fish entered and exited. I looked foolish, floating along, my mouth wide open. What would happen to my soul with my mouth gaped and flooded? Could it escape to wherever souls are supposed to rest? At least no evil could get in. How could any spirit enter a mouth dammed by river water? I decided I resembled a sunken boat, a moving reef, a curiosity to fish and invisible plankton.

An old woman who used to shop at the St. Augustine IGA before they tore it down told me that it was bad luck to die with your eyes open. She lived in Lincolnville, marched with Dr. King, saw her two sons go to jail and her daughter become a lawyer. She was old when I knew her. She taught me a lot. Such as: "You gotta close a dead man's eyes, lest he take somebody with him." And: "Open up all the windows and doors the very second a person passes. Otherwise, their soul stays stuck, locked up in the house. You don't want that." And this one, most frightening of all: "When you become pure soul, don't you dare break a mirror. If you do, your soul shatters to bits and ends up trapped in all them broken pieces of looking glass, cursed to wander not just this universe but all the verses, the multiverse."

I wondered what she'd say about this: me dying with my eyes wide open and not possessing a single anticipatory breath that my demise was imminent? But at least I wouldn't be cracking any mirrors down here.

My fingers trailed along the river's sandy bottom, touching seaweed, seashells, sea grass, unable to stop the journey.

The current dragged me away from Billy and Iris Haven and everyone among the living I loved. Edith. Lucinda. Zachary. Charlee. I might have made it all the way out to sea if it hadn't been for Billy's sweater getting snagged on the stob of some ancient submerged barnacle-studded tree.

Fish nibbled. Crabs found the bare flesh of my fingers. Seaweed collected in the hollows and curves of my body. The river rushed over me, polishing me, as if I were just another hapless river rock. In the first few hours of my death, I was in shock, unable to comprehend how—in what seemed like that proverbial eye blink—I had come to drown, with no real effort on my part, in the Iris Haven River. And also, there in the lightless water, I was terrified that my body might never be found. I was confused as to the condition of my soul and the state of my religion.

If I had been a calmer cadaver, the events leading up to my death might not have been as murky. But that was supposition. For all I knew, every living creature is struck dumb at the moment of death. Maybe initial ignorance as to the details of one's own dying is akin to the body going into shock—the truth is just too difficult to manage, given the magnitude of the change.

Untouched by God or grace, surrounded by darkness, suspended in that river I knew and loved so well, I began to grieve. On the 365th evening of 2001, I had lost everything and gained nothing.

But with dawn came a small gift: I was faceup. I could see the new day coming. I watched the light tipple the surface. I saw how it shooed away the darkness, turning the river water gold and green and distant blue. But my grief over having lost my life and then having gained squat in death was resolute. No amount of dawn could make me accept my circumstances. As the water slowly warmed, I grew angry. I was thirty-five years old—the lover to many men, a good friend to a well-chosen few, a daughter who'd been secretly wild but openly obedient, a mother who'd never stopped viciously mourning the loss of her only child, a woman who despite some tough breaks and lapses in judgment had made her own way in this world—yet I hadn't been allowed one small final act of self-respect: the conscious participation in my death. Why couldn't I remember what had happened? Or perhaps memory had nothing to do with it. Maybe there were simply two states of existence: on and off. I couldn't accept this. I wanted more out of both life and death. I wished I'd had more sex, born more babies, eaten more chocolate pie. And in death, I sure as hell didn't want to lie passively by while crabs consumed my corpse.

The current tugged, and eventually the sweater began to shred into long woolen tendrils, freeing me from the stob. I floated deeper into the river, and it was then that a rumbling began in my spine and my belly and even my knees: My soul was being wrestled from that old body of mine. This was not easy. It did not feel good. It was, like all forms of birth, a violent act. As the essential force we call spirit was torn membrane from muscle from bone, I joined the chorus, lifting up my voice in the eternal maw of the primal scream—it's silent, you know. This was a humbling experience, not unlike being born to flesh amid blood and shit. I was ripped from that pickled bag of skin and tossed like an old dirty washrag into the cold, bright air—the fog had lifted—and I looked behind me, from where I'd just come, at that river I had loved so well. I watched a flash all silver and gray arc through the air and splash back down. The absurdity of my situation took hold and I began to laugh (my laughter flew in droplets of water that struck the river's surface, ringing like chimes), because I realized that in the moment I left my body, I was not a golden spirit sprouting wings, ascending into the gates of heaven. No. Not me. I was lowly, common, prey to both dolphin and shark, sustenance to poor coastal people—black and white alike. I was a jumping mullet.

Charleston Rowena Mudd

*I*n Boston, they know me as Charlotte, for in that northern city, positioned as it is in the breadbasket of higher learning, I became a geographical liar. My goal? To hide my true origins. And not simply because people outside of dear old Dixie have unfairly pegged us all as shiftless, ignorant, backward, inbred—should I go on?—but because I, Charleston Rowena Mudd, am a Self-Loathing Southerner.

As such, I have developed various airs and voices appropriate to whatever name I'm using in whatever region I find myself in. For instance, in Boston, I truncate my vowels. "My name is Charlotte." Quick as a darting bird: five syllables compressed into one quick wobble.

But after two or three bourbons, I sometimes slip up. "My name is Chaaaarlut. Rhymes with *haaaaarlot*."

Very few of my friends back at Harvard Divinity find my seldom-revealed but ribald southern humor charming. Only

Happy Jim, a fallen Franciscan brother with the smile of an angel. An easy audience, for sure.

And now I have returned to my old haunts—the sandy coquina-laced beaches that build and recede at the whimsy of the tides, the lesser-known shores of Anastasia Island, Crescent Beach, Iris Haven, Marineland, for Christ's sake—where I am known simply as Charlee. Charlee Mudd.

And I must confess, the name fits.

I never imagined I would return to this place. I left in order to become an educated woman, to escape redneck culture, to become worldly and intellectual and Yankeefied. And I pretty much succeeded.

True, I didn't manage to totally stamp out my good manners and, as I said, the old drawl lifted its ugly magnolia-scented head occasionally. And even after coming to terms with the awful realization that rednecks are universal, as is racism, sexism, and plagiarism, I still managed to live my life using my brains versus my body. Which, come to think of it, was actually my main goal when I set out from the South. You see, at the time of my exodus at the age of twenty-nine, I was convinced that female brain-driven success was a peculiarly northern tradition. I never stopped to consider that those cotillion queens, whom I loathed both out of envy and disgust, might have had more going on upstairs than I was willing to give them credit for.

So, yes, I could pass as northern on most days. I learned to make a phone call and get to the point immediately, rather than engage in the ritualized politeness that serves as the glue binding all cultures of the South into one huge dysfunctional gossip tree. You know, *How's your daddy, your great-granddaddy, your camellias, and your mama doing?* When the point of the call was to ask, *Can you please turn down your stereo just a tad? The baby is trying to sleep.*

I could meet a man for the very first time and discuss world issues without knowing who his people were. I could bully my way up to the front of a line without ever once saying "Excuse me." I quit addressing people as sir or ma'am even if they were over seventy. This alone would have killed my mother had she been alive. I ate grits only in private. A store in St. Augustine shipped them to me. I hid them in a tin canister I kept tucked out of sight on the top shelf of my kitchen cabinet. The raised black letters on the canister identified the contents as flour. If a friend happened to spy the leftovers in my fridge, I would lie, saying that it was couscous. I once spent a weekend alone in New York City. I rode the subway. Hailed a cab. Wandered Central Park without police protection. I've been known to dine out by myself. I learned to stop asking for sweet tea—I grew tired of the dismissive waiters saying, "The sugar is on the table," and me trying to explain it's simply not the same. I paid scant attention to football, claiming not to know that the Florida State Seminoles were anything other than an amalgam of lost tribes chased into the Everglades by the U.S. Army and disease. I owned an ice scraper. I pretended to like, even understand, Philip Glass. I never ate supper anymore. *Dinner. Let's go have dinner.* I joined the ACLU.

But there is one fact above all others that illustrates how far I had traveled from Iris Haven and my Deep South roots. My fiancé, the man who dumped me two weeks before we were to say our vows in a Unitarian chapel close to campus, hailed from Nigeria. Ahmed. Ahmed Al-Kuwaee.

His was a lilting, London-influenced, perfect-grammar accent. A Muslim by birth, training, and choice, he considered my Catholic upbringing exotic, naïve. He was, as my southern cronies would say, black as the ace of spades.

We were a perfect match, a complement of Old World and New, cream and coffee, intellect and passion, seaweed and salt. But he had a secret. One that he revealed, if you will indulge me, in the most startling fashion. It was a Saturday night in early November. Already, Cambridge was locked down in wayward piles of dirty snow and temperatures so unkind, I refuse to recite them. Ahmed was to be at my apartment at 7:30 for dinner. He had his own key, which he used. I was in my tiny kitchen, which was, if the truth be known, an afterthought carved out of a closet, chopping cilantro—a must-have ingredient in the spicy Thai lemon and shrimp soup I was serving. Ahmed loved my cooking. And I admit, I'm not half-bad in the kitchen. But I digress. There I was, standing at my kitchen counter, Yo-Yo Ma unfurling in the background, me concentrating so singularly on the task at hand that I didn't realize Ahmed had let himself in until he cleared his throat.

I spun around, thrilled—I was wild for him—the knife still in hand, and then froze. Ahmed was pale. I swear. His ebony skin resembled chalk. Beside him stood a petite young thing with downcast eyes. A child, really. Shy, maybe gentle, definitely out of her element. I could read nothing else about her.

He spoke softly, a slight embarrassed smile revealing a thin flash of white. He explained it succinctly, with all the emotion one uses when reciting a textbook passage. Theirs was an arranged union, an agreement entered into before he or she had any inkling of puberty. They were married the day prior to him leaving for America and Harvard. His conscience wouldn't allow him to go forward with a Christian marriage. He asked that I forgive him.

Despite my northern, sophisticated, and tough-as-nails-in-an-urban-way attitude, I didn't take the news well. He had barely finished his plea for forgiveness, when I heard myself screech, my drawl in full bloom—anger, hurt, and disbelief fueling the elongation of my vowels—"Why, you no good lily-livered shit ass!"

He could have run me over with a Jeep and I would not have felt as injured. I feared my eyes were darting about in my head as I tried to recover some semblance of control. My best friend from home, Murmur, scattered like light through my foundering brain. She never let anyone get the best of her— she never showed it anyway. She could have a cobra sitting on her head and remain steady. I had to slip into another dimension, if only for a moment. In my mind's eye, Murmur gathered. She was smirking, not a drop of fear betrayed, not even in her squinty blue eyes. It did the trick. Briefly, a calm pushed at the thunderclouds roiling through my veins. And I did it. I got righteous.

My voice deepened. I slowed way down. I enjoyed the heft of the knife, which I gripped ever so sweetly.

"How dare you. You have taken advantage of my honor. My good nature." I pushed an errant strand of hair off my forehead with the point of the knife. "Even my honest heart." I pursed my lips as I conjured my next face-saving line, all the while struggling not to collapse at his feet and beg and howl in true belle fashion for him not to abandon me.

"You are dead to me. Do you understand? And if you don't walk out that door this very second, you will also be dead to your sweet little bride." I tossed the knife—one revolution— and caught it by the handle. For the first time in my life, I was grateful that in high school I had been a baton twirler.

Over the top? Certainly. Effective? Oh yes.

Ahmed backed out of my Cell Block C—size apartment, shielding his poor shocked bride with his own body, stunned, I believe, not only by the spin of my knife but, most importantly, by my sudden southernness.

Yes, it's true. I had deceived him, too. Told him I was from Chicago. My friends at Harvard warned me that I would rot in hell for telling such a lie and that surely he would find me out. But I felt the need to hide my origins, because he truly hated southerners, too. We had so much in common. He had seen George Wallace footage and believed everyone in the South was just a bunch of little Georges blocking school entrances throughout the region, yelling racist epithets into bullhorns, and swiping sweat out of their pale, beady eyes. Their intention? To prevent Ahmed from stepping foot into any of their hallowed halls of second-rate education.

Playing devil's advocate, I once asked him, "What about Jimmy Carter?"

"What about him?" He stared back at me, unblinking, unwilling to admit I had scored a point.

"He's from the South. He's not prejudiced. He's a good man."

"He's not truly a southerner," Ahmed said thoughtfully, stroking his new-growth goatee, seemingly at peace with his flawed logic.

Of course, my deception was minor—indeed, barely counted—when compared to him not disclosing he already had a wife. My God, he had turned me into an adulteress— and nearly a polygamist—without my informed consent.

So upon learning that my fiancé was already married, the guilt I had borne those last seventeen months transformed itself into seething satisfaction, even as my heart was shattering like a Kmart wineglass dropped onto a terrazzo floor. In the face of my solemn death threat, Ahmed had exited my apartment with a soft shush of the door, but I flung it open, and before he and she had made it down the hall to the elevator, I screamed triumphantly, pointing that trusty blade at what I presumed to be the upper chamber of his heart, "Yes, you fucking asshole, you have been sleeping with a Cracker!"

Then I slammed the door so hard that my Tiffany art glass wall calendar fell off its hook. I started bawling and headed for the kitchen, where I poured myself a water glass full of bourbon and ate cold leftover cheese grits right out of the plastic container. I planned all manner of revenge. I could have gay smut magazines delivered to his mailbox at the Divinity School. I could call Immigration from a pay phone and say I believed he was in the country on an expired visa. I could tell the FBI that he often had clandestine midnight meetings with men of Middle Eastern origin and that he once had admitted he'd like to bomb the State Department. Lies. Lies. Lies. I could, I could, I could. . . . But I did not.

Instead, I dropped out of school. One class to go—three credit hours: Christianity and Ecology. Course description: "A rigorous exploration of sound Christian environmental thought." As opposed to? And then there is the matter of my dissertation, which, if ever done, will explore the thorny subject of the historical Jesus. My committee head, Dr. Wise, was hoping for something a bit more traditional. Not my style, I told him breezily.

The truth is, despite a lifelong preoccupation with religion—and yes, I'll say it—the Holy Roman Catholic Church in all its many genuflections—I have lost my faith. I'm not sure when it left. Or was I the one who walked away? Beats me. All I know is that in my current state of lapsed faith, I cannot possibly write about a Christian Jesus. A political strategist? A social maverick? A revolutionary par none? Yes. God? No. Not right now.

I am newly home—four days—haven't yet unpacked. The coastal plain of Iris Haven feels as familiar to me as skin. But I am not the same person who left here six years ago. If we are, indeed, defined by the friends and lovers who fill the lonely hollows of our hearts, displacing for a moment our sadness and alienation (those twin sisters of original sin), then I am ash. Not bone.

Ahmed wasn't solely one more attempt on my part to wrestle free from the South's wide guilt. I loved him. When he held me, I felt free. Surrounded. The pain of past traumas receded. The fear of failure faded.

Almost two months after he jilted me, Murmur died. Alone. In the Iris Haven River. How does a woman who spent her entire life fishing and surfing and snorkeling these waters die by drowning? And what condition was her faith in as she took her final breath? Did anyone care? Did the Christian God—so important to her in girlhood—whisper into her fading ear, "My child, you are a woman of many sins: adultery, drink, promiscuity. But you indulged honestly, with a fair heart, meaning no harm. So welcome home"?

I always knew that I could gallivant anywhere. Re-create myself a thousand times over. Charleston. Charlotte. Cher. Hell, you name it. I could pass as a Yankee. I could fall in love with a fine-boned man from Nigeria, someone whose dreams were of places, colors, smells, textures more foreign to me than the surface of Mars. I could fall off the edge of the earth and never be honest about the consequences, because I had Murmur. Murmur was back home, keeping the world straight, sending me letters about new dune lines and turtle runs and the metalline sound of dragonflies on the wing at dusk. So no matter what new plot I was hatching for myself, at the close of the day, by the time I got to that last flourish at the end of the page—*Love you lots, Murmur*—I knew once again who I was. Charlee Mudd. A simple white girl from North Florida who loved grits and sea oats and, sans racism, most all things southern.

October 3, 2001
Murmur Lee Harp's Last Will and
Testament, Handwritten in Baroque Cursive
Script on a Yellow Legal Pad in Purple Ink
and Notarized by Lashandra P. Pacetti

The wind whips through my house, spins my mermaid mobile round and round. Papers fly. Dust bunnies hop. Light shifts, nearly moans. Gillian Welch wails "Orphan Girl" from the sanctity of my boom box. Her high-wire voice splits me in two, makes me shake, makes me want to testify, makes me fear that I bear no secrets.

As the world dances, I sit, fractured by song, barefoot on my front porch, my hair blown asunder, mourning Katrina Klein's death. Three years ago today. Three years. Yet the pain and disbelief are as fluid and startling as when we bore witness to her last breath. Iris Haven changed forever when Katrina died. She had not been here very long, but her soul understood. It recognized the ancient ghosts who clattered among the palms and magnolias and oaks and jasmine. Perhaps she had grown too close to them. And that's why they took her. Everyone who met Katrina wanted to claim her for their own.

I know one true thing today: My sorrow over her passing will never list, nor will Zachary's.

So here I am, wandering through my life, Katrina's life, and my dead daughter's life, hoping Zach is okay despite the sadness of this anniversary. Incense burns and swirls. I have set the turtle skull on the porch, facing east, the horizon, the sea, and maybe heaven. This morning, I discovered a dead blue jay by my back door. I buried it under the magnolia and rang my brass lady bell as I circled the trunk three times. I'm not sure why I did this, except that ritual in the face of death and re-membrance is a universal have-to-do. I knew there would be bird death today, for they are unknowing messengers, flitting between various scrims of existence. Maybe the jay was Ka-trina's way of telling me, *Remember me well, Murmur Lee. Remember me on this wild day.*

Surrounded by scent and memory, I watch surfers glide across cobalt waves. They are, for the most part, towheaded boys striped in slick black wet suits. As they ride the swells, they curve their bodies to match the shape of the waves, and when they swim out past the breakers on their boards, their arms stroking the air and ocean with athletic glee, I wish I was underneath them, a buoyant arrow gliding over the water with the confidence of a smug and happy shark.

And also, there is this: Selfishly, instead of staying focused on Katrina, I am compelled to ruminate over, of all things, my last will and testament. But perhaps this should not come as a surprise. One of the awful aspects of having someone your own age die is that it pinpricks the ego, pushing us into the fleeting recognition that mortality is not reserved for the old and infirm.

Don't misunderstand. I suffer no serious ailments. Albeit,

there's a tune or two in this life I'm wise to avoid, but other than that, I have no reason to doubt the vigor and stamina of my physical self. My mood is simply a manifestation of sorrow and practicality. Forty is just a handful of years around the corner. In two weeks, I will have outlived my mother. Never thought I'd see the day. And Katrina was two years younger than I. So a bit of planning is in order.

And let us be delightfully honest. Always in life, there are scores to settle. Good scores and bad. And what better way to grab the last word for all of eternity than by making your wishes known in a legally binding document? How fabulous to have this last will and testament read aloud, a public airing. Oh yes. And both friend and foe will recognize in these words, penned by a healthy woman who had no intention of dying, venial acts of gracious revenge.

Charlee Mudd. Ms. Charleston Rowena Mudd, to be official. I name you executoress. I trust you will follow the spirit and intent of this document without adding any undo flourishes that others might inspire.

Firstly, to my ex-husband, Erik Nathanson, father of my child, I bequeath to you Daisy Blue, my 1992 Dodge pickup, which, as of this moment, sports 97,336 hard-earned miles. It is my sincere hope that my dear truck will inspire you for once in your life to get those pretty manicured hands dirty. Also, this is what I do not bequeath to you: any portion of the air our child once breathed. I am not a bitter woman. Just practical. You don't deserve a single particle of her, no matter how tenuous or spectral the connection might be. The fact that I leave you something at all is a sign that I have (a) successfully purged your negative energy from my personal and spiritual life—it took years of tear spilling and potion rubbing to get to this point, but hey!—and (b) forgiven your treatment of our daughter and me, although I will never absolve you of the consequences.

My rifle. I love that gun. I have aimed her at rattlesnakes, rats, shadows, unwanted solicitors, and old boyfriends who came calling at just the wrong time. She has never let me down. Lest anyone forget, she was given to me on my wedding day by Grandfather Harp. So you, Lucinda, my youngest, meanest, most talented, and much-beloved friend and neighbor (You don't fool me. I know you proclaimed yourself a pacifist and joined the Mennonite church just to piss me off), the rifle is yours. Be good to her. Keep her cleaned and oiled, and she will see you through many a scrape, nonviolent and otherwise.

I hereby donate all of my books—with some exclusions, which I will note below—to the St. Johns County Homeless Shelter. Mind food is just as important as slopping down a bowl of watery soup. (Charlee, call the shelter to arrange for a pickup. No need you hauling all those boxes down the stairs.)

My literary exclusions are twofold. First, I want my Zora Neale Hurston collection to go to some deserving child who needs a healthy infusion of hope in her life. So, Charlee, go see Pastor Smith at the AME in Lincolnville and tell him I said that nothing builds hope like reading good literature and that I want the books to be given to a child of his choosing.

Literary exclusion number two: the guidebooks. *An Identification Guide to the Trees of North Florida* (also all my other wildlife guides: reptiles, birds, butterflies, mushrooms, shells, the whole shebang). *The Ordinary Person's Guide to Dream Interpretation. A Lucky Lou Guide to Hiking the Pacific Northwest. A Guide to Better Health and Fitness. How to Become a Millionaire: An Easy-to-Understand Guide. An Easy-to-Understand Guide to Self-Hypnosis. An Easy-to-Understand Guide to Self-Esteem.* And my personal favorite, *Sex Is Fun! A John-*

son & Johnson Guide to Sexual Freedom. I've got tons more, but I don't feel like writing down all the titles. So, Charlee, just do this: If a book has the word *guide* in the title, give it to Father Diaz. You know how he's always saying, with that round pious face of his, that he's simply a lowly guide leading his flock to salvation? Well, once I'm gone, he'll be able to lead them toward any number of other things, including botany, metaphysics, travel, fitness, financial freedom, hypnosis, self-esteem, and good sex. What will they need Jesus for?

All my music—Bach, Mahler, Verdi, Vivaldi, Coltrane, Monk, Davis, Hendrix, Muddy Waters, Tampa Red, Robert Johnson, Billie Holiday, Sarah Vaughn, Nina Simone, Ella Fitzgerald, Isaac Hayes, Memphis Minnie, the Allman Brothers, Yo-Yo Ma, Portishead, all of it, even the Dixie Chicks—just divide it among yourselves. And if anything is left over, give the CDs to the music department at the junior high.

I don't believe there will be a soul privy to this last will and testament who doesn't know (some of you actually remember) that after Blossom died, I went to the shore in an attempt to walk away my grief. And as I stumbled and fell and stumbled some more, I gathered every talisman I came upon—anything the ocean tossed my way—convinced as I am that earth objects contain their own power, their own constellation of tears and remembrances. So all of these sacred trinkets, once I've gone over to the other side to be reunited with my baby girl, will be burned with my body. The talismans and I, we shall become ash. Together. And you will spread our mingled dust on the beach in front of my house while the trade winds sing. I offer this partial list of said relics, humble though they may be (Charlee, forgive me, for this recitation is incomplete): seashells, dolphin vertebrae, bird skulls, petrified blowfish, starfish, sand dollars, mermaid purses, sea urchins, sea whips, sea sponges, coral, coquina rock, the turtle skull, the gator skull, the raccoon paws, plus all those bits of glass—bountiful in color: red, green, blue, white, pink—each polished to a fine satiny sheen by the ocean waves and tossed onto shore before the sea could grind them back into sand.

Desdemona. You know I can't leave her up to the Fates. I want to be welcomed by my people, not shunned, when I drift their way. So beautiful Desdemona, the woman who kept her ship safe on the high seas until finally a hellish storm rolled her onto our island, the rainbow-skirted figurehead who was dis-covered by my great-great-grandfather Harp the morning of his wife's death and daughter's birth—what shall I do with her? I have no blood relatives to speak of. And even if I did, good old Desi stays put. She belongs in Iris Haven. Therefore, I offer this solution, with the admonition that even in death, I will be watching: I bequeath Desdemona to the citizens of Iris Haven, to be preserved in perpetuity, displayed on holidays and good-weather weekends, giving newcomers, visitors, babies (I'm hoping we get a few of those out here) the chance to mar-vel over her, to ask questions about how she came to rest here. In this way, see, the old stories—the family legends, the breath of pure spirit—will never die.

My winter coat? Take it to the battered-women's shelter.

The ruby crystal-studded lavaliere made in Czechoslovakia pre–World War II? The one I wore only on New Year's and my birthday? Edith Piaf, my dear, it's yours.

My anal thermometer? The same one I used countless times to take my baby's temperature? The one that, thanks to my sentimental nature, I could never bring myself to toss? Dr. Z, you know I love you. But you also know that you get too hot under the collar over matters of little consequence. So once I'm dead to you in the flesh, you can test my theory on your very own behind (and a cute one it is) anytime the mood strikes.

And, Z, you work too much. So I bequeath to you my boat. Take it downriver, anchor it, shut your eyes, let the past go. You deserve nothing less.

My spell book. Now, this is powerful stuff. It has my recipes for dyeing cloth, making healing soups, plus various prayers and rituals that needle the universe into doing what's right. I don't know what to do with it. I'm going to leave that up to you, Charleston.

Salty's, my venerable old icehouse, where more beer has been consumed than probably anyplace on the planet? Charlee, it's paid for lock, stock, and barrel. I laid down cash for that joint. Was scared to death, but I did it. So, girlie, you who will soon have a big fat divinity degree, if you are still alive upon the occasion of my demise, the keys are yours. And if you pass before I do, well, Saint Rita, I don't know what to do.

William Speare, because you and I are lovers and friends of recent vintage, I'm not quite comfortable bequeathing to you any of the tangible evidence of my having walked this earth. So rather than a concrete offering of love and grace, I leave you a directive: Remember us. That's all. Bless the memory. Because so far, we have been very fine together.

And finally, this ounce of paradise I call home, the house I built with my own hands after you divorced me, Erik, the little palace that rises from its wooded nook behind the dunes, allowing me a respite from which I can look out over the inlet, Iris Haven, and the Atlantic? Charlee, once more, you are my heart. We have gotten into and out of many a scrape together. If you're reading this, it means I'm dead, you're not, and the place is yours. How's that for friendship? A business and a house. I always said I was going to get you to come back home one way or another.

Now, I know I'm supposed to say something about being of sound mind and body. Which I am. I've never been saner. My health, other than that old thorn, is tip-top. And while I don't anticipate an early departure (do we ever?), my mother taught me to be prepared for contingencies. To my great sorrow, I haven't always heeded her advice. But I am a woman with intimate knowledge regarding the brevity and precocious sadism ofttimes attached to life.

So today, the third of October, 2001, while Gillian sings "I have had friendships, pure and golden," I take this oath.

Please, don't anybody mess around. Simply adhere to the words, plain and simple, that I have set forth.

With the breeze and the sky and the songbirds and the darting dragonflies as my witness, I sign respectfully,

Murmur Lee Harp.

A Grocery List, Written in Murmur Lee Harp's Excessive Cursive Script, Unread, Lost Amid the Cobwebs Behind Her Rusting Refrigerator

Coca-Cola (little bottles)
Budweiser (case)
Rat traps
Candles (white)
Incense (sandalwood)
Pens with purple ink
Hot dogs
Fresh basil
Chips Ahoy! (chunky)
Cigs
Moisturizer
Pink lipstick
Sausage pizza (x-tra cheese)
Water pistol
Doritos
Salsa
Maybe some corn for supper (stop by fruit stand)

Rubbers
Tampax
Toilet paper
What else?
Toothpaste

Murmur Lee Harp

Here, the wind is visible. I watch it with the eyes of the newly born: curious, delighted, free of the yoke of judgment. It swirls and billows. Light threads its way through the wind's shifting gray tones, weaving images. I have no form, no corporeality, yet I am here: a spirit watching the film of my life, my family's life. The images waft all about and I feel my soul's aperture open wider and wider. The light fills me. The wind fills me. The past—which was life—fills me.

Murmur Lee Harp Sees a Moment in the Life of Her Great-Great-Grandfather Oster Harp

Yes, I am watching him as if in a movie.

My great-great-grandfather Harp walks the shoreline, the very same shoreline I wandered for thirty-five years. But the beach in Oster Harp's time is different. There is more of it, so wide that a plane could land with nary a problem. Not so in my day. At Iris Haven, time manifests as erosion. So while Oster Harp walks on a wide field of sand, I slip along a crescent. One day, there will be nothing: no beach, no dunes, no railroad vine, or coreopsis. The sea will claim my house. The lizards and snakes and bobcat and fox will find higher ground and will have to make due with less land from which to spin the drama of their lives. Iris Haven will become myth. And then what? What will Oster Harp's life mean once the ocean obliterates the land we lived, loved, and died on? My soul blinks open (it smells of salt and gardenia); the wind sweeps in: I am full of memories.

I watch him trip in the wet sand; he lands on one knee, rubs his shoulder against his cheek, struggles to his feet, stands unsteadily—I think the wind might just knock him flat—and then he begins again. In the viewing, I gain a sense of his heartbeat. It is warm and steady and fully content not to return to the house and the women.

He is a young man—about my age—and other than his fierce blue eyes and a faint dimple in the bull's-eye of his chin, I look nothing like him. He fidgets as he walks. His thin, strict lips rhumba, staccatolike, as if a lifetime of confessions are banging at the door, desiring to be let out, longing for the freedom that comes with being heard. The thumb of his right hand taps and retaps the pads of his fingertips—index to pinkie, index to pinkie, index to pinkie, Hail Mary, full of grace, the rosary made flesh. He doesn't fool me. Oster Harp may be a Protestant, but his mother's Catholicism runs like a neon virus in his veins.

He looks up from the rain-pocked sand and studies the night. The sun is finally beginning its liquid ascent, revealing a horizon I love so well, the one made restless by a wind-whipped sea. Slow-growing swaths of purple and gold cauterize the darkness. Yes, daylight insists on her due.

Oster listens, his head slightly tilted, to the soft sucking sound of the waves lapping near his bare feet and to the wind, which has not stopped howling since early yesterday, and the onset of the big blow. Yes, the wind song clattering over the dunes and through the embattled pin oaks and between the shredded green fringe of palm fronds frightens him because it carries in its whirling folds memories of Orchid in childbirth, memories only three hours old. He wants the wind song to stop. It rattles him the way scorpions rattle the long dark night of our fear. He covers his ears and tries to concentrate on something that bears no weight—last week's fishing excursion: the sun, the good rum, the fair seas, the decent catch, grouper and triggerfish, and the one that got away.

It's no use. The memories rush at him: The black women swooping through the candlelight—God's great birds flying through the shadowy night—ministering to his young wife, who just happens to be my great-great-grandmother. There she is—Orchid Porphyria Harp—her legs spread wide, the mess between her legs opening grotesquely, wet and bloody, the frothing mouth of a wounded animal. I wish I had been there. I would have given her a tincture of yarrow to ease her pain, and before that—at the onset of her second trimester—I would have wrapped her belly in raw silk dyed with the blood of elderberry, so that the baby would have been content to stay in the womb for the whole nine months.

This is what Great-Great-Grandfather Harp cannot accept: Childbirth split her open. And as he watched, pegged to that flickering circle of reflected candlelight on the heart-pine floor, he was fascinated. Transfixed. Appalled. Embarrassed. Outraged. Sickened. Unable to look anywhere else. This is the truth: Not once did he consider stealing a glance at Orchid's pale, crushed face. Or at her plum-sized fists flamed purple with the effort of gripping that rose-embroidered sham. Or at her small-boned bare feet held wide and aloft by two little black girls. Nor did he consider offering any words of comfort. He was too freaked-out: He was a man witnessing a train wreck; the carnage sickened him, but the passion that burns when life and death collide had hold of him by his ever-so—Gilded Age testicles.

The surf and sea foam bubble around his ankles and he shakes his head in an attempt to loosen these unwanted images, as if they might fall right out of his head and onto the sand, as if the incoming tide will wash them out to sea. No wonder birthing is woman's work. No wonder Velma looked over her shoulder, her black face glistening behind a stinking veil of sweat and candlelight, and said in a voice so calm one might think she didn't understand the magnitude of what was taking place, "You get on outta here, Mr. Harp. This may be your do-ing, but right here right now ain't none of your business."

And all of this caused by a new life pushing its way into the world!

Oster Harp knew a storm was coming. Everyone did. The weeds and grass at the bottom of the water-filled jars had be-gun to rise. And the pelicans rode the sea wind (a steady wind, which lacked the ominous quality of song) east to the far shore, across the river, and hunkered down behind the dunes in large, feathered battalions. The sun-glazed clouds traveled even faster than the great birds, pushed by forces building—indeed, boiling forth—in the Sargasso hundreds of miles to the east. But he surely did not know that a baby was coming, too.

He has not laid eyes on his child. All he knows of her is what the women told him. "A bird, a tiny baby bird," Velma cooed. "So small, you barely need more than one hand to hold her!"

And while he paced and drank good French brandy behind the closed doors of his study—all in a failed attempt to block the memory ghosts of my great-great-grandmother in labor—Velma yelled the pertinent details from her side of the door. The women swabbed his daughter in unsalted butter, slipped her into a shoe box, and placed her in a slow, warm oven in the screened kitchen that overlooked an oyster midden and the river. "Got to be kept warm. That baby wasn't ready to be born!"

As for Orchid, all Oster knows (perhaps cares to know) is what he was told by Martha Ann, Orchid's white help, and—if the truth be told—her best friend. She tapped on the door and, probably emboldened by the evening's events, took it upon herself to crack it open and peer in. "She's quiet now, Mr. Harp." Martha Ann smiled indulgently, the way women do when they are trying to pull a man into the sphere.

But Oster was not a man to be pulled. He'd see his wife later, once she was recovered and all signs of a difficult delivery were swept from the house, her countenance, her language.

From the slouch of his shoulders and the slow roll of his gait, I can't be sure what gives my great-great-grandfather more comfort: the fact that the birth is over, or that he isn't a woman and will, therefore, never have to endure what Orchid just went through. Maybe that's the key to masculine discontent: They are pissed, grateful, and in awe that giving birth is a privilege reserved for women. He stops walking, pushes his spectacles up the ridge of his nose, and squints seaward. He notices something bobbing in the roil of foam and waves. Inanimate or not, he is unsure—but most certainly something is there, maybe twenty yards out, riding the surf with humanlike determination. Perhaps a case of Madeira from a Portuguese ship. He waits and watches. He looks over his shoulder, scans the dunes, the leafless pin oaks, the sky hardening into a relentless blue. He is the only human soul present. He turns to the northwest, toward the mouth of the inlet, and perceives the faint surge of a rainbow as it unfurls across the moisture-soaked sky. A reminder of the covenant. Perhaps God is trying to apologize for the suffering he forced upon Orchid. This thought wafts by on the salt-laden wind, free of irony or complaint.

Again, he turns seaward. The object is making frenetic progress. The waves push it forward, suck it back. Occasionally, it spins, caught in the web of an eddy, before popping back into the sea's incessant ebb and flow. And sometimes, in a lull between waves, the drifting treasure simply rides the surface, partially submerged. For a moment, Oster worries that it will never make landfall, that it is too heavy, that the sea will open its jaws and swallow it whole. He is about to give up and continue his stroll, when the wind blows a tangle of seaweed around his bare feet. He glances at the green-brown ringlets that wiggle eel-like against his skin. The wind gusts, stinging him with salt and sand and its discordant song. He removes his spectacles and wipes the salt out of his eyes with a handkerchief retrieved from his back pocket. With growing impatience, he positions the spectacles back upon the bridge of his nose. He longs for silent air. He casts a final gaze seaward, blinking, eyes watering. Through the veil of gauzed vision, he sees it: a giant wave propelling the object shoreward. Oh my, this is no case of Madeira. She is exquisite. He steps closer. Even from this distance, he sees she is raven-haired, barroom-boned, buxom, of course, as are all figureheads. Her skirt, mottled with foam, seems to swirl—as if tumbled by the sea—and even this harsh world of wind, salt, and water hasn't been able to erase the fact that whoever created her possessed the whimsy of a child. Her hardwood prism-colored skirt billows as if caught in a strong gale, and along the hem, fish—their eyes painted yellow and green—happily swim. Dolphins leap over the curve of each breast.

Oster frees himself of the seaweed, rolls up his pant legs, and wades into the surf. Water surges past his ankles, slaps his calves. He takes another step and plunges waist-deep in the roiling Atlantic. The storm has rearranged the ocean floor, creating new drop-offs and shoals. His gold watch fob floats on the surface, as if riding a swell of liquid glass. The timepiece is ruined. He's sure of that. Or perhaps its gold case will keep the inner workings safe. He scolds himself for behaving so carelessly and then shades his eyes, searching for the raven-haired girl. The wind moans, high-pitched, like a bat, as it presses against the gullies and hills of the water. Oster Harp feels the tug of total immersion.

Aqua-prismed swells. White foam swirling off the wide, round hips of waves. Wind screaming along the sea's ruffled edge. A horizon splashed purple and orange and insistent blue: the morning's glow. This is the Atlantic at its wildest: post-storm, when beauty and relief combine to drive men and women alike into madness.

She is nowhere. There are no telltale signs. No pieces floating, bobbing, which is what would be found if the surf had broken her apart. She is not here. She doesn't exist. She was a cruel mirage.

The world consists of Oster and the ocean and a chain of pelicans cruising effortlessly in this siren wind. He decides to head back to shore. And to tell no one of this foolishness. His brain betrayed him. The strain of last night meddled with his good sense. A form of sea madness inflicted by stress and sleeplessness and devil brandy. That is why he keeps imagining the wind is singing. Sea madness. There is no wind song. No such thing exists. And there is no figurehead. There is just Oster and this ocean, which he struggles to take leave of. The current tugs at his legs, arms, even his chest. He pushes forward through the weight of water—his head high and proud—before being slammed soundly off his feet by a Mack truck of a wave.

Fully submerged, not to mention surprised, he swallows seawater. The current pulls him eastward, tugging at his spectacles, which he attempts to remove and pocket for safekeeping, but the water steals them from his fingers. He reaches through the murky darkness, but the sea has already spun them beyond his reach. Unknowable creatures and objects tumble past as the riptide ferries him toward Europe, the islands, Africa, and toward, he fears, the past—the pagan past that flourished before men of enlightenment sought dominion over this old earth, and, in particular, America. (Oh, yes, how different my great-great-grandfather and I are. He with his faith in a Protestant God, me having giving up on monotheism entirely. Won't we have a few things to talk about if ever we meet!) The riptide is a rapidly moving river flowing within the larger sea, carrying him quickly to another time. A place where he is not in control. A wet, dark, sun-filtered place where he is just another fish. How delightful, the notion that my great-great-grandfather nearly was transformed into a fish at death, as I momentarily was!

As if he'd been swallowed by a great whale and then belched from its belly, he pops to the surface, gagging, spitting, struggling to fill his lungs with the air of the present. Even the wind song welcomes him. The scrub oaks grow smaller and smaller, then disappear all together as the past pulls him back down, sandwiching him between waves, imprinting upon him images of a far and foreign shore. A tremendous pressure squeezes his chest. He fears he will explode. First his spine will pop, next his heart, liver, spleen. Skin will be the last to go. It will shred like the tattered remains of a forgotten flag. As the past, which Oster perceives of as death, becomes more real, he seeks intercession. He asks God to save him. And then he insanely questions the sincerity of his own request because it is, alas, automatic. His eyes burn, salt-scalded, and his chest fills with water, replacing the present air. Animals whose identities remain secret approach, silent and unafraid. His prayers issue faster, with ever-greater urgency, until they swirl and escape beyond the realm of language. My great-great-grandfather tumbles and claws, tumbles and claws. He is ready for battle, ready to kill and be killed. Indigo and ocher and black water seep into his brain, and it is then that the whale spits him out for the second time, leaving him to vomit seawater and redis-cover music and air. He is just about to thank God for sparing his life, when he looks over his shoulder and—buxom and proud, propelled by the ocean's force—the figure slams him square in the head.

No one comes looking for my great-great-grandfather. They are all too busy caring for his nameless shoe-box baby on his nameless island and pressing cold compresses against the forehead of my fever-delirious great-great-grandmother.

In my film of Oster Harp—a man I knew precious little about in life—the sky boils with giant white clouds that move quickly east to west, then finally clears into a high-pitched brightness. It is then—when the atmosphere thins into glass—that my great-great-grandfather comes to, beached, blinded by his own blood. He wipes his eyes clean with a raw hand. The rainbow has retreated, the sun ascended. The moon shines on other lands. The wind song has grown weary.

Downshore, toward the inlet, maybe fifty feet away, he spies something—blurred, thanks to his bad eyesight and lost spectacles—but he is certain of what he sees. The figurehead lies placidly on the sand, like a drowsy sunbather. Oster rises on rubbery legs and runs. He is so grateful to be alive. God is so good. He trips, falls into the soft new dunes, clamors to his feet, and begins again. He is covered in the grains of the beach: a castaway crusted in salt and blood.

When he reaches the figurehead, he drops to his knees. He inspects her, his face close in, thanks to his bad eyesight, his hands doing some of the work for him. She is more beautiful than he first imagined. Her gaze is forward-bound. She sees into the future with the grace of a seasoned sailor, unflinching, respectful of what lies ahead, a faint and wry grin gracing her solid features. He studies this seaborne treasure, pressing his palms against her ocean-cured wood, marveling at what fine condition she is in. Her rainbow skirts are dusted with barnacles. He decides they are diamonds sewn by the sea. He doesn't admit that this observation reveals him to be a man with a tendency to the poetic. He simply thinks, I'm going to take good care of you.

"I promise," he whispers, and I cannot help but believe that he is treating this figurehead—this inanimate gift from the sea—the way he wants to treat his baby girl but can't quite bring himself to. *I'm going to take good care of you. I promise.* He is speaking to his shoe-box baby. I know it. The sky knows it. All those countless grains of sand know it. He's the only one who is clueless.

He sits on the sand beside his worm-holed and water-beaten find, stunned by his good fortune, watching the ocean (all he truly sees is a wash of rhythmic color), mulling over the pattern implicit in God's mystery. The birth—however grotesque—of his first child. The covenant-sealing rainbow. His close call with drowning. The providential figurehead with a skirt of many colors.

And then it comes to him: The Greek goddess of the rainbow. Iris. Of course!

"Iris," he says. It rolls off the tongue with little effort, even a tongue swollen by seawater. A properly feminine name, without extraneous flourish. Distilled to a fair essence. Air. Iris.

So this is how my great-grandmother came to be known as Iris Harp, named by my great-great-grandfather, a man so full of his own importance that he named his baby girl before speaking to her mother. Indeed, before ever laying eyes on the child herself.

And in a fit of saccharin charm, he decides to name the island in honor of this day and his hours-old shoe-box baby. Iris Haven. It is a name that will stick, that will come to be printed on maps and deeds and birth certificates long after Oster Harp leaves this land.

The wind blows big and purple. The images of Oster and Iris Haven and my great-great-grandfather's life recede to black, and I am left here in the wind, bemused. Poor old Great-Great-Grandfather Harp must not have known that the rainbow goddess didn't simply spend her days lolling about Mount Olympus, admiring her handiwork. No sirree, Granddaddy! Iris, the rainbow goddess, had one hell of a job: She received the souls of dying women.

Did Oster Harp commit a metaphysical blunder when he named his baby and this island in honor of Iris? Did his ignorant foray into the world of nomenclature curse this place? Is that why we keep dying out here, again and again, so young? Did his gesture create a hole in the universal scrim, causing us to be called forward into the rainbow's portal, received perhaps by the likes of Iris herself?

As I boil forward, my spirit wobbly but not without hope, I want to know. And to stay safe—I do not understand what is happening in these early moments—I will practice my own form of nomenclature voodoo, whispering into this infinite dark space the names of those who have come before me. Orchid, Mother, Katrina, Blossom. Orchid, Mother, Katrina, Blossom. Orchid, Mother, Katrina, Blossom. Orchid, Mother, Katrina, Blossom. Oh, how this wind blows!

Billy Speare

You know, sometimes it doesn't matter how hard you've fucked up in life, because once in a blue moon the big guy in the sky sneezes, a big-assed atchoo, and just like that, all the planets spin sweetly into alignment. The ex-wife, the alimony, the daughter who has disowned your soul—all of it bleeds to white in the glaring, awesome light of one fine day.

July 14, 2001.

Memorize that. Write it down. Scrawl it across the sky. Tattoo it on your ass.

There I sat, at the picnic table outside my fish-camp trailer—the mercury already pegged on 90, and it wasn't yet 9:00 A.M.—drinking coffee with a bourbon back, sucking my first cig of the day, terrified at what lay before me: the *New York Times Book Review*. I never read reviews of my own work. And my agent is under strict orders never to mention them to me. Why would I care what a pissant wanna-be thinks? But the agent broke our rule and left a message on my voice mail.

"Read it, Speare," she said. "Just get the hell over yourself and read it." I swear to God, I bet the woman smokes unfiltered Camels.

And Christ, I was doing it. I was following orders and letting yet another woman fuck up my day. *The Sex Life of Me* was my fourth novel, my best, and it damned well needed to do well. I flipped through to page 16, squinting my eyes against the cigarette smoke, my hands shaking with the premonition that I was gonna get creamed.

Hmpf. Not bad placement, above the fold, a pen-and-ink drawing that I guess was supposed to be my protagonist, Jake Harris. I clutched the paper tightly, ready to ball up the motherfucker and hurl it—all I needed was the first sign, a clause that hinted, *Okay, here it comes, an unkind or stupid shot.* My lips moved with the words, but my voice was soft; dread had it punched full of holes.

"Mr. William S. Speare's genius is that he sees into the hearts and minds of even the lowliest human souls and illuminates for the reader their dark, lonely, wretched lives. *The Sex Life of Me* is a tour de force. We should be grateful that a writer of Mr. Speare's ilk walks among us, for all of humanity benefits from his abundant talent."

Shit. I took a shot of bourbon and gritted my teeth. Fucking bastard nailed me.

I reread the review, searching for the obligatory sentence that would indicate I hadn't done this or that up to snuff. But there was no snuff. It was a goddamned rave. Everything revved: my heart rate, my breath, the speed at which I downed my shot of Wild Turkey. My brain dropped to the floor and did twenty sit-ups. I had to call my editor, then my agent, had to let my ex-wife know. Even she, after ten years of alimony battles, might be happy for me. But first, I walked down to the river, still shaking, and took a good long piss, batting back tears, breathing in deep the scent of the rich river muck, knowing that nobody could fuck with me now.

This was it. The big break. What had to happen. In the July 14, 2001, issue of the *New York Times Book Review,* Dr. Gordon Laughton, a professor of English literature at Duke, pinned the *g* word to me. It was about fucking time. It had taken ten jerk-off years and tons of blood spilled on the page before some hack reviewer found the balls to cough up the proper noun. But, hey, who's bitching? At least it finally happened.

Later that day—after a dozen jubilant phone conversations and one argument (my ex told me I could kiss her ass and that, no, my daughter did not want to talk to me)—I took my boat downriver to check my crab traps. A small pod of dolphins— four of them, I think—cruised on by, and I noticed a skiff up ahead, bobbing real gentle like, and rising from it a set of legs crossed like silk against that hot blue sky. It was right then, let me tell you, that July 14, 2001, took me by the ears and screamed, *Hey, asshole, your good luck? It's not over yet!*

She was a wisp: fifty pounds of blue eyes, the rest all sass and twat. She'd anchored just to the right of the channel. She lay back against a pink polka-dotted cushion and, with her eyes closed, sang along at the top of her lungs to Gillian Welch. She was begging for someone to burn her stillhouse down. She was tanned and freckled and had on a swimsuit small enough to fit a sparrow.

I slowed my motor to an idle, just sat there staring at her. She stopped midnote, opened them big blues, looked at me bow to stern, and asked without rancor, "What the fuck are you looking at?"

"Well, that's a good question," I said, taking off my ball

cap and wiping the side of my face with my forearm. I repositioned the cap, settling it back on my head with a wiggle of the
brim. "If I were an honest man, I guess I'd have to say I'm gazing at about the prettiest little thing I ever did see."

"Is that right?" She sat up on her elbows, shaded her eyes.
As she studied me, a bemused smirk lightened her features,
solid features that—I surmised—had only just begun to sug-
gest a life hard-lived. "So, are you?"

"Am I what?"

"An honest man?"

I cleared my throat. My balls tightened. A line of sweat
eased down my cheekbone. "Hell yeah," I said. "The most
honest you've ever met."

She laughed, deep and throaty. Oak-rich. Tobacco-cured.
"Wanna beer?" she asked, but her flat tone and stubborn jaw
suggested she was challenging me, testing to see if I'd say yes,
and not to a woman I'd just met, but to the possibilities that
churned dreamlike in the air between us.

I smacked a mosquito off my forearm. She smelled like
tangerines. I tried not to, but I couldn't help it: My lips curled
into a smart-assed grin. "Your skiff or mine?"

She tossed me a Bud. "Stay where you're at and we'll do
just fine."

That's it. That's how our love affair began. In the middle
of the Matanzas River—the tide rising—she and I in separate
boats.

Oh yeah. Listen to me, Jesus. Let me say this again: July 14,
2001, was the finest fucking day of my life.

Edith Piaf

Zachary broke the news. I mean, he tried. But I was too fast. I saw the ghost before he did. *C'est vrai.*

I was doing my nails, enjoying the quiet cool morn that placidly welcomed in the New Year. Oui. January 1, 2002. The world was coming apart—war and plagues and the ranks of the have-nots were growing ever larger, ever more voiceless. But what did I care? I owned my very own piece of paradise, an old rambling beach house situated on a whisper-thin rise of undiscovered land, a refuge that seemed so far, far away from that other world. The real world. And what greater thing to do at the dawn of this New Year, before the guests arrived for hoppin' John and honey-glazed ham and champagne, but put a fresh coat of lacquer on my nails?

Holding the applicator just so, working on my index finger of my left hand, feeling pious and whole and lucky to be a woman at the dawn of yet another renewal of life's circle, I and all of Iris Haven were jolted by the wail of sirens. I looked up, at first confused by the piercing noise. What on earth? And then came the rustling, the sound of great wings, sudden and reluctant, frenzied and violent. Out of the corner of my eye, by the door, I saw the white bird. It had entered my house. I had not given it permission. This was a very bad sign. *Whoosh. Whoosh. Whoosh.* Wings tolling death. Chiming death. Announcing death. *Whoosh. Whoosh. Whoosh.*

I dropped the lilac polish. The bottle spun across my tile floor but did not break, coming to rest against the lion's paw of my piano stool. I did not dress. There was no time. Out into the cold morning, barefoot, clothed only in my robe, the door slamming behind me, I ran down the south path, through the brambles and sticker burrs, over the dunes, toward Dr. Z's dock.

The sirens and wings. What a horrible jumble. And soon added to that would be the heart-shattering song of human wailing.

As I drew near, I saw that Iris Haven on New Year's Day had been transformed into *la scène tragique*. Police, fire, ambulances. The chaos! The stupidity! There was no fire. And why two ambulances? Two. There was only one body. This came to me. One body. Not two. *Pourquoi deux?*

The whooshing of the wings forced me to cry out. I saw Z, his face stricken as he stood huddled with police officers, talking intently, like he knew something. *Oui.* He knew something huge. I flew past Lucinda's house. I saw her at her French doors, staring out, her eyes big and worried. She knew, too, but not the way I knew. Not like all of a sudden the blood inside your cells begins to vomit. And your head splits wide open in grief and disbelief. You don't know the details. Those will come later. But you do know this: Murmur. Murmur. My sweet child Murmur. I broke into a pell-mell run, cutting my bare feet on the oyster shells.

Zachary yelled, "Edith, no! Don't go down there." He started toward me, tried to head me off, but he didn't stand a chance. I hurled myself down to the river, along the dock. The bird ferried me.

There the men worked. At the dock's end. Divers yelling and EMTs scrambling and detectives with cell phones making horrid calls to horrid places about a horrid event. All on New Year's Day. They were hoisting her out of the water, bringing her into the clear, waterless air. Please, no! Murmur, Murmur. A strand of seaweed curled across her forehead, as if placed there by a careful God.

"Murmur!" I heard myself scream. My voice echoed off the water, the sky. It rearranged the wind. "Murmur!"

Her blue eyes were open. Oh God, no, not that. She was watching her own death.

"Murmur!" I made the wind shudder. But I could not bring her back.

_H_ere I sit on my beloved porch, gazing out at the haunted landscape, the real *oiseau chanteuse* spinning away on my hi-fi (I can't bear to listen to Edith on anything other than a record player), and I keep trying to scrape away my grief. Obliterate it. Shoo, shoo, grief, shoo! But it remains stalwart, an ugly, terrifying thing—a bone eater. I stare, gaunt-eyed, at the empty horizon, wondering again and again, *Pourquoi la mort? Pourquoi? Pourquoi Murmur?*

S he was the only one who came to see me in those drug-hazed days postsurgery. Charlee was gone, trying to find God in Boston, of all places. And what's her name? That little cuntress who was terrified of me? I tended to forget her name, just to mess with her. Oh, yes, Lucinda the Nameless. I really should have been kinder to her when she first moved here. The poor dear, I was the first transsexual she'd ever met. But whatever, no, she never stopped by. Not once. So I am free to say it loud and proud: cuntress, cuntress, cuntress! Now, it's true that Dr. Z visited. But it was, by nature of his training, a necessary act. So he doesn't count in this particular litany of who did me wrong.

The operation was performed in Canada. Actually, in an attempt to be *précis*, I should say operations. *Oui.* At the opulent age of sixty-two, I had my nose straightened, narrowed, and a hint of an upward curve sculpted at the tip, à la Michelle Pfeiffer. At the same time, I received my breast implants; I tend to think of this phase of my transformation as akin to being crowned. *Joie!* I am forever grateful to be free of that tedious ritual drag queens and adolescent girls refer to as "bra stuffing." I do pine, however, for a term other than *breast implants.* It sounds so, so—I don't know. Agricultural. We need a feminine word. Say *fleuraison.*

Anyway, on that very same day, January 3, 1999, my penis was—how shall I say? Amputated. Cut off. Whacked. Penile-ectomized. Surgically removed. Chop chop. Well, a portion of it. The surgeon left enough of the old guy hanging that he was able to fashion from it my new sex organ. *Oui, oui! C'est vrai!* The surviving cock was inverted, tucked, trimmed, and turned into a functioning vagina. A less-than-orgasmic but perfectly adequate cul-de-sac, if you will. Ten hours on the table and—voilà!—a whole new me. The real me. The one who had wandered for six anonymous, soul-wrecking decades inside a stranger's skin. *Je suis femme.* Hear me roar.

Friends who knew me preop urged me to drag out the change (aren't puns delicious!). But I refused, and I have never regretted the decision to cut, cut, snip, snip, plump, plump in one fell swoop. For starters, *I am* a former marine. And once a member of the Corps, always a member of the Corps. We are nothing if not tough. *Semper fi,* motherfucker, and all that.

But really, teasing aside, my time in the Corps helped prepare me for my journey into womanhood. When I, Gunnery Sgt. James MacHenry, stared through the scope of my M2 .50-caliber machine gun and engaged the enemy—*one shot one kill one shot one kill one shot one kill*—and my subconscious tried to rip into my real world the way the 700-grain bullet was ripping into the enemy who was dropping to the ground—poof!—barely a human at all, ever, just a target whose ability to inflict damage on us was now neutralized, I disappeared into a truth every marine knows: Pain is weakness leaving the body. So is death. And when my metamorphosis—thanks to the surgeon's scalpel—was complete, when I'd journeyed from redneck Palatka wuss to USMC sniper, to Edith Piaf the drag queen, to the penultimate woman I now am, the same truth saw me through the psychological and physical minefield. Pain is weakness leaving the body. You bet, motherfucker.

But back to me compressing my transformation into the span of one single stint on the table: Let us not overlook the catch-22 we call time. As a species, we may be living longer, but individually we can't count on it. *Immortalité? Non!* Look at Mur. She didn't live to see a hot flash. I have forever been blessed with a keen sense of the old mortality clock. And I would have gotten my sex change when I was twenty had it been available and affordable. Alas, drag queens don't, as a general rule, make big bucks. Especially aging drag queens. It was left to my dear estranged *papa*—a man who was so ashamed of me that he denied my existence to both friends and strangers, a prideful old fool who refused to speak to me for the last thirty years of his life—to come up with the bucks to pay for my transformation. He may have hated what I was, but he still had enough sense of family to leave me his dough. *Par conséquent,* having served my prerequisite sentence of two years in counseling and one living as a woman, I wanted all of me to exist. Without delay. *Tout de suite.* AARP, incisions, morphine drips, catheters inserted into brand-new orifices, probing latexed fingers: All of it be damned!

So, *oui,* at first friends of many ilk abandoned me. I understood. Indeed, I anticipated such behavior. Never have I felt that I deserved to be accepted. My God, we still hate one another over such mundane matters as class and race and religion. Please! The fact that I chose to live my life as a woman—no, that's incorrect, for the feminine gender chose me (my right to flourish as a female was ripped from my embryonic fingers through a laughable accident of one kinked curl of the double helix)—and that my psychological, primordial self was so immersed in my inner goddess that I was compelled to have my dick whacked off and a vagina constructed does not in any way imply that I can operate outside the bounds of normal human cattiness, meanness, and strife.

Did it hurt my feelings when not a single resident of Iris Haven, save Mur, came to visit me during my convalescence? *Bien entendu.* Granted, we have only three full-timers out here, four if you count the nameless painter, but still. And how do you account for the fact that no one from St. Augustine except for my great-aunt sent me so much as a card? It's simple: People tend to be heartless, cruel, and profoundly stupid when it comes to something as basic as a sex change. Was I surprised, embittered, angry? Not really. *Non.* I've lived too long snapped up in the amused, disgusted, and outraged glances of strangers to let my friends get to me.

So, for a few weeks in the unusually warm winter of 1999, I spent my days and nights cocooned in fresh ocean breezes, in my four-poster bed, which I had moved into the living room before I left for Canada, surrounded by pillows and lace that smelled of lavender and patchouli, my windows flung open, Edith spinning round and round on my old phonograph, her chestnut voice wafting like the scent of sex over all of Iris Haven.

Dr. Z would stop by on his way back from visiting the migrants in Elkton, Corona, Hastings. We'd sip sherry and he'd show me the strange assortment of treasures he had collected that day on his journeys through northeast rural Florida (Dr. Z is a pack rat extraordinaire; there is barely a pop top along his route that escapes his notice), and then—as circumstances would permit (meaning the alcohol gave us permission)—he would inspect my newly minted breasts and baby vagina. He'd make animal noises, as though he were a squirrel happily secreting away nuts for the winter. He'd mumble, "Wonderful, wonderful! Hmm? How did they do that? Oh, I see! What a marvel!"

I never wanted to know what he learned from inspecting my new privates. I was happy simply contributing to his education. And I didn't want to know the nitty-gritty medical details. To be a woman was enough. And the fact that I fed his infinite curiosity helped to heal me. By exposing my wounds, I was nurturing the good doctor. You see, it's a maternal thing. I'm bursting with motherly impulses. Just call me *la mère nature.*

Every evening at dusk, just before sunset, as Dr. Z and I debated whether or not I was truly a woman, given that my DNA suggested otherwise (he can be such a hardheaded bore, really), Mur would arrive, indigo skirts flowing, her arms full of groceries, clucking away about what she planned to cook.

Dr. Z and I so welcomed her presence. I craved the food and friendship. Z needed that and safe shelter. The poor man never wanted to wander home. And who could blame him? His wife had passed away of breast cancer three months earlier. I do believe he held himself responsible. Guilt at not knowing his wife was ill until the disease was too advanced to save her changed Dr. Z *profondément.* Short of stature to begin with, he grew even smaller under the titanic weight of guilt and grief. His pants had to be hemmed. Mur shortened every single pair he owned. And though he continued his antics (plastic vomit left on the bedsheet of a patient, a fuzzy fake spider slipped into the twilight darkness of my purse, a dreadlock wig artfully plopped on his head when he visited the black potato pickers in Spuds), he did not fool me. I glimpsed into his dark Jewish eyes and knew going home meant facing empty rooms that clanked with memories too bittersweet to sip. How awful for him: *avoir le coeur gros!*

But let me return to those postop evenings. Mur's specialty was soup. From my throne of pillows and lace, as she rifled through her willow basket, which brimmed with spices and potions, I would ask, "*Quelle est la soupe du jour?*"

And sometimes she answered me quite frankly. Minorcan chowder. Bouillabaisse. Roasted tomato with basil. But very often she would squint her tiny nose and say, "We'll just have to see what happens."

My point is, she fed us the most marvelous bisques and chowders and even consommé, which I had never enjoyed until I ate hers. Her soups were magic. She dusted them with secret spices, ground by her own hand, and as we slurped away—their essence easing down our gullets—a sense of well-being bloomed in each of us, and even the candlelight seemed to twinkle with uncommon ease.

Dr. Z always brought crusty brown bread that he purchased from a Latvian widow who picked potatoes for a living in Elkton. We slathered thick slices with real butter—never margarine and never guilty—and washed everything down with *champagne et vin rouge*. Dr. Z monitored my alcohol intake, since I am forever smitten with even the mildest forms of pain medication.

After dinner, as we happily digested and sipped our aperitif, we would listen to Mur read with a full measure of emotion and grace a García Lorca poem. Yes, Federico García Lorca. Mur was nothing if not multifaceted. This child of the lost Florida, the Florida of swamps and piney woods and cypress hammocks, had somewhere during her thirty-plus years run across a copy of *The Selected Poems of Federico García Lorca* (in translation, of course—why couldn't she have fallen for Baudelaire?). And she claimed that not a day went by when she did not read at least one of his poems aloud. "To the stars and bobcats," she'd say.

Let me set the stage. My living room would be afloat in candlelight, the flames twisting and twirling in the reflection of my crystal goblets. Edith, whom I had spent a career imitating in drag clubs across the country, continued her perpetual spin on the hi-fi, her voice seeming to rise out of the blood of angels. I am partial to French lace—I have arranged it *précis* throughout my house, with the utmost care taken to ensure its placement appears to be merely the inevitable afterthought of a fine mind. Shawls, runners, curtains (not one doily—I'm not a puss) added texture and depth to everything we did.

Imagine how gorgeous the night: the wind blowing in off the Atlantic, candlelight shimmying in the crystal breeze, and my beloved French lace all aflutter, like a sweet young street whore grown suddenly shy yet coy.

And then there was me, stretched out in my four-poster, a lace shawl situated just so around my thin shoulders, ensconced in lavender and patchouli, my tender (dare I say *jeune?*) breasts and vagina drugged into a comfortable haze as I listened to Mur read a type of poetry (one that was drunk on images and romantic notions of Man and the inevitable sadness spawned from such romanticism) that Dr. Z hated. Or at least he pretended to hate for the sake of argument. And there was nothing Dr. Z loved more than arguing.

Mur would clear her throat, hold the book aloft, and say, "Now, if the real Edith will excuse the interruption, I'd like to read a poem." She'd jab her head in the direction of the phonograph, which sent Dr. Z rising and huffing up from the white wicker chair that he favored and then striding across the room to the phonograph, which he never turned off—*that* was not allowed—but he did fiddle with the volume. He would return to the chair and gaze eastward, across *la mer Noire*, which would be invisible to us if the moon was new. Her eyes shining, lit as they were by a mischievous but fair soul, Mur would begin to read.

If she paused to admire a phrase or line, Dr. Z would fidget in his chair and mutter, "Crap!"

"Zachary Klein, I swear to sweet Jesus, you are the most frustrating man I have ever come across." Mur would say this without looking up from her book.

"But it's crap. He's personifying a lizard!"

"Just because you graduated from Harvard doesn't mean you can use fifty-dollar words with me or that I'll be at all impressed."

And she would continue, reading to us about, for instance, a lizard whose eyes resembled those of a "broken artist."

I would sneak a glance at Zach and discern a faint warming of his features. Those pouty lips would relax, elongate, approach a smile. A flesh-colored lizard right there on his face. He might even close his eyes. But once Mur had read the poem's closing line and we were all left to contemplate the images—an empty field, or a cuckoo that sings only intermittently, unable to break the darkness—the dear doctor would say something foolish, such as: "Well, he's certainly no Shakespeare."

To which Mur would respond, "And you're no brain surgeon."

Thus it went night after night, always a different poem, for a good four or five weeks. And always there was this: a generosity of spirit that transcended breaking bread together. *Oui*, there was my willingness to allow Dr. Z a studious glimpse at my new sex, and Mur's selfless brewing of magic soups, and our sometimes crabby indulgence regarding the nightly poetry readings. But what clings to my heart's memory, above all else, is Mur's tender insistence—even when I cried that I was too exhausted or too frightened or too sore—that I use my dilator before sleep.

Dr. Z would have disappeared into the night, ready to face his empty house, which was just a bit farther than a stone's throw away, fortified by drink and magic soup and friendship. Mur would have washed the dishes and wiped down the kitchen, and then she would come sit beside me on the bed, take my hand in hers, and say, "Edith, it's time. Just once more today and you're done."

"Please, let it go until tomorrow." I would wave her away with my free hand, which held a lace hankie.

"You cannot let it close up on you, Edith."

"I am simply too weak."

"No, you're not. What you are is stubborn. You know you have to do this." She'd fuss with my sheets and comforter. She'd reposition and fluff my pillows. Her dangling silver earrings would sparkle in the candlelight. "You know I'm right."

I would sniffle and dab tears with my hankie. "*Merci, mon amie*. But I am so tired. *Très fatiguée*."

"Edith!" Her strained patience would claw at each letter of my name.

That was my cue. I played the tragic waif, sighing, silently nodding my assent, blatantly ignoring another marine creed that I held dear: Pain is temporary; pride is forever.

Mur would float across the room, first pausing to turn up Edith's volume, then disappearing into the kitchen, where she would retrieve the hard white plastic dilator from the dish drainer. She kept it sparkling clean for me. With the serene confidence of a field commander, she would return to my bedside, plant the dilator firmly in my hand, and say, "I'll be out on the porch. Call me when you're finished." Then she'd pause, rummage in her deep skirt pocket, and pull out a square of fabric—almost always raw silk, sometimes linen—that she'd dyed herself, using plants she cultivated across the island. "Place this against your throat; just let it rest there. It will take you to where you need to be." And out the door she'd go.

This act—one might even say indignity—was the final medically necessitated task that separated my old self from my new. I was fleeing fast from any connection to my Palatka

childhood, which was spent—at my father's insistence—
killing quail and rabbit. He would have, by his own hand, mur-
dered me if he had known about those long nights I spent
hidden in my closet, guided by the beam of my flashlight,
pouring over the pages of my sister's fashion zines. And, yes,
fleeing—I hoped—from whatever sin and redemption, dis-
honor and glory Gunnery Sergeant MacHenry might have
brought upon his head as he served his country with distinc-
tion. What a long journey it had been! And now, when I was
nearly too old to enjoy the wonder of it, I was participating in
the last step in my quest to become a whole woman. My
friend, my dear Mur, would sit on the porch, smoking cigarettes, giving me my privacy and her acceptance. And I would
begin. With a magic square of fabric floating on my throat,
carefully, tentatively, I would insert the dilator into my new
vagina. Each time, I concentrated not on the act but on
Edith—Edith Piaf and her voice that swallowed the night—
allowing my suffering to swirl like incense along the winding
altar of her voice.

"Des yeux qui font baiser les miens . . ."

Lucinda Smith

Fuck! What do you want me to say? That I saw it all? That I watched the vultures gather as they brought Murmur's corpse out of the river? That I noticed how oddly masculine Edith the Sex Change looked as she barreled down the dock? That I smoked five cigarettes as I stood at my French doors and watched Dr. Z preen all official, even though I knew his fucking heart was breaking. Well, no. I won't talk about it. It's nobody's business. My pain is off-limits.

Dr. Zachary Klein

Two women. Two loves. Two deaths.

I'm a Jew. And an atheist. Where does that leave me? Whom do I dump my sorrow on? Whom do I blame?

Doctors are supposed to be healers. That's medical school lie number one. What we are, are dispensers of hokum churned out by pharmaceutical companies for the benefit of stockholders. Sometimes we ease pain. More often than not, though, we dispense a pill or pump a vein full of morphine. Unfortunately, the pain and illness still wreak havoc. All we've done is rendered the poor sick bastard incapable of caring.

Sure, sometimes we get lucky. But if death insists on its due, we're simply handmaidens.

No, I didn't cause Katrina's death. But I sure was impotent in the face of disease.

And sweet Murmur Lee? I was impotent all right, in ways great and small.

Murmur Lee Harp Sees a Moment in the Life of Her Mother, Lily Cordelia Harp

The wind has scattered me across this infinite darkness. If humans had animal eyes, they would see me, phosphorescent, a wild-flung smattering of glitter. They wouldn't give me a second thought.

Here, in this void, I witness my mother, Lily Cordelia Harp, at the moment of her greatest pain. It's not anything I want to see, but the vision insists on its due; the past is saying, *Murmur Lee, you gotta know.*

She is newlywed—pushing nineteen, looking fourteen—fresh as hyssop on a summer's day. She stands in her yellow kitchen, at the supper table, folding laundry that smells of the new sun and the old sea. Her hair is swept into a golden ponytail and her midriff top fits her snug and sweet. My mother is a pretty woman. She is petite, like me, with blue eyes—Oster Harp eyes—but I don't have golden hair. I wish I did. I want her hair. The kitchen door is open. The midmorning light spills in. She must not have closed it after bringing in the laundry off the line. Towels, washcloths, white T-shirts—my father's T-shirts. She hums. I don't know the tune. But I see the shadow at the kitchen door and I am afraid. She is not. She is unaware.

A man walks into the kitchen, just strides right on in as if he owns the place. He is ordinary-looking: brunette, crew cut, jeans and a plaid shirt. There is nothing emblazoned on his forehead that shouts, *Run, bitch, because I'm a dangerous motherfucker.*

And still, Mother is oblivious. She is loving her wifely duty, just folding those clothes and humming and pushing a fallen curl back off her forehead. He is a tall man, with long, long arms. He reaches out with one long, long arm and grabs her shoulder.

My mother screams, clutches my father's T-shirt to her chest. The man spins her around and smiles. He *smiles.* "You're what I want."

"No! No!" My mother says this quietly, as if she is praying. It doesn't do a bit of good. That man takes my mother. He hurls—yes, hurls—her onto the supper table, takes a knife out of his pocket, rips her shorts from the waist to the knee. "Bitch. Yes. I'm taking it all, you little bitch."

My mother stops praying the "No! No!" prayer and unleashes a wail that should make the sea retreat. But nothing retreats. The world outside goes about its business, as if there is not a crime against all creation taking place. To muffle her wail, he rips my father's T-shirt from her tiny hands and stuffs it in her mouth, stuffs it so hard and deep, I hear her gag and I see the edges of her lips rip.

When he is done, he takes that knife and cuts my mother. He cuts a shallow crescent at the top swell of her left breast. Her blood bubbles up like a string of garnets. "Don't forget this."

That's what he says. And then he strides out of our house—saunters, really—leaving my mother to cry the hollow ballad of women who long for death.

*H*ere I am, sand-scattered and glinting, lost, hating the pain that omniscient knowledge breeds.

William S. Speare

Two days after we met, Murmur Lee stopped by the trailer unexpectedly. She stood on my stoop in her tight jeans and tight tee, batting those sapphire blues, balancing a willow basket on the whispering curve of her hip.

"Hey," she said. "I'm sorry to disturb you, but I think you're in need of some soup. Your chakras are under siege."

"My chakras are under siege? Good God, girl, what in the hell are you talking about?"

She claimed I knew what she was talking about, and she bustled on in and set me a place at my own supper table and served me up homemade who-the-hell-knows-what's-in-it soup. She sprinkled some kind of powder that she claimed she ground from the root of a plant she discovered in the hammock.

Before dipping the spoon in the bowl and bringing it to my lips, I asked, "Are you some sort of a witch?"

She reached over and touched my hair. She gazed at me—steady and confident—and said, "No. I'm simply a good woman."

Sainthood:
Murmur Lee Harp Reveals the
Zenith of Her Childhood

L et's move past the movies the universal jester keeps running before my eyes. I want to ruminate on my own memories, not on tragedies and triumphs that happened before I was born.

Me alone in our kitchen. My cotton night shift damp with sweat. The polished wood floor cool beneath my bare feet. The light spilling in through the kitchen door—the locked kitchen door; oh yes, all our doors stay locked, and now I know why; now I know why Mother slapped my behind whenever I left the door open—and the softer light filtering through the pale yellow curtains that waft like ghosts, fluttering about the window above the sink.

Everything was as it should be. The house was quiet. Father was gone. Mother was attending to something—praying somewhere. That's what Mother did. She prayed. But she also always left the makings for breakfast at the kitchen table: a box of Lucky Charms, a white bowl with a red-checkered rim, a soup spoon, a jelly glass, and two clear pitchers—milk and orange juice.

I poured the cereal into the bowl and used two hands to add the milk. I spilled a bunch of it on the table but didn't wipe it up. Mother would clean up after me. She always did. I ate fast. I liked my cereal crunchy. When I finished, I wiped my mouth with the back of my arm—something Mother would have flown all over me for. Then I clutched my juice glass with both hands and gulped, gulped, gulped. Ladylike was not a description ever applied to me—not by parents or boyfriends, and certainly not by my husband.

Anyway, as I downed the orange juice, I thought of my ladybugs. They were orange, too, only a deeper color, and sprinkled with tiny black dots. I had spent the day before searching the vines of the confederate jasmine that sprawled and twined across our weather-worn fence, collecting the insects, dropping them into a jelly jar, talking to the tiny creatures as if they were my best friends. Mother said ladybugs were good luck. I needed good luck. Every little girl did. So I set down my juice glass and pushed my chair away from the table. I ran outside—spring was just beginning to tendril its scent into the briny air—and uncovered the jar from its secret hiding place beneath the brown crackle of fallen magnolia leaves.

"Hello, little ladybugs. How are you today?" I brought the jar close to my face and waved my stubby fingers against the glass. Here's how I know I was never a bad child, that early on I cared about the lives of unseen beings: Guilt began to natter away at my high spirits. How sad for these bugs to be trapped in a jar! But how else could I watch them? How else could they be my friends? I wanted to carry them with me everywhere I went. Even into Mr. Posey's store. But was it fair to them? And there were so many difficulties. How would I feed them? What did they eat? And if they went to the bathroom, wouldn't they mess on one another? There was no room to fly, not in this jar. Why hadn't I thought of this yesterday? Why was I so bent on collecting every single bug I saw? I sighed, rubbed my nose, fretted over what to do. There was little choice; I would have to set the ladybugs free. First, I would empty them into my hands and let them wander through my soft arm hairs—wander, wander, wander, anywhere they wanted. Some might even dance across my face. I would be magic. Blessed. Fairylike. The world—and maybe even the God that Mother was praying to right at that moment—would be pleased. And after I was covered in ladybug dots, I would whisper, "Fly, fly away." And they would, spreading my good luck on the breeze and into the secret throats of flowers.

That was my fantasy, my intent. But as I stared into the jar, it dawned on me that the ladybugs had not flittered at all. Not one wing. Not a single beat. My good-luck friends appeared to be little more than hard orange beads, curled and still and piled like dust. I shook the jar. Their bodies hissed. *Sh, sh, sh.* "No! Wake up!"

But, of course, they didn't. I had killed them. I had killed every single one. The spring sun tumbled from its blue perch. My heart lurched like a skimmed stone. I dropped the death jar into the brown leaves. With tears streaming, I hurled myself back into the house, searching for my mother. "Mama! Mama!"

I found her on her knees in her bedroom, wearing that yellow dress—the dress I loved so much, the one I would slip on over my clothes when she wasn't home and play grown-up in—praying the rosary aloud. She was so pretty in that yellow dress with the white bow positioned at the waist, an exclamation mark dotting the thin curve of her backbone. "Mama!"

She opened her eyes. They were vacant. In time, I would come to recognize that hollow stare as a signal of faith. Despite the interruption, her fingers continued to travel the rosary, insistently, stubbornly conjuring the ancient prayer. *Hail Mary, full of grace.* "What? What is it, Murmur Lee?" Her voice was soft, pillowy. I wanted to crawl inside it.

"I killed them!"

"Killed what?"

"My ladybugs." By now, snot was running down my face and I couldn't breathe well because tears had tied my throat in knots.

"Oh, really, Murmur Lee." She shook her head and her face bobbled as if she were being pulled between prayerful contemplation and irritation. "They're just insects. They die every day. Don't you know that?"

I nodded yes, but my crying escalated. What was she trying to say? Why was she so calm in the face of death? And what had become of my good luck? Wouldn't God smite me for killing his most innocent of creatures?

"Go on now. Go wash your face. I'll be with you in a little while. We'll finger-paint or something." She turned away, back toward God.

I stumbled out of her bedroom, heaving my grief into the air and down my face. I was five years old, and for the first time in my life, I feared the stranger she was praying to.

*A*nother first. Two weeks after the jar incident and three weeks after my fifth birthday. My mother had joined the choir at the cathedral in St. Augustine. She had to go to rehearsal. She just had to. And Mrs. Ringhoffer, the widow who lived in the old lodge, couldn't baby-sit that day. I don't know why. I think maybe she was sick. And there was no one home at Charlee's. So I had to go to town with Mother. I had to sit in the pew and listen to the music and look at the pretty stained-glass windows of Jesus and all the saints. And I had to keep from making a sound. Not one peep.

Ladymass. That's what they called it. A special program to celebrate Mother's Day, and, of course, to honor Mary. Only the women would sing. Of course, of course. "Don't make any noise, Murmur Lee. Just sit here and say some prayers and listen to the pretty music. Be a good girl. Mama's going to be right up there in the loft. I'll be watching you."

I'm not sure if it was her tone of voice or her vacant stare or the way she kept glancing up at the loft as if she couldn't wait to get away from me, but I knew then—even in my five-year-old heart—that Mother loved Christ more than she loved me. So I tried to look her straight in the eye, tried to keep my face steady, tried to fight my urge to throw myself into her arms and beg her to love me. I said, "Yes, ma'am" over and over. Yes, it's true: I was desperate to please her, desperate to push Christ into playing my role, that of second fiddle.

But I don't believe my good behavior swayed my mother in any way. She fingered the strand of pearls around her neck. "We'll go for ice cream afterward," she said, nodding thoughtfully, as if the promise of something sweet would seal our deal.

"Okay, Mama."

She smiled briefly—barely at all—and then, with her lime green pocket book hooked on her arm as if it, too, were an appendage, she turned on the soles of her lime flats, which matched her lime dress—all in all, she reminded me of a lime wedge perched on the lip of a water glass filled with pink lemonade—and trudged through the shadows and into the bowels of the church.

So there I sat, alone, a small fink of a child amid Christ and crosses and saints, flickering in the illuminated glow cast by the stained-glass windows—and I tried to do as Mother wished. First, I would pray. I dropped to my knees. The cold leather of the kneeling bench pinched my sunburned skin. I re-arranged the folds of my cotton skirt so there was more padding between me and the leather. Then, feeling as pious as any five-year-old possibly can, I crossed myself, clasped my hands, and started the only way I knew how. *Our Father, who art in heaven.* I asked for forgiveness for all my sins—I wasn't spe-cific—God knew about my transgressions even before I had committed them. Then I asked him to bless my parents and the dolphins and the birds and the lizards and the butterflies and my best friend, Charlee. I went on like that for a while, asking God to bless about every little thing that crawled, walked, flew, or swam.

But somewhere along the way, my mind drifted. Pleas for holy intercession died a natural death as I found myself staring—fascinated and appalled—at the gigantic broken body of Christ that floated in the air above and behind the al-tar. I could never look at a crucifix without thinking about the Easter story, which I hated. I hated that they nailed his hands and feet to the wood. It must have hurt so bad. How could people be so mean? I discreetly rubbed one knee and then the other, chilled by thoughts of an angry mob jeering at our Lord. And then it dawned on me that this particular cross— one that I had seen in Mass on many Sundays past—did not look like a man-made torture device. Not at all. This crucifix was backbone and blood. Something fleshy spun by angels. Maybe Gabriel himself. Yes, that's exactly right, I decided. Those people only thought they nailed him to the cross. But that was a trick God played. The crucifix was actually a pair of wings. Christ wings. He could fly anywhere. And I bet he did. I secreted my hand between my legs—I had to pee—and I thought about Jesus flying over us, gazing down and offering comfort to anyone who felt crummy.

I imagined him zooming over me, his long hair wild on the breeze. He winked, which was his signal that he was well pleased with my behavior. I squirmed and pressed harder at the spot between my legs. Maybe he loved me more than he loved Mother. What would I do then? Mother would never forgive me.

The women broke into song. I jumped, stunned by the sudden sound, and turned toward the loft. Their voices rose in unison—one magnificent hairy dog—unfurling and spinning along a single melody, filling every nook and cranny and spidery shadow. Nothing was left untouched. This was not just music. The ladies were giving voice and form to a full-blown haunting. The sound pierced the rough-hewn beams of the cathedral and seared itself to my bones, causing me to rattle and shake.

There was no being still in the presence of such sound. Their chant swirled through me and about me. My brain felt on fire. I tried to lift my hands to my head, but I was shaking too hard.

And then I left this earth. My body remained bent upon the prayer bench, jerking. But my soul darted upward, spiraled the length of the crucifix, and came to rest in the cold marble cleft of the Savior's chest. All it took was one more swollen refrain and he and I flew. We swept past the women in the choir loft—I waved at Mother, but she did not see me. With the crucifix wings beating hard and sure, we ascended into heaven.

It was there, on that day, at that moment, amid a vacuum of stars, that I first saw the face of God. His eyes, like my mother's when she prayed, flashed with the hollow light of faith, and all of him—his forehead, lids, lips, nose, chin— scintillated beneath a living blanket of ladybugs. My ladybugs. They flourished in his presence. They crawled and flitted and tried their wings, which caused his face to shimmer perpetually, like votive flame. I reached out to him, hoping that one of his holy creatures would light on my arm, thus conveying they had forgiven me for sending them to their deaths in that sealed glass jar. But just as my finger was about to touch his cheekbone, the plainsong ended. And in one silent blink, God and Christ vanished. I tumbled from heaven. My spirit crashed hard onto the pine pew. I peed on myself. And I cried. I floundered in a puddle of tears and piss.

That was vision number one.

Over the next few weeks, the visions piled up, one atop the other, like the dead orange beads in my savage jelly jar. *Sh, sh, sh.*

Mother, who was of the mind that I'd peed and cried simply to embarrass her, barely spoke to me. In fact, immediately after the incident, she didn't bother to contain her rage. The ladies in the loft looked down upon us as Mother made me clean up the puddle with paper towels she had retrieved from the old woman who ran the gift shop. She grabbed me up from the pew by a single arm, which caused me to whimper, although to little effect, and hustled me from the church, into the daylight and our Mustang. Displaying a strength that inspired awe and fright, she shoved me into the backseat and, with shaking hands, removed my soiled skirt and panties. "Honestly, honestly!" she kept spitting.

I wanted to try to explain that nothing that had happened in the church was my fault. But my five-year-old brain could not muster a believable defense. So I crouched, naked from the waist down, behind the driver's seat while my mother sped down A1A toward home, shouting over the sound of the wind, "What is wrong with you? How could you embarrass me in front of the entire choir?"

On an empty stretch of highway between Crescent Beach and Iris Haven, she tossed my soiled clothes out the window. I watched the way they flew—ripplelike—in the clutches of the wind and I wondered where they would land and if some other little girl would one day walk around in my brown cotton skirt and white panties, or if a rattlesnake would come upon them and make a nest.

To make matters worse, one of the choir ladies gave Mother a tape of that blasted rehearsal. She favored one song in particular. I made out the word *Alleluia,* but other than that, it was just sound to me, a sound so enthralling that it made even a five-year-old believe she had a soul.

Mother played it during her morning prayers. She would sing it at random moments throughout the day. Yes, she acquired an immediate obsession with plainsong. I suppose the ancient chant was one more way to express her religious piety. It gave her yet another avenue to avoid me, to escape my father's indifference. And now—in death—I know that this cathedral built from penitent voices and pure song provided an auditory refuge from pain.

But hear this: I don't want to give a false impression; my father was not a mean man. I have no way of knowing how deeply wounded he was by an act of violence exacted upon my mother by a depraved stranger, or how it must have felt to raise the seed of that rape, or the depth of his loss when my mother turned away from him and hid inside the crepe-paper drapery of the Catholic church. All I know is that familial involvement—if it required any effort beyond superficial niceties—was beyond him. I don't think he was really raised, having been a boarding school child from the age of seven. His parents were busy spending their money on European trips and great art. By the time they died in an auto accident on the Taconic in upstate New York—this was years before I was born—they had spent nearly their entire estate. And I guess my father didn't want anything to do with their lifestyle. Or his decent education. Because day after day, hours on end, Clement Harp guided hordes of behatted, sunburned tourists through the dark rooms and astonishing vistas of the old coquina fort, known officially as the Castillo de San Marcos. By the time he traveled the half hour home to Iris Haven, his feet hurt and he was, I believe, fed up with humanity. So he would turn on the TV, drink a few beers, and go to bed. Sometimes I wondered if he knew my name. Or my mother's. Whenever he spoke to her, he called her Mrs. Harp. Never Lily. "Well, Mrs. Harp, what's for supper tonight?"

So it was to the Catholic church that my mother directed her passions—a Catholic church that my father refused to acknowledge in any manner discernible to a small child. He never went to Mass. He never bowed his head in prayer over our supper table. He never took God's name in vain or praise. Perhaps the rape had burned God out of him.

So. For a blessedly short time, in the spring of 1971, while half a million antiwar protesters descended on Washington, D.C., and South Vietnam invaded Laos, and Charles Manson was sentenced to death, and Lieutenant Calley was court-martialed for the massacre of twenty-two people at My Lai, my mother's passions centered on plainsong. Every morning during the month of May, she flung open the windows of our white clapboard house, which was built by Great-Great-Grandfather Harp; the Atlantic breezes swept through the rooms, dispelling dust and shadows, lifting the polyphonal strains of plainsong from the tape player to corners unknown.

And every morning, I succumbed to ecclesiastical visions. I saw the face of God—daily. I felt the fires of hell—daily. Saint Francis and Saint Martin took me shopping and instructed me that blackbirds, like God, always knew what we were thinking. Christ told me that every time I saw an ant, I should eat it. Angels picked lice off my tongue. Mermaid saints sang, but when they opened their mouths, there was no sound. Only rain.

The bodily manifestations attached to my God sight wavered with the light. A simple shaking fit would sometimes escalate into something more violent. But how violent, I am unsure, since I could never sit on my own shoulders and watch events unfold. But I do know I bit my tongue. My muscles grew sore. And I almost always peed a river.

For the first couple of weeks, my bouts with religious ecstasy remained a secret. Only God, Christ, and the saints knew. Mother hadn't a clue. Avoiding me and praying the rosary while listening to her music was all-consuming. And while she prayed, I grew ever more convinced that God loved me best. How else to explain my visions? I may have been a little girl, but not a stupid one. Clearly, there was a connection between my visions and my mother's morning insistence on playing plainsong. I never jerked and spazzed and went shopping with the saints any other time.

And I was desperate not to be found out. While we were healing leper children in downtown Jacksonville, Christ himself told me that our meetings were top secret. And although Mother wasn't a woman who flaunted her emotions, I feared she might fly into a jealous rage if she knew my relations with the Holy Trinity and all the saints were more intimate than hers.

The only part about all of this that proved tricky was my soiled underwear. Because I was old enough to be able to clean my own bottom, I could more or less take care of myself once I rallied. But the evidence remained on my ruffled cotton panties. So I told God that this particular bodily manifestation confused me and I prayed to him to make that part stop. But he didn't. He did keep Mother shortsighted, though. Each time she did the laundry, she fretted to herself that it made no sense I had started to wet myself again and that perhaps she needed to take me into town to see Dr. Sinclair.

So I became a morning hermit. I skipped breakfast and stayed in my bedroom, with its pretty chenille sailboat spread and matching blue curtains and waited patiently, daily, to be swept away by plainsong.

I developed a ritual. Upon waking, I recited the alphabet, counted to one hundred, prayed for the souls of my parents, and listened for the sounds of my mother making breakfast, Father attending to bathroom chores, and finally the revving engine of his pickup. The tires' crunch against the oyster-shell drive was my signal that it would soon be time. I would crawl out of bed and lie on the floor—I didn't want to mess the sheets. There, while staring at the ceiling, I would try to push away my anticipation, joy, dread, and fear by thinking pious thoughts. There wasn't much else to do, since I wasn't in charge.

Mondays always presented a slight alteration to my ritual. That's because it was Father's day off and I would have to pick up other signals that Mother was about to crank the chants.

One particular Monday, the clue was the annoying drone of the lawn mower. Father had decided to cut the grass in the cool of the day. To be utterly honest, we didn't have much to mow. Iris Haven was not, and is not, a place where you'd find a sodded yard. But we did have to knock back the sand spurs on a regular basis. So that's what he was doing on an early blue morning in May, trying to get a head start on the sticker burrs on his day off, leaving Mother to attend to her devotions in private.

I threw back the covers, shimmied down to my panties, lay on the floor, and clasped my hands in prayer. Within moments, the mower noise receded as our house filled with the strains of chant. The voices of the monks mushroomed all about. My muscles contracted, spurting my spirit into the air. Before I could say squat, Saint Francis and I were walking on water, right in front of my house, and he was telling me that fish hated little boys with red hair. I told him I did, too.

Unbeknownst to me, while I tripped over the waves, Father stood outside my window, contemplating sand spurs, and the wind blew open my curtains. I guess his disinterested gaze must have followed the wind, and that's when he saw me jerking and frothing to beat the band.

He did not come running. There was no scooping me up, no carting me to the truck and speeding to the hospital. No hand-wringing supplications to science or God. No. Nothing like that. According to a confession Mother made to me when

I was twelve, Father—sweaty and burr-pricked—tapped on her bedroom door (this must have killed him) and said, "Sorry to bother you, but there is something wrong with your daughter." That's how he always referred to me, as my mother's daughter.

Mother, as it turned out, had a different opinion about my condition, one that I surely did not anticipate. First, when she saw me sprawled and floundering in the middle of my bedroom floor, her maternal gene flashed into action, erasing the anger she had discreetly aimed my way for the last two weeks. I know this because I came to in her arms and was amazed at the sight of tears trickling down her worried face. She told Father—who, to his credit, hovered in the doorway—to phone Dr. Sinclair. But I, despite my condition, let loose with a mighty wail.

"We have to. We have to find out what is wrong with you," she said, brushing my sweaty brown bangs out of my eyes.

"No, Mama, no. Nothing is wrong with me."

"Well then, what just happened here?"

I couldn't go to the doctor. He'd know that I was completely healthy, and then my secret would be splayed out for all the world to see. It wasn't fair. God was forcing me to break my agreement. But perhaps if only my family knew the secret, I would be okay. What a world—shatter my promise to Christ or lie to my dear mother. Either way, I was going to burn. And when I told her the truth, she was going to hate me with a vengeance that would make the past few weeks look like a birthday trip to Weeki Wachi. I burst into torrential tears, the sort only a confession can unleash. And once I started crying, there was no turning back. The words rushed out of me before I could cork them. "I've been talking to God."

Mother's face went blank. She exhaled hard. "What?"

I stuttered through my tears, "Every time you play that music, I talk to God. And Christ. And all the angels. The saints, too."

Mother pulled her rosary from the back pocket of her Bermuda shorts, grabbed my chin, tipped it upward, and asked, "What do they say?"

Aha! Here was my chance not to rat out Christ totally. I would tell her only bits and pieces. But not everything. Just enough to get by. I looked into her blue eyes, which were identical to my own, and said in the tiniest voice I had ever used, "They love us." I gulped, searching for the right words. "They love everybody."

Mother brought her rosary-clutched hand to her mouth and gasped. That perpetual dull, haunted light in her eyes bounced around. "Really?"

I nodded yes. Never before had my mother spoken to me so earnestly. I loved her. More than anything, I wanted to please her. God was giving me this chance. I could see him, in the clouds, pointing the way, whispering to me that the water was clear and pure and deliciously cold. "You can do it," I heard him say. "Make her love you." So I dived in.

"Christ says you're special."

Mother squeezed her eyes shut and pulled me hard against her. Her breasts smelled like talcum powder. Then she pulled away, grabbed me by my shoulders—now she was the one crying; tears streamed across the bright bruise of her rouge—and said, "Show me. Show me what happens when you talk to God."

I couldn't. I was exhausted. I didn't want to wet myself again. And for the second time in my life, I was truly scared of God—perhaps he and Christ needed some time to get used to the idea that Mother was in on our secret. I stared at the ceiling, widened my eyes as much as possible, and tried to think of a way out. God wasn't offering any advice this time. So I took my best shot. I looked into my sweet mother's face and said with angelic solemnity, "God wants me to wait until morning."

Mother almost stopped believing right then. I could tell by the twitch. Her upper lip shook when she smelled a rat. But, ultimately, her faith did not fail her. That unearthly smile resurfaced and once again her countenance grew distant, be-atific. "Oh, yes, sweetie, of course. I'm sure he's . . . well, terri-bly busy. In the morning, then, yes?"

"Yes, Mama."

She stroked my cheek. This was not something I was accus-tomed to. I pulled away. "You are"—her face collapsed into what I thought was a mixture of sadness and grudging love— "good."

I nodded shyly and looked over her shoulder. Father was gone. I slipped my hands into hers. She squeezed. The rosary beads dug into my right palm. I knew if I hung on long enough, they would leave little dimples in my skin and that I would like that. Mother tilted her head and gazed at me with an expression I had never seen: something rich and dangerous, maybe pride.

Forgetting for a moment about my missing front tooth, I shot her my most winning smile. Finally! For the first time in my life, I thought, Mother and I are in cahoots.

I swear to you: Seeing the face of God was not as thrilling.

Charleston Rowena Mudd

When we were five years old, I tried to kill Murmur. I mean it. I really did. Everybody thought she was such hot stuff—having visions, seeing God, healing the sick. The responsibilities of a child saint are huge. She simply didn't have time for me, so she stopped being my friend.

Truth is, no one had time for me. Not even my own mother. She was always saying *Murmur Lee this* and *Murmur Lee that* and running up to the cathedral every time Murmur put on a show. She never missed a Murmur event, even though she exhaustively explained to my father that the whole thing was a farce and a crime against God. But whether they were believers or not, Mother wasn't alone. Everyone—even people who weren't prone to insanity—went Murmur-mad for a few weeks in the spring of 1971. I suppose I was among them.

But I had good cause. We were the only two children on the island. We had pricked our fingers with a hot needle and mixed our blood. We told each other everything. One time, just to make our bond even tighter, we showed each other our private parts. Every afternoon, Murmur and I played together, building sand castles or dressing up our Barbies in clothes we made ourselves, or cooking up mud pies and having fake teas.

Well, all of that came to a screeching halt once the adults decided Murmur was in touch with Jesus. My mother always baked cookies on Thursday mornings, and Murmur and I would reap the benefits of her labor as soon as they were out of the oven. She stopped baking as soon as Murmur got in touch with Jesus. Every Saturday morning of my life, my parents took me to town and we ate breakfast at Woolworth's and then they took me to the park, where I rode the carousel and ate pink cotton candy. Sometimes I threw up. Well, all of that ended as soon as Murmur got in touch with Jesus. Murmur and I had a secret hideout. We discovered an old Indian oyster midden hidden in the oaks on the western end of the island. We'd go out there and say curse words and stuff like that. Well, all of that ended as soon as Murmur got in touch with Jesus. On Friday nights, Murmur would come to my house or I'd go to hers and our parents would order us pizza and we'd have a sleepover. Well, all of that ended as soon as Murmur got in touch with Jesus. The final straw was when my parents announced that my birthday party was to be postponed yet again—I'd had the mumps on my real birthday, so we'd chosen May 17 as the new date. Mother had taken on extra responsibilities at the parish—there were strangers to be hosted and greeted and fed, so no party for me, and no new date was announced—and all because Murmur had gotten in touch with Jesus.

It was a weekday. Iris Haven was overrun with miracle-seeking pilgrims. I waited until I was sure Murmur's morning performance was over and the pilgrims had started to clear out.

I remember so clearly what I was wearing—a mint green shorts set that Mother had bought for me at a department store in Jacksonville. The bottoms had an elastic band around the waist, which I didn't like, and the cotton made a soft scratchy sound when I walked, which I did like. Scratch scratch.

Mother had returned home from Murmur's place and was on the phone, gossiping about what had happened that morning. I guess a woman with a bad back from Hastings had been in attendance, and when she left, she claimed to be suddenly without pain. As I sneaked out the back door, I patted my pocket to make sure my secret weapon was still there.

I marched myself over to Murmur's, full of confidence and resolve. She lived at the end of the lane, in a big windy house her great-great-grandfather had built. It was haunted. Everyone said so. But ghosts didn't scare me. In fact, I liked them. I went to the kitchen side of the house and knocked pretty as you please. Mrs. Harp opened the door and didn't even give me a chance to speak. That's how little I mattered. She said, "Murmur Lee cannot play with you, Charlee. She's resting."

"But Mrs. Harp, I just have to see her. I won't be long. Pleeeeeaaase?" I was cunning and mean and guiltless: I was on a mission.

She looked at me the way adults do when they don't want to give in to a child's demands but a voice in their head is saying, Oh, go on, what harm can it do?

"All right, Charlee. But make it fast." She stepped aside and I shot in.

Murmur was on her bed, perched in repose like a perfect little angel. She didn't fool me. She was a hellion. We both were. Saint, shmaint. I walked over and shook her shoulder.

"Leave me alone. You're not supposed to be touching me." She opened her eyes and stared at me with blank disdain.

"I'll touch you whenever I want."

"Nah-huh."

"Uh-huh."

I grabbed her hair and pulled as hard as I could.

"Ouch!" She dug her nails into my arm. "You're not supposed to be here. Go away. Leave me alone! I have to rest."

I pinched her skinny leg. I thought about tearing the scab off her knee.

"Stop it! I'm gonna call my mommy!"

" 'Stop it,' " I mimicked. I tried to grab her nonexistent titty—this is an innate move all girls are born knowing. "She's not here. Hahahahaha!" I loved the lie. I jumped on the bed and pinned her down. "I hate you! You're not my friend! You've never been my friend!"

Murmur's lips pinched up and I knew what she was getting ready to do. She could spit like a boy. "Don't you dare!" I slammed my hand over her mouth. She bit me. I grabbed for the weapon in my pocket. Since I no longer had her pinned, I lost all leverage. She tried to throw me off. I hung on. We slapped wildly and grunted and struggled—all of this done in a desperate hushed fury because, if the truth be told, we really didn't want to get caught. Neither of us did. This death match had been long in the making. She bit my left arm. With my right hand, I scratched her throat. We went tumbling off the bed. Boom! I hit my head really hard on the nightstand.

Still we fought on, crying and scratching and slapping. I managed to get back on top of her. She reached up and tried to choke me. I said, "Eat this and die!" I pulled a plastic Baggie filled with an entire package of Ex-Lax pills out of my pocket and jammed them down her throat. She made some kind of awful noise, which scared me.

"What in heaven's name!" Mrs. Harp was a small woman,

but she pulled me off of her daughter with one arm. I never heard her coming.

Murmur spit out the Ex-Lax, wailing all the while. Her cheek bled from a cat scratch I'd gotten in as we fell onto the floor. "She—she—she tried to kill me!"

"Hush, Murmur Lee!" Mrs. Harp's steel grip was not an enjoyable experience. I tried to squirm away, but she only squeezed harder. "Charleston, have you lost your mind? What are these pills?"

"Ex-Lax," I mumbled.

"Jesus, Mary, and Joseph!" Her grip tightened with each name. "Murmur Lee, did you swallow any of those?"

"I don't know," she whimpered.

Mrs. Harp's pale freckled face was flaming red. "I want you to go home this very second and tell your parents what you did. You tell them they'd better punish you. You need a good spanking. I'd do it myself if I thought you were worth my time. And tonight after services, I am personally going to speak to them. You are in trouble, Charleston Mudd." Then she shoved me and said through gritted teeth, "Now you get on home."

I looked at Murmur as I made my way out the door. Her shirt was torn. Ex-Lax tablets clung to her chin like big fat zits. Her tears diluted the blood that slowly trailed down her cheek. I shot her the meanest smirk I had. Saint, shmaint.

Mother and father put me on restriction for a week. So what? No one was playing with me anyway.

Later that night, I heard them in their bedroom. They were laughing about what I'd done. Father said, "Mm mm mm, well at least there is one person around here who is unimpressed by little Miss Murmur Lee."

I put my pillow over my face and sobbed. I mean huge,

unladylike, convulsive sobs. My father was wrong. I was wildly impressed. Murmur was so special that the Pope himself was probably going to call her to Rome. All the evidence pointed to it. She'd never given me one hint about any of this God business. Maybe she hated my guts. When did she start hating me? I wondered. I didn't want her to hate me. And I sure didn't want God to make her a saint. It wasn't fair. He needed to find some other little girl to make a saint, because without Murmur, I didn't have a friend in the whole wide world.

A Letter Written by Father Matthew Jaeger
to Bishop Haywood F. Carroll, which
Father Jaeger Never Mailed, Opting to
Hide It in a Secret Pocket He Whittled
into the Cover of His Favorite Book,
From Here to Eternity

Bishop Haywood F. Carroll
Miami Diocese
Pastoral Center
9401 Biscayne Boulevard
Miami Shores, Florida

Dear Bishop Carroll:
Please forgive me for contacting you directly
(astonishingly presumptive of me, I know; hopefully
after reading this, you will agree I have no choice),
but since Bishop Beaver isn't expected back from
Rome for another two weeks and because of the
seriousness of what is occurring in my St. Augustine
parish, and after much prayer, the Lord has
directed me to speak to you—without the benefit
of Dan's wisdom—about a matter of urgent
importance.

I offer this in a spirit of full humility and wonder.

A situation has arisen in my flock that necessitates our immediate and focused attention. It is a delicate matter, rooted in the purity of our Lord, and one about which I seek the full range of your counsel.

It is my opinion (offered humbly and with no small measure of trepidation, since I've been unable to speak to Dan about this at all—seems his Roman holiday is keeping him quite busy) that because of the nature of what I am about to reveal, the church must vigorously assert itself, bringing to bear all of its sanctified powers and rights in order to keep at bay the wolves who would otherwise inevitably close in, seeking profit and fed by Satan's greed.

I don't quite know how to approach this matter delicately, so I shall plunge ahead, asking forgiveness if my discourse appears brash. (Thank you, Bishop.)

We have here in St. Augustine a young female—a mere child, the offspring of a devout, observant, and working-class but tithing mother (the father, I'm afraid—well, frankly, I don't know what he is)—who, simply put, is being blessed (evidently) by Christ and a fair number of saints with the most amazing visions. These wondrous moments (I shan't call them miracles; that is for the church to decide) have resulted in what appear to be healings. Notice, Bishop, I say "appear to be," for I in no way would proffer myself as an expert on such matters. And believe me, I understand quite thoroughly that these are delicate matters I speak of, but speak I must!

For the sake of this discourse, I will detail for you

some of the mysteries that have resulted from being
in the child's presence.

A. A single male, age forty, after having shown no
interest in the many lovely young ladies in our flock,
has promised to find a suitable Catholic woman of
similar age to marry. Since the start of the child's
"visions," he has attended our singles' Bible-study
group regularly (no absences, not a single one).

B. A ten-year-old boy, upon witnessing the girl's
holy agony, informed his mother that he no longer
needed his inhaler, and he hasn't suffered an asthma
attack since.

C. The cathedral's janitor, a Negro who, if I
venture to guess, must be seventy if a day, claims that
after being in the presence of our subject, the arthritis
that had plagued his hands for the past twelve years
vanished. And I will personally attest to the fact that
our floors have never looked better.

D. A young couple—married for well over a year
and committed to their nuptial responsibilities—had
been unable to have a child. After bearing witness to
our subject's agony, however, the wife is finally with
child.

I have, of course, closely monitored the events
taking place in St. Augustine. Indeed, I have kept
copious notes (even some photographs), which I will
share immediately upon request (forgive me for not
sending them under this cover, but knowing how busy
you are and the fact that a paper trail in these
instances is most helpful, I thought it prudent to
refrain from sending the material to you until you
officially ask).

Bishop, here is a curious fact. The one detail I can confirm with righteous confidence is that all of our subject's visions and agonies take place in conjunction with ecclesiastical music. Gregorian chants, to be exact. Each time she is exposed to these sacred strains—music that most certainly pleases the ear of God—she ascends to an altered state, during which time she appears to reside in the realm of Christ, the saints, and a choir of angels.

Her mother (a pious woman if ever there was one) is holding up the best she can, given the circumstances. And even though the mother limits how often the girl is exposed to the chants, I'm afraid the word is out. (As you know better than I, people have a longing, a hunger, a spirit-based craving to be in the presence of Christ.) So, despite the best efforts of both her mother and myself, I'm afraid the floodgates might soon break and we will be awash in pilgrims seeking all forms of spiritual and physical healing. And then there is that pesky aforementioned problem of wolves.

I think you will agree that the situation is urgent and demands immediate and wise guidance. Which is why I am consulting you, what with Dan off to Rome. Of course, this revelation would have come directly from Dan had he been around. As it is, with the good bishop away again, I am shouldering the full weight of this extraordinary series of events. The magnitude of what is occurring here in St. Augustine simply does not allow me the luxury of remaining silent or waiting for Dan's return.

Bishop, I shall promote the status quo until hearing

from you (and I shall pray that I'm able to keep things under control).

May God be full in the hearts of your South Florida flock. And congratulations on Miami being named an archdiocese. (Just between you and me, this is long overdue.)

Sincerely yours in Christ,
Father Matthew Jaeger
St. Augustine Cathedral

Disgrace:
Murmur Lee Harp Reveals the
Apex of Her Sainthood

I was a fat little kid until my mother, with the help of Father Jaeger, who so wanted a saint on his hands, turned me into a freak show. There's nothing quite like regular doses of brain electricity zipping through your body, contracting every muscle, to turn the chubby into the buff.

But first, let me tell you about that letter: dribble, dribble, and more dribble. Keep the wolves at bay! Protect me from the blessed hordes! Ha! My dead ass!

The world has rarely seen a duo such as my mother and Father Jaeger. Their egocentric piety, fed by a hunger for limelight and power, propelled them into a brand of ecclesiastical madness that my own vision-seeing insanity couldn't hold a stick to.

For instance, they put me on display three times a day. "The people have a need and you have been gifted by God," my mother said as Father Jaeger stood serenely by her side.

Morning and noon sessions were held at my house. The evening gathering took place in the cathedral. The faithful would gather, their rosaries in constant movement, inching silently—like beaded snakes—through miracle-seeking fingers. Candlelight fed and sucked the dancing shadows. Prayers curled about, mingling with the ascending trails of incense and votive smoke. Lame adults, cross-eyed children, and people who should have known better waved crucifixes, crossed themselves like muttering medieval hermits, and doused their tear-stained cheeks with the cool burn of holy water—all of them kneeling and genuflecting and supplicating and crying and sloshing Hail Marys into the Christ-crowded air.

To this extent, I was a willing coconspirator: How astounding to be the focus of my mother's ecstatic passion, how bone-breaking delicious to be the object of her approval! So participate I did, no whining, no squirming tantrums. With all the dignity and simplicity one fully expects from a blessed child, three times a day I dutifully pulled on my plastic underpants and frilly dress and lay down on a mattress covered in white silk—a rosary clutched in my tiny hand, eyes closed as if in prayer, listening to the faithful file in (some started sobbing as soon as they saw me lying there in my lace dress, holding rosary beads).

The sessions were eerily predictable. The insistent drone of prayers scratched the thick air as I, motionless, waited for someone to balance the needle in the proper groove of the vinyl album, waited for the polyphonic chords of plainsong to rise like fog, thus obliterating both prayer and smoke, waited for my veins to grow plump and wild on the juice of ancient chant, waited, yes, for my body to seize and for my soul to be stomped upon by angels.

Oh, how I remember those angels. Their wings sharp, their feather tips as finely hewn as scalpels.

I bled. I know I did.

For reasons I really can't fathom, Father Jaeger never mailed that nauseating letter to the bishop. Why didn't he send it? Wouldn't he have gotten extra credit for having a child saint in his flock? Maybe he decided to catalog more miracles (in the child's presence, two bunions, one backache, and three warts were healed), build a stronger case, and it all got away from him. Or maybe he simply lost his nerve.

All I know for sure is that things changed once a certain Father Arturo Vincenzo Parisi arrived from Maryland—simply a short layover, a courtesy visit before continuing on to his new post at the newly created archdiocese in Miami.

Father Parisi was a skinny man—I liked that—and, according to the adults hovering about me, barely old enough to drink (now that I was virtually a saint, they held grown-up conversations in my presence). His deep-set blueberry eyes (nearly black, that's what they were) glared out at the world as though he had been flogged as a boy and no amount of Christian forgiveness would wash away his need for revenge.

Children have crushes, you know. This idea that we don't become sexual beings until puberty is hogwash. And I, in my rubber panties and sweet ruffles, took one look at Father Parisi and fell head over heels. I wanted him. And I wanted him bad, with all the passion that children possess but usually successfully hide from adults. His rakish blackbird hair, those glowering black-blue eyes, that sharp blackbird nose, his thick lower lip, which had nothing in common with a blackbird at all: He was my boyfriend. Crick, crack, easy as that!

W hat a fine saint I would be. And Parisi would love me with such true fire that he would wait for me to grow up, and then somehow God would allow us to marry and I would be so unbelievably beautiful (they would redo Barbie in my image) that we'd be graced with a houseful of sweet babies.

These were my thoughts as I laid there in the cathedral in my ruffles and lace and plastic panties—eyes closed, hands clasped, rosary wrapped tightly between my fingers. I knew Parisi was gazing at me. How could he not?

I could hear Father Jaeger scurrying about, whispering orders. And then my mother's voice and her hand on my forehead: "Sweetheart, we're ready."

This is what I remember. The choir began to sing (oh, yes, they brought in the choir to impress Parisi) and then Parisi started shouting in a thick Italian accent full of vowels that seemed to dance, "Stop! Stop! You crazy fools! You are going to kill the bambino! Towel, give me a towel! Oh sweet Jesus!"

Parisi knelt beside me and wiped my face with a towel damp with holy water. I gazed up at him—he was prettier than God, with that narrow little face and fat lips—and tried to look saintly, even though I was lying in my own piss and he was mopping up that and my drool. "This child! She needs a doctor! This is no vision. This is epilepsy!"

The only miracle in all of this was that the good priest was well acquainted with musicogenic epilepsy. A man in his village back home went into fits every time he heard a particularly sad, high-pitched Andalusian folk song about two ill-fated lovers. According to Parisi, everyone thought the man's fits stemmed from a broken heart that had been administered to him at the tender age of seventeen by one of the village's most amply hipped girls. It was spring—the time of festivals—and music was in the air, according to my lover-priest. And as fate would have it, a physician with the Royal Institute of Medicine happened by the village on his way to somewhere more important and witnessed the villager suffer a grand mal seizure in the courtyard while a street singer wailed about love gone wrong. The doctor suspected immediately what was afoot, being that he was a student of rare and obscure maladies. Now I ask, was that—the doctor's presence in that two-bit village—a miracle, too?

Or do we sometimes just get lucky?

Two trips to Maryland and Johns Hopkins later (Parisi insisted, as he held Johns Hopkins in high esteem, having lived in Maryland just prior to accepting his post in Miami), my mother and Father Jaeger were finally convinced that, indeed, I was not special in the eyes of our Lord, was not experiencing and never had experienced anything remotely akin to a religious experience, and that I should be kept away from people for as long as it took for everyone to forget about this embarrassing incident.

As a result of my fall from grace, my mother retreated back into prayer, with nary a glance my way. My father remained his distant good self. My pastor, Father Jaeger, never spoke to me again. My visions withered into painful memory. My physicians at Johns Hopkins instructed my mother that never, never, never was I to hear plainsong again. My crush on Father Parisi would have followed my visions into painful memory except for the fact that I was forever grateful and only superficially bitter that he'd found me out. And, I must say, the experience really did conjure in me a hunger for God. It was a hunger that would stay with me up until my teen years, when it was supplanted by my appetite for sex.

A Letter Written by Father Matthew Jaeger to God, Never Mailed, Just Balled Up and Then Burned in the Rectory's Kitchen Sink

Dear Heavenly Savior,

Oh blessed one from whom all grace flows, what have I done? What on God's green earth have I done!

I made a total sniveling fool out of myself in front of Father Parisi, who, I'm sure, has already reported this directly to the new archbishop in Miami. Of course, he'll tell Bishop Beaver immediately upon the latter's return from his big fat Roman holiday.

No! No! No! He has probably phoned Beaver in Rome already. These things—these stupid, ridiculous, embarrassing foul-ups—are like viruses.

I'M PROBABLY BEING MADE FUN OF AT THE HIGHEST LEVELS OF THE CHURCH AT THIS VERY MOMENT!!!!

Oh dear God, what should I do? I was operating out of your divine goodness, and now I am a

laughing stock! Give me a sign. Tell me how I should
proceed. Must I endure this humiliation the rest of
my days? Dear Lord, I am at prayer all the time. I am
listening.

Your faithful servant,
Matt

Four Journal Entries Written by Murmur Lee Harp During the Time of Her Independent Scholastic Study of the Medical Phenomenon Known as Musicogenic Epilepsy

December 8, 1985

Dear Journal,
I came upon this in my research today:

> PLAINSONG,
> OTHERWISE KNOWN AS
> GREGORIAN CHANT,
> IS DIATONIC.

What in Saint Rita's name is diatonic? you may well be asking. Aha, I have the answer!

> DIATONIC: MUSIC USING ONLY
> THE SEVEN TONES OF A STANDARD
> SCALE WITHOUT CHROMATIC
> ALTERATIONS.

That's it! The key to my soul: no chromatic
alterations. But it gets better:

PLAINSONG HAS A FREE RHYTHM
DETERMINED BY THE TEXT.

Oh yes! Rhythm determined by text. It's wholly
beautiful: a metaphor for life. At least my life. And I
hope it will be a metaphor for my marriage. You
know, free and kind of wild and every day
determined by the earth's pull, by what has already
been written in heaven's palm.

Erik doesn't know about the epilepsy. Why should
I tell him? I mean, no one living—other than Charlee,
and her lips are sealed—knows about it. To say the
words musicogenic epilepsy is to open the door to it.
And that door was slammed shut when I was a child.
Even this research spooks me, but my need to
understand the brainstorms that will evidently
erupt—no matter how hard I fight against it—with
the simple hearing of one sweet strain of ancient
chant overrides the fear.

No. He'll never know. I'll put a dusting of
cayenne in his coffee every morning so that he'll be
content in his ignorance. That's what we women have
to do: sprinkle minor spells here and there to keep
the status quo.

More later.
Signed,
Murmurmurmurmurmurmurmur Lee

January 1, 1986

Dear Journal,

The latest turn of the screw is this: I've become
obsessed with whale song. But the problem is, I
fear—rationally or not, I don't know—that their
music might be so similar to chant that it will toss
me back into that land of electrical overload, that odd
world of false angels and saints. So I won't listen to
it. Which means, like chant, I study their music
without ever hearing it.

Is this similar to a blind man who paints? A deaf
man who dances? A mute who sings in her dreams? Is
this some kind of curse?

I read about a Stanford scientist who believes
humans are coming to an appreciation of music—its
aesthetics and its composition—later than other
animals. Isn't that fabulous? It means that the highest
mammal on the food chain is actually playing an
eternal game of catch-up.

And I believe it. Look at the whales. They were
here way before we were. Which means—duh!—they
were composing music BEFORE we were. They didn't
start singing because they heard some boom box
blasting off the bow of a ship. It's true! Everything I
read about whale song suggests that not only have
they been composing and performing for eons but
also that the structure of their songs is extremely
similar to human song. Same-same. They use similar
rhythms, phrasings. Their compositions rhyme. They
mix percussive and pure tones. Their songs even
follow the ABA form, continuously playing with

variations on themes. Just like Thelonius. Just like
Parker. Just like Davis.

Perhaps this explains the Bachs and Mozarts
among us. Perhaps their DNA retained more of the
whale coding than that of most humans. Yeah, good
old Bach, who would nearly faint at a sudden trumpet
blast. And Mozart, whose strange laughter could
shatter crystal. God, I wonder what THEIR brains
looked like!

Mur

March 6, 1986

Dear Journal,
Now listen to this. If humpback whales compose and
perform what amount to symphonies, and if whale
pods teach and exchange songs, and if even your most
garden-variety songbird trills Western music scales the
likes of which inspired Chopin, and if wolf packs at
the full moon howl wolf songs that are complex,
conjoined, interrelated, and ancient, then why are
humans so arrogant as to believe we have the corner
on song?

I mean, maybe—just maybe—we're all whistling
the same tune, that there is some deep primal gateway
to the brain that leads to the most ancient core of
our being and it is from there that we respond to this
universal pan-creature music.

If you really think about music and song—why
they exist and all that—the questions become

awesome. What is the purpose of language? And what is the difference between language and song? And why does music played slowly in a minor key cause us to feel blue? Why? And how about major-key quick-tempo tunes? They get us all revved up.

This is important stuff. This is primal crawling out of the muck stuff. Wolves don't howl wolf songs because God flicks a switch in their cerebral cortexes. They howl because a series of events causes them to WANT to sing. That's the same reason humans belt out tunes.

What is all this about? I want to know why I respond to music the way I do, why chant makes me mad. What is really going on inside my brain?

We know the symptoms. That's it. We've given them fancy, difficult-to-pronounce names. But we don't know the whys, the hows, the whats. Yes, we may all be singing, but we don't yet recognize or even admit to the universality of our song.

Mur

April 10, 1986

Dear Journal,
Sorry to say I didn't obtain this from the primary source, but from a journal on musicogenic epilepsy. The author claims that the first known reference to said malady was back in the sixteenth century. Evidently, some poor guy seized every time he heard a lyre. But better than that is this: Old William

Shakespeare himself makes reference to it in The Merchant of Venice: "Some that are mad if they behold a cat, and others, when the bagpipe sings i' th' nose, / Cannot contain their urine..." That's what the article claimed Shakespeare was talking about. Sounds about right to me.

As my wedding date nears, I find myself spending more time reading about this and worrying. Am I worrying about the epilepsy—something that hasn't reared its grand mal head in years—so that I don't go mad thinking about what all can go wrong once I say I do? His parents are insisting we get married in their church. I explained to Erik that I'm not a believer, that for me, God exists in the mud and the yellow eyes of birds. He just laughed and said, "It's what Daddy wants." So First Baptist Church, here we come. If I believed in hell, my having a Christian marriage ceremony would certainly land me there. Well, at least I don't have to worry about going grand mal when they play "The Old Rugged Cross."

Mur

Charleston Rowena Mudd

I think Murmur married Erik Nathanson because she went temporarily insane. It happens. Perfectly rational children become teenagers, and suddenly their genitals take over. And also, Murmur's parents—while nice enough—never seemed to want her. Really. Once her stint as a child saint ended, life was back to Murmur and me, with her parents providing food and shelter and a minimum of interference. Maybe that's what Erik provided: the interference she always craved. All I know for sure is that my sassy friend, who could spit in a snake's eye and live to tell about it, folded like a Chinese fan every time he walked into a room.

Erik was a golfer who dabbled in law. His trust fund financed his undisciplined life in the courtroom, on the greens, and especially at the clubhouse. I was never a member of the country club, but word gets around: Erik dipped his stick all over town. His minor success as a lawyer was the fortunate result of his daddy being the past mayor and Erik being a

charmer. Men liked him as much as women. They admired—
no, coveted—his looks: the square jaw, the diamond face, the
bright eyes, which never gave away what he was thinking (yes,
people constantly gave him the benefit of the doubt, blithely
assuming he had a clue). Mostly, they wanted his hair. It was
Breck hair: longish—about chin level—blond, and full of
body, actually silky, the kind of hair women dream of having.
In my seasoned opinion, at his best Erik was a dumb blond,
but because he had testicles, his idiocy went unnoticed, or was
excused, at least.

Some people interpreted his mental dwarfism as southern-
boy gall. Stories—appalling in my view but offered as
praise—swept through town like an outbreak of pinkeye.
Take this little jewel, for example: Erik had been practicing for
only eight months when he stood before Judge Cooksey and
informed him that he wanted a three-day postponement because the weather was a perfect seventy-four degrees, with not
much humidity, and he didn't want to waste his time in the
courtroom when he could be out on the links. The judge
granted the postponement. Erik's client, a kid charged with his
first count of shoplifting, looked at the judge, then at his
lawyer, then over his shoulder at his mother, and burst into
tears.

Erik was older than Murmur by five years. They married
the summer of our high school graduation. They lived in St.
Augustine Beach, right on the water, and stayed there until the
fall, when the house became a weekend getaway and they
headed to Gainesville and the University of Florida, where
Erik would—by the grace of that fine hair and good straight
teeth—squeak up a law degree. (I'm harsh on Erik, I admit.
But believe me, this isn't an apology, nor even a sugar-coated
diatribe. It's the Yankee truth.)

Consider this:

They had been married three weeks. Erik clerked in his dad's law office weekdays and golfed on weekends. Murmur didn't have much to do that summer other than keep house and please her groom. I was biding my time until mid-August, when I would head to Tallahassee and FSU and enroll in something—what, I didn't know. Psychology. Sociology. Business. Political Science. Philosophy. God, there were so many choices. The only thing clear to me was that I was going to go to college and that while there a miracle would occur and my future would become self-evident. So Murmur and I decided that until the reality of fall descended and we were plunged into adulthood and college, we would work on our tans, drink beer, join Amnesty International, cut our hair really short, read Proust, avoid anyone who strolled around in public in warm-up suits, write letters to the editor, in which we would point out the ludicrous editorial policies of the *St. Augustine Record*, and avoid Bobby Meyerbach because he stank.

I arrived at their house one morning in June at around 10:30. Erik's Porsche was parked out front. I didn't know what he was doing home, but I figured it wouldn't stall our plans, or Murmur would have phoned. I made my way through a winding path lined with potted herbs, the Crayola faces of zinnias, an immutable sundial, and a rusting fish basket filled with seashells. Since Erik was home, I decided to behave like company. I knocked on the front door, which Murmur had painted Chinese red shortly after moving in, because she said red doors welcomed in good spirits and scared away evil ones. No answer. Brushing aside the nagging thought that Murmur had ruined everything by getting married, I rang the doorbell. Still no answer. I walked around the side of the house to the kitchen door. She'd painted it blue. I didn't know why. It was open, and I said to hell with Erik, and I walked on in. I started to call Murmur's name but stopped short. The kitchen opened into a dining room. Behind the old pine dinner table hung a large mottled mirror. Murmur and Erik were reflected in its beveled light. He was dressed in a Brooks Brothers suit, she in denim shorts and a paisley halter top, which he gripped by one hand and yanked.

"Don't! Erik, we're just going to lie on the beach. We want to get some sun. That's all."

"You will not go out there looking like a tramp. You're my wife now. Murmur the tramp is dead. Remember that, you little bitch. The tramp is dead."

"Erik, I am not a tramp. Baby, I love you." She reminded me of a little girl seeking an angry father's love and forgiveness. I didn't want to bear witness to this, but I couldn't move.

Erik grabbed her by her hair. He wound it around his fist and pulled it taut. "You were a tramp when I married you. Now you're not. I'm the reason, the only reason, you're not still a beach whore." He let go of her hair and jabbed his finger in her chest over and over, forcing her to back up, moving her out of the mirror's reflection. "You will do as I say. You will not defy me. You are mine now. Do you understand?"

Unwilling to hear Murmur's answer or witness her humiliation, I decided I had only one choice, and that was to make myself known. "Murmur!" I called, trying to keep the frantic warble in check. "I'm here! You ready?"

She did not respond. But Erik did. "Charlee!"

He strode into the kitchen, all smiles. "Hey, how you doing?" He leaned in and kissed my cheek. "I was just on my way out. Murmur is in the back, doing something. I don't know what. Give her five minutes or so." He plucked an apple out of the fruit basket on the kitchen counter and rubbed it against his starched white shirt.

"Okay." I scratched an imaginary itch on my arm. "I'll just wait here."

"Good." He scanned the kitchen. "Where's my briefcase. Ah." He grabbed it off the kitchen stool. He patted the backrest. "Have a seat."

I did as I was told. I took some solace in the fact that he didn't seem to have a clue that I'd seen the little spat. He fiddled with the lock combination on the briefcase and said, "Oh, by the way, you and Murmur aren't going to the beach today. Just stay up near the house."

"Sure."

He shot me a big grin, a pretty-boy movie-star grin, and his eyes betrayed nothing. "See ya."

"Yeah."

Just before he stepped out the blue door, which, I decided, needed to be red—evil spirits and all—he checked out his hair in a small mirror that hung precariously from the doorjamb by a blue silk ribbon, and then he was gone.

I stayed seated on the stool, scared to move.

"Charlee?" Murmur yelled.

"Yeah?"

"Let's do something besides the beach today. I'm not in the mood." She sounded, I thought, falsely chipper.

"Okay. Fine by me." I don't know why I decided to play along. I guess I felt guilty for having spied on her—even though it wasn't intentional—and, in all honesty, I was chickenshit. I mean, we all do it: wait for the person in crisis to fess up before we say anything.

"How about some tunes?" she yelled, and before I could

respond, Marvin Gaye's silk rope of a voice filled the house: "... That this ain't the way love's supposed to be."

I slipped off the stool and wandered through the dining area and into the living room. Murmur stood at the French doors, gazing at the Atlantic, her bluebird eyes framed in fresh mascara.

"Marvin Gaye is dead," I said as I walked over to her and put my arm around her tiny shoulders.

"I know." She kissed my cheek. "By the hand of his own daddy. How awful is that?"

We stood there watching the waves rumble and recede, listening to Marvin sing about sex and love and all its possibilities, and for the next eight years, we pretended she was married to a good man.

*T*his is what I remember about Murmur's daughter.

Blossom Cordelia Charleston Nathanson was seven years old when she was diagnosed with leukemia.

She had her mother's bluebird eyes, her father's outstanding hair, and was clearly her mother's daughter in terms of goodness and smarts.

She could count to a hundred when she was three and a half.

By age four, she was protecting lizards and beached sea life from the hunter-destroyer ways of little boys.

She loved to dance. She would bounce on chubby toddler legs whenever her mother cranked the stereo. With her face jam-smeared and her tiny hand clutching something—she was always grabbing—she'd squeal and grin and bounce almost in rhythm to the tunes. And later, about the time she hit five, the child could twist and shout better than her mother.

I had big plans for Blossom. She was, after all, my god-daughter. And the way my life was going—since I had become more interested in racking up academic degrees than finding a husband—she might also have served as my surrogate daughter, one I could heap praise upon, offering the sort of insider advice that mothers sometimes can't because they have no objectivity, and experiencing the wholly unreasonable pride that springs from watching a beloved child come into her own.

This is what I remember about Blossom's mother.

Her love was not stagnant. It was active, purple, fierce. Illness didn't change that. In fact, as Blossom grew sicker, Murmur's mother love boiled with a rage that transcended what most people would call good sense. She became mythic, an earth mother who refused to back down from her insistence that the universe straighten up and heal her daughter.

For six months, she did not sleep. With grace and power and haunted eyes, she demanded answers from doctors who were crazy enough to not return her phone calls when it looked like their tools weren't capable of stopping the onslaught of Blossom's disease. Murmur screamed at the moon, cursed the sky, begged the wind, wept bitter tears, which fell into the sand and oblivion, and then she cleaned herself up and was at Blossom's bedside with teas and lotions and toys before the child had any notion of waking.

I was in the hospital room and witnessed this:

Blossom—bald and skeletal and surrounded by flowers and stuffed animals and finger paintings her classmates had drawn for her—reached for her mother's face and asked like a straight shooter who knows no pity, "Mommy, am I going to die?"

Murmur's face softened into that transcendent place, the one where the ego isn't allowed, where our own sadness and fear have been sacrificed to serve the higher need of someone in trouble. "No, baby, you're not going to die. You're going to live forever in so many ways. We have a lot to do, you and I."

And then the two of them broke into spontaneous laughter. The dying child and the shattered warrior-goddess mother, laughing in anticipation of a future they would never have.

Yes, that's what Murmur gave her daughter in the final days of her life: faith that there would be a future. All dying children should leave this earth believing, as Blossom did, that tomorrow is going to happen.

I don't know, maybe Murmur was a saint after all. Her granite-hard belief in nature's capacity—but more importantly, willingness—to heal experienced stress fractures but never cracked. She got mad, desperate even, but her faith remained solid; she never stopped believing that the universe would not forsake her. Right up to the end, there in the house on St. Augustine Beach, while Blossom slipped into a coma she would never wake from, Murmur was offering prayers to whatever god might listen. She was frantic. She was broken. But she kept believing. Yes, she was a saint.

This is the awful truth: No matter the prayer or mode of delivery, no one was listening. Or if they were, they didn't care. Evidence? The child died. Nothing Murmur or the doctors did worked. Not the lotions Murmur concocted from herbs sown by her own hand. Not the scraps of raw silk she dyed in soft tones from wildflowers sown by her own hand and then placed in Blossom's palms, on her eyelids, in the painful crooks and crevices of her body. Not the soups brewed so lovingly and made with ingredients sown by her own hand. Not the prayers she made up, nor the old ones, the Catholic ones that she'd long ago abandoned. The universe would not listen to her on the subject of Blossom. Like one of those little hunter-destroyer boys who squash frogs, rip the tails off lizards, and stomp ghost crabs under a milky white moon, it was as if the universe saw Blossom's beauty and potential and couldn't bear it. So it snuffed her out. No amount of chemo or tinctures of organically grown herbs were going to change the jealous mind of the universal soul.

But Murmur, Murmur, my dear friend Murmur, simply looked out at all creation and tried to will a miracle.

This is what I remember about Blossom's father.

Erik Nathanson left the house two days after his daughter was diagnosed with leukemia. Openly, unapologetically, he shacked up with his girlfriend of three months. He never visited Blossom in the hospital. He never visited her at home. He didn't phone her. He did not attend her memorial service. He did not hold Murmur's hand and take on even one ounce of her grief, nor did he share his. He simply went away.

Six months after Blossom's death, he filed for divorce, citing abandonment. Erik Nathanson might never have read a book in his life, he probably didn't know how to pronounce *faux pas* or understand the true meaning of *son of a bitch* when it was uttered by a woman, but he did know how the good ol' boy legal system in St. John's County operated. He was one of theirs. He drank and dined and played golf with them. He shared whores and stock tips with them. He watched their backs and they watched his. He could keep Murmur in court until the St. John's River finally flowed the right way. He got the house, the cars, the silver, the furniture, the monogrammed towels, the china and rugs and wastebaskets and lamps and brooms and cleaning rags. And, as if this could get any worse, he walked away—in the eyes of the court and good Judge Cooksey—not owing his wife one dime of support.

Murmur died believing in ghosts and hauntings. I hope she was right. I hope that she'll rise from whatever netherworld she's at and exact her pound of flesh from Erik Nathanson. She surely never got it in life. For God's sake, if the universe cares one iota about balance and harmony, she'll be given a chance to haunt the holy everlasting life out of him.

And don't you know that Murmur could whip his ass with some medieval hauntings. She could make his pecker shrivel up into a droopy little thing that would resemble a rotten baby tomato. Or she might throw down on him—all over him—the worst case of herpes the world has ever seen. Or she might—and this would be best of all—cast a spell that would force him out of his self-absorption and into an eternal wrestling match with the moral ghosts of his past.

Murmur Lee Harp
Sees Her Daughter

*T*his is the strangest sensation, to be scattered asunder by a steady wind and yet feel whole—indeed, unified—all the while. It's just me and the whirling air and the picture show that flickers here and there, sudden and bright. I am loving this: the universe flowing through me like a river, offering glimpses of a beautiful and imperfect life.

There she is, my baby!

Blossom's blond curls tickle her face and she giggles—the sound strikes like temple chimes—and I heft her into the cloud-whipped sky. "Wheeeee!" we both say, and I fold her into my arms, lift her tiny tie-dyed T-shirt, and deliver a squeal-rousing raspberry to her belly. This is why I got married, I think as I set my baby on the sand: to experience mama joy. Blossom had to be born. She was always there, waiting for the right time, scanning my world so she'd know when to leap. I run my fingers over her head and wonder if all mothers feel this way, that destiny tapped their shoulders and whispered, *Hey, here's the one you've been waiting for.*

Blossom reaches up and takes my hand. I gaze at her, and an absolute tidal wave of emotions—both gnarly and soft—wells inside me.

"I love you, pumpkin." I squeeze her fingers.

Her face changes—it dances with an infusion of new light. She slips her hand from mine and toddles away, a fast little ghost crab steering through the sand. "Daddy! Daddy!"

She is about to bust—that's how in love she is with her father. I reach into my pocket and finger the old worn stone I keep there. Erik kneels like a catcher who's waiting for a fast-ball. Blossom tumbles into his arms. I wave at him, laughing, but a strange unease tugs at my backbone. Blossom pats his face, her fingers wide. I rub the stone again.

Please don't let anything change, I pray.

The wind switches direction, and just like that, Blossom and Erik fade to black. In their sudden absence, I feel as if a confession is in order: I didn't know who I was praying to back then and I don't know now. The wind gathers me in, hard and tight, and spins me like a well-shot marble. I am being pressed tighter and tighter, smaller and smaller.

I am a spirit ball now, rolling through this vast blackness.

A Letter Murmur Lee Harp Wrote to Blossom Cordelia Charleston Nathanson Harp and Tucked in the Pocket of the Dress the Child Was Cremated In

My Dearest Bloom,

Oh, Blossom, how I love you!

No matter what happens or where death takes you, baby, you must never forget the many gifts you gave me. And I will not forget, either. I will remember each one every second of every day. They will be my catechism, guiding me through a life without you: the sweat that beads along your hairline and trickles down your neck in summer's deep heat, the delight on your face when someone you love walks into the room, the way you pronounce dalmation (A Hundred and One Damnations!), the purity of your love for your daddy (he does love you, baby—he's just going through a spell), your eyes moving under closed lids as you dream, the kindness you've always offered the universe—no wonder dogs and spiders alike are attracted to you—how your feet tap the earth with such wild joy when you dance, your endless stream of questions, the way your arm hairs gleam translucentlike in the sun, the very pretty shape of your nails, the way you sigh when you mull over a math problem, the ferociousness of your tears, the rebellion etching your voice when you sass me, the way you gaze into space, lost in thought, when you think no one is looking, your odd fear of lightning bugs and your obsession with mockingbirds, the excitement in your voice when you talk to me about this or that at school, the fact that you still seem to like lying on the beach with me at night and naming the stars, the many different things you want to be when you grow up (that's a sign that you see the universe as a giant YES), your disdain for pancakes but your love of syrup, your old soul demeanor with Dr. Simon—your sweet and steady countenance demands respect and challenges him not to give up on you—your wholehearted generosity in putting up with my lotions and potions and talismans, all of you. Really, Bloom, absolutely all of you. There will be no forgetting on my end of things. You might think I'm weird, but even your sour breath in the morning is a scent I treasure.

This is what I want you to remember above all else: You are my heart, Blossom—the reason I breathe.

I don't want you to be afraid, baby. This is new territory, don't you know! But never doubt this: You will always be surrounded by love. I'm not far away. Ever. I wish this was different. I want to hang on to you all my days. I will never understand why the universe is taking you. It must be because you are so beautiful. And as much as that tears me up, we must believe that this is a good thing. Because only good things happen to you. Remember that, Blossom. You are charmed. In this life and the next.

When you do go over, I pray that you will haunt me, that in the early-morning light, and eveningsong dusk, and the starry darkness, I will from time to time feel you near. And despite my deep-in-the-gut longing for you, I will glean joy from this idea: You are everywhere, Bloom. I will experience you in this world no matter what. In the sun I will see your smile. The moon? Your sweet blue eyes. And your laughter, that will unfurl for all time in the surf song.

Go with God, baby. And do so with the happiest of hearts.

I love you I love you I love you,

Mommy

Lucinda Smith

The fucking problem is, I hate fucking seagulls. They're fucking flying rats. They fucking eat rubbish. But it's the only fucking series of fucking paintings I can sell to the fucking tourists. Assholes.

Even Murmur, who acted like she loved everybody and everything, took potshots at the big fat ones who shit all over the rocks in front of her house.

Just for the record, I am totally pissed at Queen Murmur. I mean, there is nothing more selfish than suicide. The sweet talkers around here are full of shit. I don't believe for one minute she went out on that river drunk and fell overboard. That woman never made a sloshed false step. Loaded, she could walk a high wire in a full gale and never fall.

I know exactly what happened. I'd bet my golden ovaries on it. Women in love: They're real suckers.

The first hint of Murmur in love occurred July 28, 2001,

during the weekly yoga class I taught at her house. Me, Murmur, crazy twat-confused Edith, and Dr. Z. What a crew.

I was standing by the sink—Murmur's house was mainly one large room—lighting my fourth cigarette of the day, and Z walked in wearing pink tights and a Miami Hurricanes jersey.

"Jesus Christ," I said, blowing smoke at him. "You look like a fucking fag on acid."

"What?" he asked, feigning ignorance and tossing me a bottle of orange juice. "Here, drink this. It'll help stave off that cancer you're working on."

I popped the lid. Z bopped about the room, picking up one knickknack after another: shells, framed snapshots, cobalt vases (Murmur favored cobalt; she said it possessed special powers), all the while carrying on a stream of conscious dialogue, which I refused to follow. Just as he tucked a remarkably lifelike rubber coral snake beneath one of Murmur's throw pillows on her bed, she walked out of the bathroom, dressed all in purple, her brunette straw hair piled atop her head.

"Oh, look, an elf," Z said as he zipped over and kissed her on the cheek.

She looked him up and down. "Well, aren't you something! What are you supposed to be—the Easter bunny? I swear to God, Zach, you crack me up." She straightened the neck of his jersey with all the gravity of a housewife adjusting her husband's tie. "I'm so glad you're in my life."

He squeezed her waist and nuzzled her neck. Poor bastard. He was totally hot for her. It was utterly and fucking hopelessly obvious.

I stamped out my cigarette in the sink. "You people are fucking crazy."

"And you're not?" Murmur laughed. She broke off a tip from an aloe plant that she kept on her kitchen counter, along with a dozen other cobalt planters filled with herbs. "Something is wrong with my stomach," she said before sucking on the aloe. "You are gorgeous today, Lucinda. I wish my skin was as clear as yours."

I turned away. Picked my butt out of the sink. Tossed it in the trash. It embarrassed the shit out of me when she talked that way.

Murmur walked over to her fridge, which the salt air had turned into a standing rust box. "Where's Edith?" she asked. Then she opened the door, bent over, peered in. "Anybody want a Co-Cola?"

Z was nearly drooling as he took in Murmur's ass. "Freak." I hit him in the chest.

"Those things will kill you," Z said.

I lit another cigarette, inhaled hard and deep. "You think every fucking thing will kill you."

"Cokes, cigarettes, and aloe. That's all," Z said as he adjusted his balls. "Murmur Lee, I don't think you ought to be ingesting that stuff. I know you're the witch and I'm just a doctor but—"

"Nonsense." She stuck out her tongue, squeezed the aloe, and a silvery droplet made its mark. "What I want to know is," said Murmur, closing the fridge door, a Coke bottle in hand—she favored the small bottles, said they tasted better— "what do your Mennonite friends, Lucinda, think about your smoking?"

"They're pacifists. They can't complain about anything."

"That is not true!" Z shook his head and his thick black hair bobbled.

"Look, who's the fucking pacifist here? You or me?"

"Quit fussing and help me move the couch against the wall," Murmur said, her slash-of-blue eyes shining.

As Z waved her away and manhandled the couch by him-
self, Edith called from the bottom of the stairs, *"C'est moi! Ici!"*

She ascended. That's what Edith does. She doesn't walk or
climb or enter. The bony old man who thinks he's a woman ascends stage left, stage right, even from the fucking rafters.

"Bonjour!" She fluttered into the house, wearing peacock
blue silk pajamas and a matching head scarf. Her matching
slippers were hand-beaded. *"Bonjour! Bonjour! Bonjour!"* She
kissed each of us on the cheek.

I studied my pathetic trio of students and thought, I'm
twenty-four fucking years old, and what do I have to show for
it? I paint fucking pictures of fucking birds and wander into
Mennonite meetings once a fucking week, and live in a shack
on a nearly deserted fucking island with only a few fucking lu-
natics to keep me fucking company. Well, it beats living at
home with my fucking psychiatrist parents. Talk about fucking
quacks. I started another cigarette with the ember of the one
I'd just lit. A nervous habit. I blew the smoke through my nose
and then said, "All right, you weirdos, let's get started."

"Wait, wait!" Murmur held up her hand in a gesture that
looked as if she were about to bless us. "I have a question.
Would you mind if I brought a guest next week?"

"Fine with me," I said, "as long as she pays."

"Lucy, it's her house. She can invite anyone she wants." Z
stretched his left arm over his head, then his right. His jersey
drifted above his navel. I thought, Jesus, Doc, I don't want to
see your fucking hairy pot belly.

Edith arched one very nicely penciled brow. "I don't believe
the intended guest is a she."

Z, who can go from a good humor to a flat-out sulk in under one second, cut his eyes at Murmur, who was beaming like
a fourteen-year-old who'd just discovered sex and weed.

"Yes, Edith," she said, "you are absolutely right." She stroked that hollow spot at her throat. "My new friend is a he."

Z planted his hands on his pink-shod hips and asked, "He?"

Murmur danced her fingers coyly along her jaw. "Yes. I have met a man. A very nice man. And I thought if it was okay with all of you, I might invite him to yoga."

"There's not enough room." Z's protest was immediate.

"Oh! *Mon amie!* We'll make room!" Edith glided over to Murmur, held her by the shoulders, and, with tears in her old gray eyes, exclaimed, "Finally, romance in our midst!"

Z flopped down on the couch and glared at the Atlantic.

Pussies, one and all, making me sick to my stomach. "Fuck it." I stretched my arms over my head. "We can talk about this later. We need to get started, or we'll never get out of here. Murmur, go put on your damned music."

"We certainly are in a mood today, Lucy," Murmur said as she bolted over to the stereo and cranked up the CD. We fell into our respective places: me in front of the sliding glass doors and Edith, Murmur, and Z strung out behind me in a ragged line. We began with sun salutations, repeating the movements, breathing, slowly increasing our speed and heat. Why was I so fucking cursed? Who in the world has ever heard of doing yoga with the Allman Brothers blasting in the background? But Murmur wouldn't allow me to play my soothing *om om om* music. She said she didn't trust it, whatever *that* means. And when I suggested we skip the tunes all together, she pouted.

So there we were, the four of us, battered all to hell by this fucking weirdness called life, attempting to get in touch with our chakras to the gut-thudding strains of "Statesboro Blues." *Ommmm* and Duane Allman's rock 'n' roll blues riffs didn't exactly make for unruffled mind/body/spirit partners. Although I have to admit that meditating to "Stormy Monday" is not a totally unpleasant experience.

"Breathe in through your nose and hold it," I instructed, cigarette clenched tighty in my molars as we stood in the *urdhva hastasana* position. I took in as much air as my smoke-cured lungs could bear—but not enough, sometimes, is too much—and then started coughing and could not stop. My eyes watered and my face turned red. Just before I doubled over, my cigarette shot out of my mouth like a flaming arrow, hit Murmur in the chest, landed on the floor, rolled, and came to a rest at my toes. We all collapsed, fucking laughing our asses off, except for Z, who just glumly looked on, heartbroken.

When we recovered, I lit another cig and we began again. *Vinyasa.* Corpse pose (we were all pretty good at that one). Child's pose. Downward-facing dog. Whatever! Edith, actually, was the most limber of the bunch. Murmur had too much Cracker blood ever to be an accomplished yogi. And Z? Well, I will give him credit for trying, even if every time we attempted a standing forward bend he would, first, fart and then, second, try to explain why such a position was physically dangerous, saying that none of us should ever try it again.

Now, I might not be the calmest yoga instructor in the world, but I am pretty damned perceptive. In the four years I knew Murmur, I thought that one of the many things we had in common was an uncanny awareness of the undercurrents we all swim and drown in daily. But on that Saturday morning in July, love had blinded Murmur.

Here was Z, a man who was crazier than hell, but loyal and good. A widower once over, whose affection for Murmur was as true as any I've ever fucking seen. A few times I thought she might even want to jump in the sack with him. Hell, I've seen stranger things. But she always insisted, "Me and Dr. Z? Not!"

Still, she was gentle with his feelings, never flaunting any of the men who drifted in and out of her life like smoke. Until that day anyway. At the end of the session, as always, I had my motley crew lie down, close their eyes, and drift into relaxation while their bodies cooled down. I wanted them to maintain the positive energy they had built up over the last fucking weird-assed hour and to release any tension they might be holding. I rang my singing bowl. It sent currents of ancient song through the room.

"Let yourself go. Feel the energy. Become aware of what your mind is doing. We are calm. We are at one with the universe." "Stormy Monday" washed over us. Edith's head scarf fluttered in the breeze. I lit two incense sticks. "No more tension," I said. "Only light. Let yourself accept this sense of well-being."

"God, I haven't felt this good since yesterday afternoon when Billy fucked my brains out right there on the kitchen floor."

I stopped waving around the incense and took in the reactions. Edith was in la-la land. Murmur the sex elf was oblivious to the razor she'd just swiped through the air. Z kept his eyes closed, but his body tensed.

"Just shut the fuck up, Murmur," I said, jamming the incense into its balsam holder.

"Oops, sorry!"

Before "Stormy Monday" and our relaxation period were over, Z gathered up his tacky towel with the image of a fat lady in a bikini emblazoned on it. He tried to tiptoe out.

"Where the hell you going?"

"I've got tons to do. I've got to drive into town and get some paint for the sleeping porch, and I promised Katrina's mother I'd stop by and help her around the house." He kept moving, heading straight out the door.

"See you later," Murmur called breezily.

"*Au revoir!*" Edith warbled.

As soon as I heard the Roadmaster crank, I marched over to the stereo and flicked it off. "I swear to God, Murmur, why don't you just stab Z and get it over with? It would be less painful."

"Uh-oh," Edith said, stretching like a cat, pushing her fake boobs skyward.

"What on earth are you talking about?" Murmur rolled onto her stomach, propped herself up on an elbow, and rested her chin in her palm.

"Z! You 'bout killed him with that 'fucked my brains out' business. It's one thing to invite someone to yoga. It's entirely different to talk about fucking him."

Murmur batted her lashes at me. "Why, I did not hurt Dr. Z's feelings. There is absolutely nothing between us. Never has been. Never will be. Besides, who could be mad at me for being in lust! You could not believe what we did last night."

"Jesus!" I shook my head and reached for my cigs. "Sex has turned you into one selfish bitch."

Now Edith was all ears. She sat up and tucked her legs together, anglewise, like a proper lady. "Oh, do tell!"

"Y'all make me sick. I'm leaving. Just think about what I said, Murmur." And with that, I grabbed my cigs, mat, singing bowl, and incense and headed out, pissed to hell and back that not only was Murmur getting fucked but that she was doing so with no grace whatsoever.

*T*hat's it, the beginning of Murmur's end. She fell hard for a jerk. A badass boy writer who thought he was a gift from God. Fell so hard, she turned her back on her friends. And when he dumped her (I just feel he did, even though he'll never own up to it, but I know it the same way I know seagulls are nothing more than evil, no-good, fat bastards), she could not live with the consequences of her actions.

I would have done anything for her. Nut-twat Edith would have, too. And as for Z, his heart was so thoroughly on his sleeve, his shirt bled. He would have welcomed her back in faster than he could check his fly. I wouldn't have minded if those two had gotten together—I'm a big-enough person to admit that—because even though I loved her (platonic, of course; I gave up sex when I quit pork), I know that Z could never have screwed her over so bad that she wanted to die.

But Billy Speare did. He screwed her in every way possible. And Murmur lost her goddess spirit in the process. Bang, bang, bang. Fuck, fuck, fuck. So she drowned herself.

Motherfucker. To hell with my Mennonite ways. I will never forgive Murmur for leaving me.

Dr. Zachary Klein

Katrina and I were high school sweethearts. Met in biology class. She and I were assigned the same dissection frog. That's right: We fell in love amid the stench of formaldehyde and the sorry sight of frog guts.

She was frail and blond and shorter than I. The height, that was a big plus. The vertically challenged Napoléon in me couldn't do tall girls. Physically speaking, Katrina was barely more than a dewdrop. Even her bones were tiny. I always teased her that her parents should have named her Willow.

We went to the University of Florida together. She got her degree in education. Me, biology. When we graduated, she returned home to St. Augustine and landed a job teaching first graders how to make block letters and count to ten on the stiff fingers of stick men. I wandered off to med school.

Truth is, I was not faithful. Couldn't be. I was sex-addicted. Aren't all young men? Testosterone is a mighty drug. But I remained true in other ways. Never tumbled into a moral dilemma or made a decision about my future without asking myself, What would Katrina do? She was my heart's compass early on.

And I didn't dillydally in Cambridge. As soon as I got my degree, I came back here, started a family practice, bought an old house within earshot of the ocean at Iris Haven, and asked Katrina to marry me. Talk about pins and needles: She didn't give me her answer for three days.

Turns out that her parents did not want her marrying a Jew. But their delight over the idea that their daughter would be a physician's wife outweighed their bigotry. Too bad for them that they didn't realize I'd never be in the game for money. Treating Medicare and Medicaid patients—most of whom are migrant workers—doesn't put you on the pathway to six figures, a fat stock portfolio, a manse in the burbs, a Jag, a flop-top Mercedes, and membership in the country club. I don't know what it puts you on a pathway for, except out of the social circle of other physicians.

But that's okay. Listen, what we got was a simple, happy life. Katrina loved her students. I felt I was doing God's work out there in the camps, tooling around in my Roadmaster. Three years. Plenty of laughs. Lots of sex. No children. And then, six months of a deathwatch.

When the diagnosis came down, everybody assumed I'd take care of her. Her parents, her sister, her friends, her colleagues. *Oh yeah, Katrina is married to a doctor. He'll make sure she gets the best care. He'll stay home and nurse her through the worst of it.*

I let everybody down. I'm not a man. I'm a coward. I don't know what we would have done without Murmur Lee.

In high school, Murmur Lee and I ran in different circles. She was one of the wild girls: keg parties on the beach, lots of dope, most likely plenty of sex. Me, I was a dweeb one hair short of a pocket protector. When I moved out to Iris Haven, though, things changed between us. Especially after I married. She, Katrina, and I ate dinner at each other's houses. Edith would often join us. Sometimes Lucinda. We became buddies, a circle. Polite, loose, kind, easy.

I discovered the lump in Katrina's breast. We were making love and I felt the malignancy—hard, like a cherry—beneath my fingers. I knew the second I touched the tumor that if it were not death I was feeling, then it was something damn close to it.

Sure. I've read my Kübler-Ross. Denial, anger, bargaining, depression, acceptance. Yes, Katrina and I went through all the stages of grieving. Except I stopped at depression. I'll never accept that she is gone. And as for Murmur, perhaps I'm still stuck in denial.

No one can ever accuse Katrina and me of not trying. We did everything in our power to kill the beast. I believed in science. Chemo. Radiation. Double mastectomy. Bone-marrow transplant. T-cell therapy. Science will save us. Science will save us. Oh yeah, science will save us. That's what I kept telling her. Instead, I should have shouted, No! Enough! Stop! Science is a religion as iffy as voodoo! Bring in the rabbi! Bring in the priest! Bring in the goddamned faith healer!

Katrina knew it wasn't working. But she stuck with every form of torture I threw at her. She let herself be dehumanized, experimented on, all in order to appease me. Hers was an act of love, mine the ultimate selfishness. I put her through hell because I couldn't face the prospect of life without her. Coward.

After all the traditional treatment modalities failed, we traveled to Durham, North Carolina, to seek absolution and healing from the physicians at Duke. Thirty days of hell and isolation as we thundered through a botched T-cell transplant. Our doctor sat with us in the sunroom, its walls a sickening bile yellow. He spoke to me, not Katrina. I wanted to bust his ass. You know what? He couldn't even look at me straight on. Only pretended to. He stared at a spot below my eye. A cheek doesn't give away much, doesn't expect much. His voice was smooth. How else do you deliver a death sentence?

"The cancer has metastasized to Katrina's brain. We can go in and—"

Katrina lifted her twig hand, a hand full of IV holes, and said, "No." Then she turned and looked at me with those sea green eyes that bulged from her crumbling face and said softly, as if she were trying to ease my pain, "Sweetheart, I can't do this anymore."

I wanted to say, No, no. Hope is not lost. Don't give up. Don't do this to me. Hang in there. Let them cut on you. Just one more time! I reached for that twig hand and held it gently, hoping to find strength there. She was the strong one. Always. But there was nothing left—just clammy skin, heartache, resignation. And without finding in the parched lines of her palm some slight sign of a stubborn insistence to live, I couldn't utter one more hollow promise carved from the cruel inexactitude of science.

So I brought her home to die.

And it was there, in our house, on the banks of the Iris Haven River, that I abandoned her. I hired twenty-four-hour hospice care. I left early every morning and worked well past sundown. Sometimes I drove the Roadmaster through the two-lane farm roads around Elkton until midnight. She was always asleep by the time I returned. I wanted it to remain that way, with me never seeing her when she was lucid. I was angry, bitter, lost. And, oh yeah, a coward. All that I had ever believed in—the empirical world of logic and proofs and clinical fact—turned out to be useless against invisible sharp-edged cells so glutinous, they ate my wife from the inside out.

I made it her fault. *Damn you for giving up, Katrina. Damn you. I'm sorry I ever fell in love with you:* Those words became my cancer, eating away at my brain, my heart, my gut, endlessly. Day in, day out. If I could remain angry, I could stave off facing the inevitability of her death. Maybe I could even stop loving her.

Into this void stepped Murmur Lee. I didn't ask her. She just decided. Every morning, I slipped out of the house before sunrise, did my work, and didn't look back. I didn't say to myself, Take the day off. Spend it with your wife. Feed her some warm broth.

Murmur Lee, on the other hand, informed her crew at Salty's that she wouldn't be around much. She let the bar—her livelihood—operate under its own goodwill and that of its patrons. She exhibited saintlike compassion, and I hated her. All that goodness shone like a spotlight, making it impossible for me to hide my flawed nature—lousy husband, ineffectual physician, profoundly disgusting excuse of a human being.

One morning, I overslept. That was a fatal error. I stood in the kitchen, downing my coffee, while the nurse dealt with Katrina on the sleeping porch. Murmur Lee slipped in through the back door, not bothering to knock, dressed in too-tight blue jeans and a Harley T-shirt.

"And how are you today, Zachary?" she asked, all business, unloading groceries, books, CDs, herbs, and lotions from the willow basket she carted about as if it were a child.

I didn't answer. Instead, I stood there, cup in hand, fuming, watching her move through my kitchen. My space. She straightened a photograph of Katrina and me that hung on the wall above the wine rack. She wiped spilled pepper off my dinner table and slapped it from her hands into the wastebasket. She threw open the refrigerator door and began rearranging its contents. As fast as a match to gas, anger flew all over me. I was angry enough to do something rash, like throw my coffee cup across the room. She was all bent over, fanny in the air. She had a nice ass.

"Why are you doing this?" I asked, not bothering to conceal the nails in my voice.

"Well, the orange juice needs to be kept cold. And if I can get some of this yogurt down her today, we'll be doing really well."

"Stop it, Murmur Lee. You know what I'm talking about."

I turned away, tossed the rest of my coffee in the sink, tried to steady myself by rinsing the cup.

She walked over to where I stood, leaned against the counter, wiped her chin on her shoulder as if she'd spit on herself, and said in a near whisper, "Look. The hospice nurse is great. It's not that. She can handle all this by herself. But maybe . . . maybe I just need to be here. I've got my own reasons. Okay?"

I stared down at the stained white porcelain and at the coffee pooled near the drain. I wanted to smash everything. Anything. Something. Without looking up, pushing my fingers through my hair, I said, "Fuck you."

And I didn't so much as glance at Murmur Lee. Nor did I kiss my wife good-bye. I gave that up once she made the decision to die. I simply walked outside, got in my Roadmaster, cranked the engine, and tried to drive into a different day.

So it was Murmur Lee who read Agatha Christie and Loren Eiseley to Katrina. Murmur Lee who fed her when she was too weak to feed herself. Murmur Lee who helped the hospice nurse change the sheets and clean my wife. Murmur Lee who rubbed potions into her drying skin.

And it was Murmur Lee who gave me the greatest gift one could possibly ask for: a way out, and a way back in.

She ignored my rude, boorish behavior. She came by every morning, full of positive energy and small talk. I couldn't get out of the house early or fast enough. I ignored her, turned my back to her, told her to get the fuck out many, many mornings. All she ever did was cock her little-bird blue-eyed face and offer a blessing: "You go on now; we've got things covered here."

And I did. Her blessing carried me into the potato fields, where I treated strangers, curing their skin rashes, treating their gout, setting their bones, and easing the sore throats, infected ears, and wheezy coughs of their babies. I could heal a stranger in nothing flat.

But for my wife? What could I do for my wife?

This is what I will never forget about Murmur Lee: She proved to be far more stubborn than I, way more hardheaded. She put up with my anger and abandonment, waiting me out, minute by minute, hour by hour. Don't know how she did it. Four A.M. and I'd be leaving the house? She'd be there. Eleven P.M. and I'd be just slinking home? She'd be there. There was no beating her at whatever game she was playing. So I gave up. Or maybe, like Katrina, I just got tired. All I know is that after three weeks of this baloney, I started coming home by six o'clock every evening.

And that's when Murmur Lee began shining the light

down the path in earnest. She'd greet me as I walked through the kitchen door, shooting me through the heart with those deadly bright eyes. Anger and the fatigue it inspired had made me helpless against this woman. She'd say, "Come on, time to see your wife," and I'd do it. Dull, dumb, but I did it. I'd follow her out onto the sleeping porch, where Katrina lay, surrounded by freshly cut lemon balm, candles, Murmur Lee's potions, lotions, and scraps of cloth she'd dyed herself and which she claimed offered comfort. Who was I to argue? The volume on the stereo was turned low, but someone was always crooning: Ella Fitzgerald, Frank Sinatra, Rosemary Clooney. For some reason, Murmur Lee thought torch songs would ease my wife. Or maybe she played them for me, for us. I don't know.

She'd motion for me to sit, and I would. Katrina would open her morphine-clouded eyes, and recognition would flutter—in her and in me. A part of me, an old, almost-dead part, so wanted to hold my wife, comfort her, tell her how much I loved her. But any of those things would have split me in two. Anger was safer. So all I could do was stare into her once-lovely face and try to force my mind into a cold, dark, silent void.

But then Murmur Lee would begin to ask all the questions Katrina would have if she'd had the strength. "What did you do today? Did you see Mr. Acuff? Does he still have that awful cough? And what about Mrs. Williams? Is her daughter doing any better? Did her boy get out of jail?"

Astonishingly, I would answer. I would keep my eyes on Katrina. Sometimes hers would open and she'd smile slightly as I spoke about my day. And while I did, after being prompted enough that I started speaking on my own, Murmur Lee would slip out.

And that's how it happened, how—with Frank singing, "Don't change a hair for me," or Ella: "Walk my way and a thousand violins begin to play," or Rosemary: "You go to my head and you linger like a haunting refrain"—I would hold my wife's hand, touch her face, kiss her cheek. The first time I did this, I hadn't touched my wife in three months.

After a week of being just so with her, I tried to take one more step in. On that bleak path, crowded by dying candle-light, lost in the sound of surf and silken voices, while Katrina slept, I took off my shirt and tie and slid out of my trousers. A good husband, a real husband, a man and not a coward, would lie down with his dying wife. I pulled back the white cotton sheet. Katrina's skin was translucent, her bones a collapsed and brittle nest. She was drying up. I could have grabbed an arm, a leg, a toe, snapped it in half. Did she need me? Had she already traveled well beyond any comfort or love I could provide? I started to stroke her cheek, when a gust rattled a shutter. The sound startled me. I jerked, knocking over a cobalt bottle of some sort of potion Murmur Lee had concocted. Katrina didn't respond. If I woke her, would she even know I was there? Did any of this matter? I pulled the sheet back up over her. I sat down in the chair beside the bed. What idiocy. Why, for even a few seconds, had I entertained the notion of behaving like a husband? I sat there staring at my nearly comatose wife until the candles burned down and darkness swept in.

At first light, I woke. The porch was cluttered with Murmur Lee's junk—plants and fabric and chains made of bells. The sea wind blew hard. I leaned forward, resting my head and arms on the mattress. Katrina was wide-awake. Not dead. Still not dead.

"Good morning, baby," I said.

A slow skeletal smile spread across her twisted face. "Zachary, you're still here!"

"Of course I am," I said. "I'm not going anywhere." She reached over and touched my hair. We both knew it was a lie.

Other than one's own inefficacy to prevent death, the worst thing about watching a patient die is knowledge. As a physician, I know what happens when the body begins to shut down. I know about opportunistic infections, and fluid building in the belly to the point that an emaciated patient looks pregnant, and tumors that gather in colonies like impenetrable opaque soap bubbles atop mastectomy scars, and lungs so crowded with cancer cells that the tissue itself begins to pop open. Pop, pop, pop, pop, pop! But silently, unseen.

What I don't know, however—indeed, what none of us knows—is what truly happens once that last breath has been inhaled. Forget the near-death experiences, when people talk about the tunnel and light. The brain plays all sorts of tricks when it's in distress. We don't know what's out there. Maybe faith is nothing more than the crutch of the weak. Maybe nothing happens. Maybe you just die.

October 3, 1998. We knew it was nearly over. Even Lucinda—the baby who would be a hard-ass—got over herself long enough to come to the house and sit in the living room with Edith while Murmur Lee, Katrina's parents, her older sister, Opal, and I watched over what proved to be Katrina's final day.

Howard, Katrina's father, kept pacing and looking out at the Atlantic and uttering totally idiotic, inappropriate things, such as: "You need to check out that new steak place in town. They serve a filet that puts Bonanza to shame."

And her mother kept picking at a spot on her sweater sleeve until she'd successfully created a small hole. When she wasn't picking, she was fussing with her daughter's bedcovers and saying worriedly, "Where's that ice? She needs more ice." Or: "Don't you think it's time we gave her a sponge bath? I'm sure she'd feel better cleaned up."

As for Murmur Lee, she rubbed my wife's feet with eucalyptus oil. She rubbed calendula oil through Katrina's thin, brittle hair, which had slowly begun to grow back. She placed strips of soft raw silk in my wife's palms.

I sat in the chair next to Katrina's bed and monitored her vitals. The objective measurements would see me through. The oils and lotions and silk would see Katrina through. I took a washcloth out of a bowl of ice water, wrung it out, placed it gently on her forehead. When I did, her lips moved. She was trying to speak. Her parents did not notice. But Murmur Lee did. We looked at each other, both of us beyond tears, both of us sensing that we had reached the edge of a high cliff and one of us would have to leap. I did. I stepped into the void, leaned over, placed my ear near my wife's lips. "What is it, Katrina? What can I get you?"

It took a long time. I am not a good man. But I am patient. And I admit that her faint respirations against my ear felt like salvation, which is a lot for a Jew to say. Howard was talking, her mom was jiggling the water pitcher, Murmur was warming oil between her hands, and Opal was staring with raw eyes at the floor. Katrina opened her mouth, a bald little baby bird, searching for a breath.

I stroked her head, kept my ear to her lips.

"Katrina, I'm here. Whatever you need, you let me know." Something had happened. When I jumped off that cliff, I landed in her world. We were on the same path now. Yes, we were struggling along, but we were together. I felt a trot rising.

She rasped so softly, I could barely hear her say, "Zachary."

"What?" I already knew. "Tell me."

Her lips moved, but no sound came out.

"Katrina. Tell me."

She breathed out as hard as she could, I think, and then said, "Let . . . me . . . go."

I rubbed her cheek and finally did what had been threatened: I split in two. "You sure? Katrina, are you sure? Be really, really sure."

She squeezed my hand, opened her drug-hazed eyes, and saw me. I'm sure she saw me. "Please. Zach. Please."

"Oh, baby." Suddenly, there was no oxygen in the room. There was no way to breathe. And no way out. Whatever anger and confusion and denial had sutured me together those past five months snapped wide open. My two cracked halves splintered. I was useless. A pile of thorns. "Okay, sweetheart. All right." I rubbed her forehead and I rubbed her hands. I could hear our feet pounding down that path.

Murmur leaned in close and asked, "Is it time?"

I said yes, automatically, as if I were a zombie. I goddamned said yes. I took the eucalyptus oil from Murmur Lee. I stroked Katrina's head, stared into her, deep down into her. She closed her eyes again. Murmur Lee shuttled my wife's family off the porch. "Zachary and Katrina need some time together." That's what she told them.

In those few irreversible minutes, I did it, goddamn it. I became a husband again. I removed the bedcovers and anointed my wife head to toe. As I rubbed the oil into her translucent skin, I whispered over and over, "I love you, Katrina. I love you. You are my life. I love you." I massaged her twig neck and twig arms and twig legs and twig toes and twig fingers. Someone, I don't know who, it must have been Murmur Lee, slammed in Sinatra and there he was, crooning that old saccharine tune "It Had to Be You." Without thinking, I started singing along, softly at first and then fully, without shame, every single word. Yes, in the final moments of my wife's life, I serenaded her.

I sang and sang, and when finally there was not a patch of skin I hadn't tried to soothe, I walked over to the stereo, restarted the song, turned up the volume, and sang some more. I filled the syringe with just enough morphine to help her leave this wasteland, this carnival built of pain. Beneath the song's sweet façade, I heard our feet—Katrina's and mine—barreling down the path. I pumped the drug into the portal taped to her leg—the veins in her hands had long ago collapsed. My hands—healthy, strong ones—shook. I recapped the needle, set it on the side table, crawled into bed beside my wife. I rested my head against her chest and counted. One. Two. Three. Four.

Yes, four respirations. No doubt.

Frank and I were about to launch into a new verse when the music was suddenly sucked from the room. And when the music ended, so too did the sound of our feet—beating, beating—down life's path. I held my hand above Katrina's mouth. Nothing, not one puff of air, shallow, scraping, or otherwise. I reached for her wrist, searched for a pulse. Even then, I pressed my face against her lips, praying a miracle would grace us, since science had failed us.

There we stayed, a married couple in love, me holding her

while from time to time I checked for a pulse, a respiration, anything.

I did not hear Murmur Lee enter the room. All I heard was her voice: "Z, you gotta let go. It's time. Z, it's time."

No, it was not time. It would never be time.

Even as I eased out of my wife's bed and lifted the sheet—let it fall over her still face—I was fully aware that I could not take a single step down the other path, the one she would never grace.

Murmur Lee Harp Reflects on Her Life as a Catholic, a Witch, a Parent of a Dead Child, the Wife of a Bad Man, and the Friend of a Tragic Couple

I guess I'd better admit it: I was never a very good witch. Look at the evidence. Despite the fact that I sewed a lizard—which, as far as I could tell, had died of natural causes—into the pocket of my husband's favorite pair of trousers, he still gave in to his bleakest tendency—that of an emotionally dead asshole—when Blossom got sick. I couldn't rustle up one decent cure or potent prayer for my own daughter. And as for Zachary and Katrina? No amount of me dancing naked under a full moon eased either one of them.

Also, I guess I should admit this: Maybe my talents as a witch were forever undermined by the fact that once you're a Catholic, you're always a Catholic. That's bitter knowledge. But I think it's the only thing that can explain my inefficacy as an earth mother and my holy bent to die in the months after Blossom's death.

Those were razor-wire days. I had to remind myself to breathe. That's how deep my grief ran. If I could stop breathing for long enough, I, too, would take up the ghost and, thereby, be reunited with my baby. I performed this oddly voluntary act of inhaling and exhaling out of habit—not conviction—and I hated myself for not having the courage to stop the intake of breath altogether.

So I resorted to courting death, but in the most Catholic of fashions. Suicide by accident. I drove too fast, under the guise of trying not to be late to wherever I was hurtling off to. I took fistfuls of sleeping pills chased with Wild Turkey, because surely I needed a good night's sleep. I stood under trees in lightning storms.

Oh, yes, lightning. I placed lots of faith in it. I did all the things that Florida natives know not to do in electric storms. I talked on the phone, stood on an aluminum ladder and pretended to be cleaning out my house gutters (yes, in a jaw-rattling thunderstorm), took showers, went swimming, ran over to the golf course with an umbrella and club in hand.

Death by lightning was particularly handsome, since it conjured connotations of being struck by the hand of God. And truly no one, *no one*, could ever possibly connect a lightning strike with suicide.

Nothing worked, of course. But there was an upside to my constant suicide-by-accident attempts. It kept me busy. I could—at any time of the day or night—slip into the garage, unearth the chain saw, and try to teach myself to use it as I cut down a perfectly fine kumquat tree. You should have seen me wander across Avenida Menendez at rush hour.

What was the other thing I did? Oh, yes, I walked. I wandered the shore, just like Oster Harp, and I collected every manner of trinket the sea gave up: shells, polished bits of satiny glass, dead creatures. I prayed over them. They became my rosary, my idols, my reminders to breathe.

I don't know how long I tried to die. Or why I stopped. I guess the walking, walking, walking simply delivered me beyond a place where death seemed like a rational answer.

This was the day. I woke predawn, to find myself smack-dab in the middle of one doozy of a lightning storm. The darkness pulsed as if it were being zapped with a cattle prod. What a good time to take a walk! I pulled on shorts and a tee and headed down to the water. Rain slashed my face. I couldn't keep my eyes open because the wind was pushing the rain horizontally. The blowing sand scoured and stung my bare legs. I tripped over a coquina rock, fell, hit my head. When I hit, nothing gave. My skull took the entire force of the blow. There was no reason to get up. I lay there, the cold, salty surf rushing over me. I knew I was bleeding, because there is nothing quite like salt water lapping at a fresh wound. Maybe now I would finally die. And while I waited, I listened to all the world. The ocean's jazz. The wind's howling blues. The thunder's insistent, surprising tympani. The silent phrasing of the rain.

We're not talking epiphany here. We're simply talking about me lying in that zone where the earth doesn't know if it wants to be the sea and the sea doesn't know if it wants to be the earth, and I let their flux and confusion and want fill me up.

As storms tend to do, it moved on. And the sun slit open the darkness. And I was better.

That's all that happened.

And then Katrina got ill. By then, I had regained my faith in folkways. So I fed her secret soups, and slathered her with lotions and oils I'd conjured from rosemary and lemon balm and aloe, and stood over my stove for hours at a time, dying natural cloth with bloodroot, broomsedge, black oak, bayberry, blackberry, bracken, coreopsis, guava, grape, goldenrod, dandelion, elderberry, mulberry, sumac, horsetail, hibiscus, holly, onion, indigo, privet, palm, madder, marigold, camellia, nettle, nandina, juniper, gardenia, sorrel, Saint-John's-wort, rush, Spanish moss, pomegranate, persimmon, tansy, zinnia, fig, peach leaf, tupelo, willow. I used many a mordant agent: alum, chrome, iron, caustic soda, even my own urine. As I did with Blossom, I cut the cloth with shears I'd blessed with basil water. I cut long strips, short strips, ovals, rectangles, hearts, zigzags. I tried to squeeze from growing things their essence, tried to transfer each of them from one living thing to another. It took Katrina nearly two years to die. Maybe if there had been no cloth, she would have only lasted a year. Maybe Blossom wouldn't have seen the pink moon.

But this is my point: Zachary was angry at me. That was good. I was more than happy to take that on, to deflect his bitterness and rage from Katrina, or whomever else he might land on.

After Katrina's memorial service, Z and I sat on his dock, drank beer, watched the sunset. I was dressed all in white—I never wore black when death lingered. He was gaunt and skinny. I don't believe the man had eaten a good meal in six months.

"Z, I'm taking some of your trousers home and hemming them. You've lost so much weight, your pants are dragging in the dirt."

He glared at the chaotic light of the setting sun and said, "Why'd you do it? Why were you so good to me? I've been such a rat bastard."

I chewed on my lip for a few seconds, mulled over the very real option of lying to him, and then thought, Oh what the hell. "It wasn't out of the goodness of my heart. I did it in order to stop hating my husband. And I think it worked. I mean, I'm still not above burning a dead bird with his name stuck in its beak, but I figured out something these past few months. He didn't abandon Blossom and me because he hated us. Or because he didn't care."

Z's jaw tightened, and I feared he was grinding his teeth so hard that it might cause a brain aneurism. "Well, Murmur Lee, I'd sure like to know what the hell you'd call it."

"Quit grinding your teeth, Zachary."

He shot me a look that brimmed with the kind of annoyance you can only summon if you love someone.

"Leaving was easier than sticking around. He couldn't watch his child die. I don't think he ever loved me. But he did adore Bloom. I will insist on that. I'll argue until the whole world pukes that he loved his little girl. His leaving us is the one true sign I have of that." I stared down into my beer, knowing that I had finally spoken the truth.

Z reached toward me. He was about to put his arms around me, give me a big old hug, but he stopped short. Of course he did. He wore his fear the way women wear love. He breathed in deeply. I shook my beer to see if I had anything left other than backwash.

"I would sure like some oysters," he said.

"Me, too."

And maybe it was then, with my folk wisdom once again intact and my Catholic propensity for confession satiated, that I decided Zachary Klein was one of the finest men who ever walked the planet.

Charleston Rowena Mudd

Ghosts. This place is crawling with them. And I'm not talking about your run-of-the-mill goblins à la Stephen King or Steven Spielberg or even Edgar Allan Poe. I'm talking about energy and memory. About the simple act of rounding a street corner and suddenly being twelve years old again, watching an ambulance blaze past, ignorant of the fact that it is ferrying your father to Flagler Memorial Hospital, where upon arrival he will be pronounced dead. About a pink spray of crepe myrtle plunging you back to a sun-dappled afternoon in your childhood when you and your mother lay on a chenille spread in the backyard, watching the sky, naming the clouds, the blossoms and afternoon light casting lacy shadows across your mother's pretty face. About how Murmur's clothes in the laundry hamper, her stubbed cigarettes in the clamshell ashtray, the scraps of handwoven cloth in the wicker basket, and the pair of sneakers crusted in sand by the front door all evoke her essence, her living warmth, her refusal to truly die.

About how every time the phone rings—her phone—I jump and then have to fight the threat of tears because my brain hurls me back to the early-morning call from Dr. Z, who informed me in sonorous tones that my best friend had died in an accidental drowning. Yes, energy and memory—the knowledge that the past isn't through with me—are driving my highbrow, Harvard-educated self half-mad.

The land and seascapes are gorgeous here, but they, too, glow with ghostly auras. I find myself traveling to and fro around St. Augustine with blinders on, trying not to notice what has been torn down and what has been built in its place. Gee, there used to be a charming little beach cottage on that dune. Now a five-thousand-square-foot monstrosity looms over flora, fauna, water. And there, across from Fort Matanzas, my parents and I picnicked on the beach against a backdrop of undisturbed coastal plain, land that offered habitat to all manner of wildlife: bobcat, dune rattler, rabbit, meerkat, skink. The dunes and scrub are gone now, replaced by condos and tennis courts and swimming pools. Nowadays, the predominate wildlife chumming these shores are weekend drunks.

I feel as if I'm being batted about in a world of strange gravity, a universe where flowers bloom underground and blood lies motionless in the vein. I left these windy shores to escape the South and the ghosts of my upbringing. But when physical reminders—tattered remnants or spanking new monoliths—tap at memory's door, I am, by turns, grateful and distressed that I have returned home.

But whose home is it? Whose space am I inhabiting? Whose life am I living? I occupy Murmur's house. I sleep in her bed. I listen to her CDs. I pour through her photo albums. I drink her beer. I tend to the many details of her will. I watch the sunrise from her front porch and the sunset from her back.

I use her towels and her sheets and her soaps. I haven't even bought my own toilet paper yet. I exist in the shadows and frames Murmur left behind. Remember what happened in Hiroshima and Nagasaki? The heat and impact of the A-bombs were so intense, people evaporated. But their shadows—the outlines of their corporeal souls—remained behind, testaments to the tenuous thread that tethers us to life, on sidewalks and city streets and park pathways.

Without any real sense of who I am—the labels by which I defined myself are all extinct; I'm not a scholar, or a student, or a theologian, or a southerner, or a northerner, or a bride—I find myself swallowed up in Murmur's wake, in the ripples she left behind. Everywhere I look, I see the outline of her soul.

Yes, Murmur may have left this earthly plain, but her influence lives on as a haunting of epic proportions. She floats and furls amid my scattered heart, enjoying—I think—a hearty laugh at my expense. She must have had quite a time writing that will of hers, leaving her junk heap of a workhorse truck to her lazy, no-good, child-abandoning ex-husband, her guidebooks to Father Diaz, and that dump of a bar to me.

Salty's. Let us just say that nothing like it exists in Cambridge. With the dissolution of my engagement, with no living relative to rely on, with no true friends, when I fell from the lofty snobbery of well-educated Boston, I landed with a splat. What am I going to do with a bar? Especially this bar. Salty's is a tacky testimonial to Old Florida, pre-Disney Florida, the Florida of coffee-stained, nicotine-sticky, dashboard-faded, uncluttered road maps that led visitors to the underwater big-fish wonders of Marineland, the amazing gators at the Alligator Farm—which climbed slides and zoomed down them, to the delight of Yankees and schoolchildren alike (that has since been deemed cruel, and all they do these days is lie around in fetid water, waiting for a possum carcass to be tossed their way as they grow fatter and fatter—and farther south, into the Central Florida citrus hills, whose geometry and color needled even the most urban visitor to contemplate the beauty agriculture surprisingly inspired, and maybe the adventuresome traveler would gas up at the full-service station and press on even farther, venturing to the bottom of our world—a watery land many a Florida native had never seen—a place where mosquitoes and good fishing and Miccosukee Indians held at bay the now-ubiquitous pesticide-soaked golf courses.

Structurally, Salty's is a garage—a wide garage, to be sure—and on cold winter days, the sliding doors are kept closed in a futile attempt to beat back the nor'easter gales. Otherwise, the place is wide open, sandy, shady, and horribly hot if the wind has died.

Situated on A1A, at the base of the Crescent Beach ramp, its clientele is an eclectic mixture of folks who rub shoulders only within the confines of this dilapidated but remarkably functional icehouse. On weekends, the place jostles with locals, old salts, surfers, families on vacation, and marine biologists from the Whitney Marine Laboratories just south of Iris Haven.

Junk covers the walls and all of it is for sale. Rubber flip-flops, beach towels, beach balls, suntan lotion, sunscreen, aloe vera cream, Frisbees, batteries, postcards, cold drinks, chips, beef jerky, Styrofoam coolers, sun visors, baseball caps, University of Florida crap (UF Gator this, UF Gator that), big dill pickles. If you are going to the beach and can't find what you're looking for at Salty's, you don't need it.

Furthermore, it is widely known that Salty's serves the coldest domestic beer (not a single bottle of imported beer has ever crossed this bar's threshold) within a twenty-mile radius. There is no wine on the menu, although the license allows for it. Rumor has it that Murmur feared wine would class up the joint. But being a good businesswoman and not wanting to ignore the tastes of some of her female customers, she stocked wine coolers.

The finest thing about Salty's in my humble, worldly opinion is the food. The kitchen serves up the greasiest hamburgers this side of Eden, grilled hot dogs with sweet relish, and on special days—traditionally, only Murmur could call a day special—grouper sandwiches. On weekends, breakfast is served: bountiful omelettes with cheese grits and biscuits and strong chicory coffee. Every Sunday morning, the hungover scientists from the Whitney descend, chasing their coffee with Budweisers and Bloody Marys they prepare themselves.

Let me, this very moment, drive home a point that should already be startlingly obvious: I had no earthly idea how to run a bar, nor any real interest in learning the ropes. Even though I had reentered the belly of the beast (I hadn't seen a Rebel flag displayed on a pickup in five years, and, I can tell you, when that open Jeep zipped past, the Stars and Bars whipping in the breeze, I choked back both shame and anger), my intention was to remain intellectually stimulated, socially and politically aware, and sophisticated, with an earthy flair. How I would manage this feat of intelligent grace as a barkeep was beyond me. But I was fairly certain it would involve being rarely present.

My plan was to throw the entire ordeal into the capable hands of Hazel Bing, Salty's veteran bartender, a woman I knew through reputation only. Murmur raved night and day about her. Indeed, on several occasions she said that without Hazel, Salty's would have most likely run to ruin years ago. Murmur described her as kind, gracious, generous, beautiful, funny, and smarter than a hungry rattlesnake. What could go wrong? With Hazel on my side, I'd be able to steer clear of the bar's day-to-day drudgery. This would allow me the time I needed to wind my way through the stomped-on, broken-in-two organ I once called my heart—a necessary task if I were to recover some semblance of self-confidence and self-control. Once the task of rebuilding my heart and soul was accomplished, I would—if my conscience allowed it—sell Salty's and begin anew. Perhaps I'd chuck theology and pursue brain surgery.

By the time I had gathered the spine and nerve to think about my responsibilities vis-à-vis Salty's, I had been home for three weeks. My biggest accomplishment was fulfilling Murmur's wish that she be cremated and that her ashes be kept in a small stoneware crock her grandfather had thrown himself. The ashes were to remain there until the weather improved—when spring had sprung—at which time we were to conduct an ash-spreading memorial service in front of her house on the beach. In a letter dated one month and two days before her death, which she put on file with her attorney, Ms. Cate Mc-Gowan, she expressed these wishes and added the admonition that she didn't want any variety of priest present. My, how far we both had journeyed from our Catholic roots. Still, I am, by turns, grateful for her guidance and needled by her prescience.

My return home was an astonishingly low-profile affair. The first person I phoned was Edith. I informed her that I needed some time alone before I'd be ready to see anyone. She didn't like it, but I think she understood. I hoped that she would put the word out to leave me alone, but evidently she skipped Dr. Z, who stopped by unexpectedly, offering his help with the cremation arrangements and cautioning me that most people who worked in funeral homes were necrophiliacs and that I would really have to put my foot down. Other than for the phone call informing me of Murmur's death, I hadn't spoken to Zach in any appreciable way in years. I had forgotten how weird he was. So when he told me to put my foot down with the necrophiliac morticians, I began to laugh insanely, but inside my gut was ripping apart. And, lastly, I steered clear of Salty's for as long as I could possibly manage, because of who all and what all I might find there. Ghosts come in all shapes and sizes, including that of old boyfriends and the women who stole them from me. Besides, I hate to fail. But I couldn't shake the post-traumatic stress–induced certainty that failure was the only card on my table.

Unbeknownst to me, while I hid out in Murmur's house and dutifully tried to meet the letter and intent of her will, Salty's had remained open, not even closing for a day or two in the immediate aftermath of her death. I would learn later that since no one knew what would become of the place—the existence of Murmur's will was a surprise to everyone—Hazel Bing and the regulars held a wake of sorts and voted to keep the place running until the law, the bank, the IRS, the ex, or whoever shut them down. They decided that was what Murmur would have wanted. They surely didn't expect a stranger—namely, me—to walk in some sunny Monday and announce that she owned the joint.

But a Monday morning it was, sunny, with a definite bite in the late-January air. Even though I had endured four Boston winters, the North Florida cold—so wet and breezy—still shocked me. I sat on Murmur's plush couch, with its menagerie of pillows that gleamed like topaz squares against the agate cloth, nursing my second cup of coffee, telling myself that I must ditch the half-full Coca-Cola bottle she'd left sitting on the kitchen counter (mold) and the ashtray festering with stubbed-out Virginia Slims (stink). I had left them there—just the way Murmur had, just the way I'd found them when I first walked through her front door—in a desire to stop time, to memorialize, to honor. I looked at her mermaid mobile slowly spinning in a mist of cobwebs and then her kitchen sill with its collection of cobalt glass bottles that pinched and released rays of early light, and I said to the house, "Shit."

I walked over to the kitchen counter, poured the Coke down the sink, and tossed the bottle, the ashtray, and its contents into the trash. The illogical constellations of guilt and grief engulfed me.

"Sorry, Murmur," I whispered, realizing that those of us left to struggle and flounder in death's wake really must make a conscious decision to move on or drown. And I wondered, Is that what Murmur did? Is that why she made a will and penned a letter to her attorney detailing her wishes? Did she know her time was up? Had she made a decision—watery and vague, but a decision nonetheless—that she'd best set her affairs in order? How does a healthy thirty-five-year-old woman come by that sort of precognition? Does the soul recognize that the light is about to be snuffed out? Does God, that Grand Jokester, ruffle through your dreams, seeding innuendos of death?

I scanned her one-room wonder of a house, aching for her to walk through that door and say everyone had gotten it wrong. I wanted time to reverse itself, for it to shuffle to a stop and then step backward, backward, backward until it stumbled into New Year's Eve and Murmur in her boat in the Iris Haven River.

"Shit," I repeated. Nearly a decade had passed since Blossom's death and yet reminders of her life were still everywhere—photos on every wall, table, and bookcase, even a lock of blond hair tied with a blue ribbon hung from the archway leading to the kitchen. How in the world did Murmur stand it? I wondered as I swept through the room, placing each image of my goddaughter facedown.

I passed Desdemona—that figurehead from a long-ago shipwreck that Murmur kept poised by her rocker, positioned in such a way that her wooden gaze forever looked out to sea— and paused. Using my shirttail, I wiped off a sprinkling of dust that had settled on the bridge of her nose. And with that, a thought: a good cleaning. That's what Murmur's house needed. Maybe it would be an exorcism of sorts. I'd scrub away the residue of the past, forcing both immovable and movable objects to shine. The floors would smell like lemon and the linens the sea. Everything—no matter its size or import— would get buffed, polished, washed, or otherwise affirmed. My instincts were like mushrooms casting spritely spores of renewal all about. It would be some kind of start. Of what variety, I was unsure, but that was one of the things my mother had taught me: "When in doubt, no matter what you're wavering about, if you can't kneel, then clean." I would drink good bourbon and play John Lee Hooker and Muddy Waters and Memphis Minnie really loudly in Murmur's honor. And I would clean and drink and maybe get drunk and cry.

But first—without question—I would cast one more

demon behind me. I would drive down to Salty's and introduce myself and inquire as to Hazel Bing's whereabouts, and I would start to set Murmur's business in order.

As I changed clothes four times, unsure of how I should present myself upon laying claim to Salty's, my mind tumbled through all the people I might run into. There was my old beau, blue-eyed Ulysses Finster, a commercial fisherman and one fine lover, who had dumped me for Beulah Masters. Beulah was from an old Minorcan family that took no prisoners. Once she set her sights on Ulysses, I knew it was over. And while losing him hurt my pride, I didn't remain wounded for long, since I had plans that didn't include anybody from around here. Then there was Rusty Smith, an old school chum who claimed to be an environmentalist but who had made millions selling North Florida coastal scrub to developers. Oh, and let's not forget Helen McAlister, a queenly member of the St. John's County Chamber of Commerce, a good old gal who called black people "niggers," Italians "wops," Cubans "spicks," Jews "kikes," gays "fags." If there was a racial slur anywhere within a ten-mile radius, she'd be sure to use it. And all of these people were going to laugh behind my back, telling one another they'd all known I'd be back, that there was no way no how I'd be able to hack it up north. I decided upon the first pair of jeans I tried on—they were brand-new and still smelled like the store. I checked my teeth for any residue of the toast I'd eaten for breakfast. I told myself it didn't matter what anybody said. I had come home for Murmur. Only Murmur. My return had nothing to do with not hacking it.

As I drove the fifteen minutes from Iris Haven to Salty's I amazed myself. Why, on God's green earth, was I this nervous? I was nearly a Ph.D. I'd nearly completed my dissertation. I'd nearly graduated from one of the finest schools in the country. I'd nearly married a very smart man. My eventual matriculation was a distinct possibility. And Salty's was just a bar. A silly little bar given to me by my best friend, either as a joke or a ploy to bring me home. As I rounded the bend at Devil's Elbow, I squarely settled into my dilemma. Murmur's ghost could haunt me until doomsday and I'd be all right. She could cloud my peripheral vision with the memory of her laughter and infect my blood cells with incurable grief. Still, I'd forge on. I wasn't scared of Murmur; I just wanted her back. But those other skeletons—they inspired fear, dread, self-loathing. I could feel them like a hot breeze on the back of my neck, rattling around, rising up from my past, demanding my attention, my time, my guilt. What did they want? Absolution? Forgiveness? Loyalty? I hit the tattered outskirts of Crescent Beach, fearing I could never appease them.

I arrived at 9:58 A.M. The place was locked up tight. I peered through the front window. A woman—let us say in her fifties, a peroxide blonde with a bosom to match—stood behind the bar, smoking, watching TV. I tried to push open the side door. She glanced at me, stone-faced, and then back at the tube. Well, that wasn't very polite. I knocked on the glass and flashed a quick smile. She shook her head. *We're not open*: She mouthed the words, exaggerating each shape, as if she were sure I was a moron.

Pointing at myself the way a person would if they were trying to communicate with an orangutan, I said slowly, taking
care with each fragile syllable, "I'm Charlee."

She rolled her eyes, shook her head the way people do
when they're faced with a hopeless situation, picked up her cigarettes and coffee cup, and disappeared into a back room.

Somebody in an old ruby Buick sped by, honking. A mini-
van family with Ohio plates pulled into the public parking lot
and began unloading beach chairs, coolers, a boom box, and
sundry other items. It looked as if they were moving in. A
small boy kept screaming, "Mama, I have to pee! Now!"

The father, with his stork white legs, wrinkle-free khaki
shorts, and penny loafers complete with brown socks, looked
totally unprepared for his Florida vacation. The mother, on the
other hand, was ready for nuclear attack: beach cover-up, chemical tan (which actually should be called a chemical orange,
since the people who use that stuff appear jaundiced), floppy
hat, shades, enormous striped bag, and jewel-encrusted flip-
flops. The four children squealed and squabbled. The little boy
who needed to pee was jumping up and down, holding himself. Mom looked in the side-view mirror and ran her tongue
over her upper lip.

Dad shouted, "Shut up or we're leaving." Then he rummaged in a cooler, retrieved a Bud, flipped the pop top, took
a good long fortifying swig, wiped his mouth, and said,
"Let's go."

By now, it was 10:08 and the place still wasn't open. The
sign on the door indicated that Salty's opened at ten o'clock.
Eight minutes late. I'd have to make a note of that. I banged
on the door and shouted, "Hey, it's Charlee Mudd. Let me
in!"—to no avail. So I said, To hell with you, too, then followed the family down to the beach. The wind was brisk and I

was cold. Toll takers were set up at the ramp, and I wondered why the folks from Ohio hadn't simply driven onto the beach, rather than lug all their stuff from the parking lot. I asked the tollbooth operator, an elderly woman with Pepto pink lipstick and leathery skin what time Salty's usually opened. "Well, their sign says ten. But they mean eleven. Eleven Crescent Beach time."

"That's no way to run a business," I said, to which she responded by shrugging her shoulders.

With my arms wrapped tight for warmth, I walked toward the Atlantic. The rollers were breaking evenly, in rhythm with the wind, and I knew that even though the water was cool for my tastes, the surfers would be unable to resist the even, slow swells. I turned around and surveyed the beachfront. So much had changed. Where once there had been dunes and sea oats and pin oaks shaped by the easterly breeze, condos rose, piercing the eggshell sky, their empty-eyed windows mocking those of us who equated progress with destruction. As I stood with my back to the wind, looking first north, then south, I decided every single condominium on every single shoreline in America should be named Tree Hugger, You Can't Win.

A late-model brown Chevy Caprice with Virginia tags barreled onto the beach and lurched to a stop. Before the driver, a seventy-something man with thin gray hair, had turned off the motor, an equally old passenger in the back flung open the door, toddled a few steps, bent over, and picked up fistfuls of sand, a look of wonderment lighting his gnarly face. He watched as the wind whipped the white crystals from his fingers. He patted the sand, laughed, and tossed more handfuls through the sky. I thought, Oh my gosh, this beach, this ocean, this place, has transformed him into a child. I fell prey to my sentimental streak, batting back tears as the visitors from

Virginia—one woman, two men, all of them in the twilight of their lives, linked arms and stumbled in a ragged circle, laughing and reconnecting with—I decided—a youthful joy they thought they'd long ago lost.

*T*he sun had traveled to God's belly button—that's what my mother always said about high noon—before I ventured back to Salty's. The wind had turned my carefully tossed strawberry curls into Medusa ringlets. I smelled like a dead fish that had been dipped in perfume. Thanks to an errant wave and my lack of attention, my jeans were wet from the knee down and I squished when I walked. But I no longer cared about making a good impression or what the skeletons might say (my confidence was fleeting, I knew, but at least I'd found some). I'd had a lovely stroll along the beach, and my irritation at having been ignored upon my arrival at Salty's had not abated. Indeed, it had mushroomed. So while I am an extremely pliant person when unperturbed, once annoyed, I can get very, very grumpy. The cold, the wet, the lack of dignity— all of it took on greater significance in light of the snubbing. Oh yes, I had a thing or two to say to the peroxide blonde.

Two pickups were parked out front. The garage doors were open. A black man and a bearded white man sat opposite one another. The peroxide blonde held court between them. Thank God, I thought, I don't know any of you. Both men drank beer out of icy mugs. The bar was U-shaped. I pulled up a stool on the short end.

The peroxide blonde tossed a Budweiser coaster in front of me. Rhinestone studs—pink, white, and baby blue—sparkled along the outer curve of her left ear. She was, I suppose, the

kind of woman that some men call "handsome," meaning it as
a compliment. Here's the snapshot: big bosom, good legs, well
preserved, bones like a bull, the air of a good-natured middle-
aged whore.

"What can I get you?" she asked, looking not at me but at
the TV. I had expected a southern accent, but what I heard was
South Philly.

"Budweiser. Draft." Why blow my cover right away? It
might be fun to sit here incognito. I might learn a thing or two.
The two men shifted on their stools. The bartender set the
mug down, wiped her hand on the towel tucked into her waist-
band, and eyed me as she backed up to her position between
the men. The white guy sneezed, wiped his nose with his giant
hand, and rubbed it across his T-shirt. My, how couth. I sipped
my beer, miserable, wondering how best to confront the peroxide babe. Rude behavior is inexcusable. I set my jaw hard and
looked at her straight on. She turned away. The black man
studied his nails. The white guy huffed as if it were the end of
the world and he didn't care. No one looked at anyone. I became increasingly self-conscious. My crazy hair, my wet jeans,
my body odor. No one would take me seriously as the boss of
this joint. No one would respect me. Murmur, what have you
gotten me into? The four of us remained locked in an unnatu-
ral silence—I was obviously ruining the party. The only
sounds were A1A traffic and the country twang from the
CMT channel the bartender was glued to.

After about five minutes, which ticked by with the speed of
a boulder on flat ground, the white guy erupted. "Well, fuck,
man"—he punched the air—"whaddya gonna do?"

I had no idea whom he was talking to. And I was afraid. I
glanced over at the black man, whose skin was much lighter
than that of my former fiancé's. He rubbed a small scarred

hand over his knobby cheekbones—the tip of his middle finger was missing—drained his beer, stared into the empty mug, and said flatly but with iron resignation, "Sell the boat. Head south."

"Now, Paul Hiers, you are going to do no such thing." The bartender pulled a cold mug out of a cooler and poured him another draft. "You'll hate it down there," she said, exchanging the empty mug for the full one.

"Yeah, asshole, what do they have down there that we don't?"

Paul Hiers took a healthy drink, let it settle, looked out at the road, and squinted his Byzantine eyes. "Jobs."

"Huh!" The white guy slapped the bar, as if Paul Hiers's answer was the most fascinating news he'd heard all day. He swung around—his beard was kinky and not as clean as I would have liked—and planted his elbow on the bar. I believe I saw him teeter. "What do you think?" he demanded, pointing a half-cocked finger in my direction.

Despite my syncopated heartbeat, I was determined to play it cool. Seemed the peroxide blonde was the least of my worries. I slowly lifted the mug to my lips and took a deliberate sip. I knew I was being tested, and I didn't much like it. In fact, the part of me that wasn't scared found it boring. Academia is ripe with such schoolyard behavior. I tried to bluff my own damn self by silently wagering that this guy—mean eyes, bushy beard, and all—was no match for me.

"Silas," the bartender said in a tone that was both scolding and amused.

"What? I'm just trying to get the lady involved in the conversation." His face opened in mock innocence.

I rubbed the tip of my ear, acting as if I were lost in

thought. Then I shot a sideways glance. "Well, before I tell you what I think, I need to know the problem."

"Is that right?" An eager smirk cracked the darkness of all that crazy facial hair. He sat up straight, stared at the ceiling while his barrel chest expanded with the intake of a deep breath. Then he took turns with his unfriendly gaze, aiming first at Paul Hiers, then the bartender, and finally me. "Paul Hiers here is a fourth-generation shrimper. It's all the mother-fucker knows how to do. And just because we've fucked up the fishing around here and there ain't no damn shrimp, he wants to throw in the towel and get himself a job carrying luggage for rich white folks visiting Miami. But what he don't know is that nobody is gonna give his black ass a job because he don't speak S-span-nole. Ain't that right, Paul Hiers? Ain't that the problem?"

Paul Hiers nodded as if his head were a vertical metro-nome. "I reckon that's about it."

The bartender watched me through the swirl of her ciga-rette smoke. Silas leveled a deadly glare. Paul Hiers thought-fully nursed his beer.

"Well, sir," I said to Paul Hiers, trying to muster my old southern moxie, "if this gentleman's assessment of your dilemma is accurate, then I have to say with all due respect, you're fucked."

Even the bartender cracked up. Silas, his glower suddenly transformed into a puckish glow, howled as he again slapped the bar. Paul Hiers finally looked at me straight on and grinned.

"Honey, what's your name?" the bartender asked.

"Charlee Mudd. I grew up around here and, well, I'm look-ing for Hazel Bing."

The bartender's eyes betrayed a sudden tear. She rushed over, grabbed my hands, and said, "Oh my God, you're Charlee?"

I'm sure that for a moment or two my face betrayed me as it dropped into that elongated, slack-jawed repose of the dumbfounded. "Don't tell me. Hazel?"

"Yeah!" she said, smiling wide, her teeth perfect and white except for the glint of gold crowning a molar. "Jesus H. Christ, it's good to meet you."

"You, too," I said. And we both meant it. We meant it for Murmur. Because she had loved both of us.

We ate greasy hamburgers that afternoon and laughed a lot as we recounted our favorite Murmur memories. Customers came and went. I was thrilled, because I didn't know a soul. The afternoon took on a rosy glow. Croley, an eighteen-year-old sun-bleached surfer showed up for work at four o'clock. His duties were many: bar back, cook, janitor.

When Hazel introduced us, he shook my hand and said, "It's wonderful to meet you, ma'am. I'm so sorry for your loss. We all miss Murmur terribly." Other than for the "ma'am" reference, I was immediately charmed.

Silas remained bombastic, with an edge that glinted mean, defensive, and overly friendly, having the scintillating speed of light spinning off a disco ball.

Paul Hiers struck me as shy, kind, with lots to hide. And I wondered, but did not ask, why he traveled to Crescent Beach to drink, when he lived thirty minutes north up in Lincolnville.

Hazel seemed eager to share with me all she knew about

the operational end of Salty's, and I promised her that I wouldn't change a thing. "Why fix something that's not broken?" I asked.

"Exactly," she said. And then she leaned against the bar, sighed, and whispered, "At least she went out the way she wanted. I mean, she loved that river, that place. It would have killed her to die, say, on the highway or in a hospital."

"Shit," Silas said, and his face clouded.

"Shit what?" I asked.

"Nothing."

"No, what?" I leaned over to him. He scared me, but there was an intensity playing right below the surface that pulled me in.

"It's just that there ain't no fucking way she died by drowning. Not Murmur. I don't believe it for one flat second."

"Oh, don't start this again, Silas. Please don't," Hazel said, shutting her eyes as if to force away his words.

I reached over and patted her arm. "No, no, I want to hear why he thinks that. Silas, what do you mean?" I couldn't tell him that I knew it, too, that my friend, who grew up loving that water, swimming in it as if she were half fish, could never have drowned. But I couldn't give voice to this because I could not deal with the alternatives. Maybe Silas could do it for me.

He clenched his teeth and his fists opened and closed, opened and closed, as if he was struggling not to punch something.

"Silas?" I said, bearing down.

"There's just no fucking way, okay? The gal knew how to swim. She knew the river. Shit, I wouldn't be surprised if she could have walked on water."

I felt myself—my fears and intuitions—slip toward something dark, something so awful, I refused to acknowledge its existence. "But Dr. Z said it was an accidental death. When he called me, that's what he said."

"Look, Silas," Hazel put both hands on the bar and tilted her head the way birds do when they are trying to listen to a faraway cry. "She went out there on that river on New Year's Eve, got drunk, fell overboard, and that's that. You've got to let this go."

"She's right, Silas," Paul Hiers said from his side of the bar. "Even if it isn't what happened, she's right."

Silas's eyes lit with an old anger, an ancient anger, one that I suspected would never be extinguished until he felt the truth was served. I looked at the three of them, not understanding the undercurrents of this conversation. "But what about Dr. Z?"

"Oh, fuck Dr. Z. He don't give a flying flip."

Croley, who'd been lingering toward the back of the bar, piped up then. "You know, a lot of people say it was suicide. That something caught up with her and she just couldn't keep going."

As if I were having an out-of-body experience, I heard myself say, "That's not true, Croley. Murmur could never do anything like that. She wouldn't. It had to be an accident. Somehow, it was an accident."

Hazel breathed out hard and whispered, "Great."

I heard a commotion behind me. Before I could check it out, the commotion sat down two stools over. He jingled a large ring of keys, mumbled under his breath, and took out a pen. He reached for a bev nap and scrawled something on it. His unkempt gray-streaked sandy hair smelled of Ivory soap. With more than his share of a five o'clock shadow, he appeared to be a portrait in studied sloppiness and noise. Yes, his hair was a mess and so was his face, but his smooth hands and neatly trimmed nails betrayed him. This guy was no blue-collar bloke.

"What'll it be?" Hazel asked, reverting back to her stone face.

Paul Hiers whipped around on his stool, suddenly fascinated with the country-music video on the now-muted TV.

Silas stood up. He was a big guy. I didn't know what he did for a living, but his arms and chest brought to mind those beefcake boys of professional wrestling. And he was tall enough that he eclipsed the Florida Gator banner hanging on the wall behind him. He threw down money on the bar, then stared at the smooth-handed man with all the disgust one might convey when being forced to gaze upon an open sore.

The man steadied his focus on the far wall.

"I didn't think so," Silas said, hurling the words as if they were fists. Then he walked out, patting my shoulder as he passed.

"How much do I owe you?" Paul Hiers asked, not turning around.

"Don't worry, I'll put it on your tab," Hazel said. "Billy, I asked you before: What will you have?"

"A Coors, I guess."

I caught Hazel's eye. I mouthed *Billy Speare?* She gave one quick nod. Paul Hiers stood and said, "Later, ladies."

"Bye, sweetheart." Hazel winked as he walked out.

I don't know if it was Silas's insistence that Murmur's death was not an accident, or his violent reaction to Billy Speare, or Croley claiming it was a suicide, or my inability to cope with the fact that Murmur's last boyfriend had just stridden into the bar, but what is surely true is that the earth was rumbling beneath my feet. I had to get out of there. The day had gone on too long and the sunset was being crowded out by ugly questions that I could not, would not, contend with.

"We'll talk later, Hazel," I said.

"Sure, honey, anytime." She set Billy's beer in front of him and took his money.

I walked out into the chill air of the dying day. Why hadn't I introduced myself? Why didn't I simply walk back into the bar and say, "Hello, I'm Charlee, Murmur's best friend. She told me all about you"? I looked over my shoulder. Hazel was reaching for the remote. Croley was mopping the floor. And Billy . . . well, I had the strangest sensation that he was one of those ghosts—a reminder of a less-than-gentle past—who would extract from my flesh something excruciating, something damning, something that would propel me into an abyss both hollow and dark.

A Note Written by Murmur Lee Harp
and Passed to Charlee Mudd
in Their Eighth-Grade Homeroom,
Written in Valentine Red Ink,
Hearts Splattered Across the Page

Bobby Cramer is to DIE FOR!!!!!! He is soooooo CUTE. OH GOD!!!! Did you see him smile at me when we walked in? We have to make sure we get right behind him in the lunch line. Oh God, I LOVE HIM SO MUCH!!!!!!!!!!!

A Love Note from Murmur Lee Harp to Lawrence Fairhope Davis, Written Eight Months After Her Divorce and During Her Brief Employment at the Catholic Day School Located in St. Augustine's Old City (It Should Be Noted That the Affair Ended Shortly After Murmur Sent This Epistolary Rumination on the Nature of Love)

Dearest Larry,

Consider this a message from on high, a message not necessarily aimed at you—perhaps any male from the Midwest will do—but since you're the only person from the Midwest I've ever been intimate with, well, you know:

TEN THINGS MIDWESTERN BOYS DON'T KNOW

1. Girls are sensitive.
2. Girls innately demand that a handful of very specific situations be honored with a plethora of ancient, indelible protocol—protocol (some might call it "ritual") that has been handed down from one womb to the next since the rise of Eve.
   Example: If a boy and a girl have recently spent

three hours exploring, licking, sucking, and
penetrating each other's bodies, then the very next
time they lay eyes on one another? Well, this
encounter is very important to the girl.

3. After lovemaking—especially lovemaking for the
first time—the girl is apt to feel mighty happy but
also a tad vulnerable. It is proper—essential,
even—for the boy to help her feel pretty about
herself the next time they see each other. This is
especially true if something has prevented them
from seeing each other in the days immediately
following the lovemaking (say a horrible illness—
the flu, the plague, mono—has struck them down).

4. If ardent, erotic notes are sent to and fro in campus
mail (dangerous) in the wake of the lovemaking,
rather than a missive in which one of them explains
that the encounter was one big horrible mistake and
mustn't ever be thought of again—well then, once
in each other's presence, a sweet acknowledgment of
their tenderness is quite necessary.

5. Girls who have recently been ravished by someone
with whom they are smitten require this: When the
girl and boy see each other for the first time after
lovemaking (fifteen seconds of running in and out
of a house as if all asses are on fire, with barely a
nod of a hello, does not count), the girl needs the
boy to send some ardent signal, even a subtle one,
that she—and their shared passion—is valued.

6. After seeing a boy for the first time after
lovemaking, the girl does not want to be made to
feel as if she is simply one more haggard colleague
passing in the hall. The girl does not want to feel

that in order to have a conversation with the boy
(Hello. How have you been? What's new in your
life?), she must do something stupid or dramatic,
like run her car into a tree. If the girl feels this
way, it will inevitably cause her to spend yet even
more money with her therapist.

7. When a boy sees a girl for the first time after
they have made love, the following actions are
considered good form. The boy should tell her
hello and that it's really nice to see her. The boy
should give her a hug—even if it's only an aw-
shucks midwestern hug. The boy should tell her
she's pretty, even if she looks like she is in the
throes of the flu. When the boy and girl first come
back into their shared orbit, the boy should be sure
to take five minutes out to sit down with her and
have a pleasant chat.

8. All these things are important because they convey
to the girl that what they shared in her bedroom
while they were all slick and erect and wanting was
something the boy does not regret.

9. The boy should not make the girl do all the work.

10. If a boy makes any or all of the aforementioned
blunders, he usually has a chance to undo the
damage. But it must be done quickly. In fact, it
should be rectified no later than the following day.
If blunders are allowed to stand longer than that,
the girl will decide that the boy deeply regrets
having ravished her, that the coupling meant
nothing to him, and that she must chalk it up to
simply one more mistake. She will also decide that
in the future, the boy is to be given nary a nod.

A Letter Murmur Lee Harp Wrote to Her Husband, Erik Nathanson, Two Days After He Walked Out on Her

Erik:

These things I know:

Your daughter, whom you abandoned in the weeks and days leading up to her death, will never welcome you into the gates of heaven. Indeed, she will make sure you never get that far.

Your betrayal of me—with someone half your age, how laughable is that!—is a function of your illness. You are mentally ill. I don't know the diagnosis (sociopath? psychopath? evil motherfucker?), but the symptom is as follows: You attempt to destroy everyone who loves you.

And finally, I leave you with this: Sex with you was always boring.

Sincerely,

Murmur Lee HARP

(I also changed Blossom's surname)

My Dearest William,
I was shocked when you entered me and filled me and
stayed deep inside me . . . shocked because of the
absolute wonder of it.

Wanting,
ml

Billy Speare

Thanks to the review in the *Times*, *The Sex Life of Me* took off like a bottle rocket in Baghdad. Six months earlier, Knopf had put me on the road. Thirty-six cities in thirty days. One hotel room after another—they all looked alike. Cities looked alike; bookstores looked alike. And so did the handful of lonely little old ladies who came to hear me read. Three to five blue-haired biddies at each stop. Washed-out, watery eyes, thin-toothed, thick-ankled. And every one of them in a book club. Hell, I started to think that Knopf had hired them. So I drank my way across America, all on my publisher's tab. Maker's Mark, Wild Turkey, Jack Daniel's. As long as it was whiskey, I was all right. The liquor helped me not care that the asshole interviewers hadn't read my book, or that the old biddies said they would wait to buy it until it came out in paperback, or that the airlines lost my luggage not once but three times.

Oh yeah, that was all behind me. Thanks to one well-placed

brilliant review, I was almost a hairbreadth away from making the List. *Best-seller, here I come:* That's what God began to whisper in my ear morning, noon, and night.

And it got even better, because my good fortune with *Sex* paled (well, almost) in contrast to the extraordinary time I was having with Murmur. After that day on the river, it wasn't long before we landed in the sack. She was a sexual leviathan, hungry all the time, pushing for more.

Oh yeah, buddy, the first time: candlelight dinner and the works at her place. I can't recall what we ate. It didn't matter. I was focused on those firecracker blue eyes, which sparkled with bad-girl playfulness. I watched her shovel something in her mouth and I thought, Oh what she could do with a long, hard prick.

We rumbled over to her bed—a big, high altar of a bed, covered in peacock blue silk—as soon as the dishes were stacked. We kissed gently and we kissed hard and my fingers explored way up there and her hand worked my member. We went on and on like that, but my fucking dick would not get hard. It was the damnedest thing. The thought crossed my mind that maybe she'd put something in my food. I did everything I knew. I sucked her. I boldly watched her. I fantasized that I had three chicks doing me. Nothing.

I was embarrassed, but mainly I was angry. I mean real anger. Like I wanted to shoot out the lights. So I took it out on Murmur. I made her come so many times, she finally begged me to stop.

Next morning, though, it was a different story. I reprised my manhood with a dick as hard as an old oak log. She took it all, with her legs up over my shoulders. Yep, it's what I thought when I first laid eyes on her: She was all twat.

So after a good long, hard fuck, there we were, wrapped in

each other's arms and a postcoital glow, our first romp in the sack, and she etched my cheekbone with a finger that smelled like sex and asked, "So, what do you write?"

I pinched her nipple. "I write," I said, kissing the tip of her puck nose, then her freckled shoulder, "great"—kiss— "fucking"—kiss—"novels"—kiss. Throat, neck, lips.

She leaned up on one elbow and rested her pointed little chin in the cup of her palm. "I know you write. But what I want to know is, do you write anything I would have heard of?"

Well, that certainly put it on the table. "My most famous book is a collection of short stories called *Good People from a Bad Town*. But the *Sex Life of Me* is well on its way to outshining *Good People*."

"Wow, that's amazing. You don't strike me as a literary type." She fumbled with my chest hair. "The way you were talking last night, I figured you wrote travelogues or something."

"Oh yeah?" I rubbed my hand across her breasts. She was staring to piss me off. "What would you know about literary types?"

She flicked her tongue across my lips. "What I know just might surprise you."

I pulled her close. "Listen, if we're going to keep up this sort of activity, you need to read my books."

She pressed her pelvis into my groin, arched her back, fiddled with something beyond her tousled hair. "Nope. Not yet."

"What? Why not?" What the hell was she talking about? I rolled her off of me and slapped her ass.

"Because I want to know you, the real you, before I start reading all that fiction you evidently churn out. I'm interested in what's up here, and here, and here," she said, touching my head, my heart, my dick. "And then we'll get to the rest."

I wasn't sure what to think of that, or even how to respond, so I kissed her deep and long. But we didn't fuck, because I was tapped out. The limp dick from the night before would certainly not see the light of day. Again, she arched her back and presented to me the slender curve of her neck. I kissed it. She tasted salty. Then, exhibiting an innate feline grace, she sat up, stretched her arms over her head, yawned with a manly timbre, and slid onto the floor. That's how high the damn bed was—when she sat on the edge, her feet didn't touch the ground.

"How about some coffee, bacon, eggs?" She stood naked before me, her hips just a slight swell and her breasts small, firm, with dark owl-eyed nipples. I had a sudden urge to cry. This woman was so honest, without pretension. I lay there looking at her, thinking, Why the hell hasn't a woman this fine been snatched up by somebody by now?

"Why don't you have a man?" I asked. "You're gorgeous and funny and smart. Seems like men would be knocking down your door."

"Ha!" Her face turned sly. She walked away but said over her shoulder, "Who's to say they aren't?"

Bitch. I laughed, got out of bed, and followed her to the kitchen. I wrapped my arms around her, cupped her breasts, pressed myself against her back and behind. I whispered into her ear, "You rock my world."

She reached back and squeezed my dick. "You're pretty amazing yourself," she said. She spun around and touched my face. "Why don't you go take a shower while I fix breakfast?"

"I've got a better idea. Why don't *we* take a shower and then we'll both fix breakfast?"

"Is that right?" She had two dimples, both of them at the corner of her left lip.

I leaned over and gently kissed her cheek. Then I took her

by the hand and led her into the bathroom. I shampooed her hair and slathered lavender suds between her breasts, down her thighs. I rubbed her shoulder blades and the small of her back. I knelt down and washed the spaces between her toes. I massaged the valleys and rises of her bone-thin ankles and lightly traced a grim mouth of a scar on the back of her right calf. Hers was not a perfect body—I mean, she wasn't fourteen anymore—but that's not what I was looking for. Murmur's body reflected her soul—a little wild, a tad bit off center, honest, basic, full of yearning.

We toweled off, slipped into tees and jeans. I can't remember what we talked about. That's because our words were unimportant. Imagine that—me saying words were unimportant. But that morning, in that kitchen, what mattered is that we spoke about things of little consequence. Ours was an easy conversation, one that flowed illogically, simply, like a stream sliding over river rock. We ate eggs and drank strong black coffee. We laughed. We found ourselves humming along to an old Beatles' CD she'd popped into her stereo. She dabbed toast crumbs off the corner of my mouth and I put a slice of bacon between my teeth and leaned into her and she bit clear through it. We told each other stories. I don't remember those, either. All I can recall is that for the first time since my divorce ten years past, I felt as if I might actually become, under Murmur's influence, a decent man.

Murmur Lee Harp Sees Her First Date with Billy Speare

Here I am, still dead as rain, floating along, scattered one moment, gathered the next. Sometimes I'm hard and tight and fast-moving. But there are other moments when I feel as if the universe has tossed me like a handful of salt just to see how far I'll fly.

I'm a little scared. I mean, can this be all there is for all of eternity? Is this what spirits do? Forever? Blow about like pollen in a dimension composed solely of wind, watching from time to time film clips of their lives? Where's God? Where's a little band of angels trumpeting golden horns and shaking silver-dollar tambourines? Where are the legions of those who have come before me? Where is Blossom? Where the hell am I?

The wind folds me up, kneads me like dough, and there, at my new center, is Billy Speare. He is knocking on my opened door, a bouquet of store-bought daisies in his fist.

I say, "Welcome!" and float over to the door—radiant in

my yellow strapless sundress, which shows off my trim figure. He kisses me on the cheek. "Come in, come in. What can I get you? What beautiful flowers!"

I fuss in the refrigerator, searching out the coldest beer. I fuss at the sink, trying to arrange the daisies quickly but with flair as I stick them in a blue vase. I fuss with my hair. I fuss with the marinara sauce on the stove. I fuss with the silver beads around my neck. I fuss with everything my hands touch. I am a mess.

He walks through my one-room house (that's a lie—my bathroom is its own space) and says, "Wow! What a view, what a great place!"

"Why, thank you. I built it myself, you know. After my daughter died and my husband left me. I had to do something. Here. Here's a picture of my little girl." I grab a framed image of Blossom off the bookcase. She is five and is dressed like a mouse for Halloween.

"She . . . she died," I say stupidly, trying to figure out if I'm repeating myself.

"I'm sorry," he says. "That must be really hard."

"It is." I put the photo back and curse myself because old grief tears suddenly threaten to spill down my face. I manage in a steady voice to ask, "Do you have children?"

"Yeah, I do. But I don't want to talk about it."

I look at him real hard, trying to divine the problem. I get nothing.

Next thing I know, I see us in bed. He pleasures me. He seems unconcerned with his own needs. I am so impressed. I think, Here is a man who might actually love women. Right then, naked, in my bed, doing it with a man who—if you really, really think about it—is a stranger, I decide to give him all of me in every way. It's time, I say to myself; it's time. You've got to get over being scared to commit. This guy is loving you up. Walk out of the pain of Erik Nathanson. Walk out of the pain of Bloom's death. Walk out of the sorrow of fucking a man just to know you still can. Walk into life.

His head is between my legs. He is loving me there. Yes, right there. I say, "Stop. Baby, please, stop. I want to talk to you."

He licks me all the way up to my forehead and then pulls me tight. "What is it, girl? You have such a crazy name. Murmur Lee," and he begins to laugh, and I interpret this as joy.

"Do you love your mother?" This is a serious question. I run my finger along the outer curve of his ear. I stare past his shoulder and into the black, star-torched night. Erik hated his mother, accused her of many crimes, including stupidity, clumsiness, and forgetfulness.

"What kind of question is that?" he asks. "Here we are, making love, and you ask me about my mother?"

I squeeze him tighter. "Yes. Tell me."

He doesn't respond right away—there is maybe a five-second pause—and I'm determined not to fill it with anything except for a silent expectation that he will answer. "I suppose you can say I loved my mother. That's what we do. We love our parents no matter what. It's obligatory." He cups my breast. "But it's not like we had a good relationship. She was a bitch, Miss Murmur Lee. A grade-A jagged thorn of a bitch. I was happy when she died."

I close my eyes three times, pretending it's the stars, not me, blinking. Grateful for the darkness, I spin around in his arms, giving him my back. For a few moments, I ponder the possibility that I am a cursed woman. How could I have met and immediately flipped for yet another man who doesn't love his mother? I fight back tears and panic. I hold on, wrapping my arms around his. But he seems so nice, I tell myself. So very, very nice.

"Murmur Lee, you okay?" he asks.

"Oh, yes, Billy," I say, knowing it's a lie but trying to please, fully throwing myself into the familiar comfort of old patterns, "I'm just about the happiest woman you've ever seen."

Oh no. This is bad. I spin round and round, shot full of holes. The truth stings. For all my bravado, all my independence, all my spell casting, all my book reading, all my talk about the Universe and what she wanted, I see now that when it came to men, I never knew how to behave.

I hate this place. I hate this knowledge. I want to go home. Where is Bloom? I want my daughter.

The wind slams me high into this eternal night. Up, up, up—I am encased in light and moving fast. My life scatters all about, splintering like shattered glass.

Edith Piaf

Two days after they pulled Mur from the Iris Haven River, she visited me in a dream.

I was on the beach, naked, gazing down at the celadon water that rushed over my bare feet. Ten feet away, a dolphin lay sleeping on the shore.

"Edith! Edith!"

I spun around. There she was, dressed in Prada. In real life, she never wore designer labels.

"*Ma chère!* I thought you were dead."

"We are both dead, Edith. You and I, we are dead." She touched the back of her hand to my face. She smiled so sweetly, and I thought, This rest has done you a world of good.

She patted her head. "I lost my hat. I need my hat."

"We'll go up to my house and find you a new one," I said, and as I turned to go, my legs twisted at the hip and then all the way down, like a licorice stick, snapping completely off. A wave swept in and carried them out to sea. There I was: a torso stuck in the sand. I began to weep.

"Don't worry. You won't need them." She removed her hair as if it were a wig.

"But Mur, I don't want to be dead."

She threw up her hands as if to say, *Hey, what can you do?* and walked away. And I was left on the shore, unable to move, the sleeping dolphin my only companion.

Lucinda Smith

I don't fucking know how long it had been—three, maybe four days—since Murmur's suicide, and I just fucking couldn't take it anymore. I went out to my studio and looked at those paintings—stacked, in some cases, six deep—of fucking seagulls and I held my hands to my ears and screamed.

Then I fucking went out to the toolshed, found a shovel, and started digging in the middle of my backyard. I dug and dug. The sand was full of crap—broken glass, petrified shells, pop tops, plastic toy cowboys.

"Motherfucker," I kept saying. "You goddamned mother-fucker!"

I brought out my paintings, every single last one of them, and tossed them in the pit. They looked insane down there, all stacked up, hither-zither, and I thought, This is the best work of art I've ever created. I started singing—and I mean loudly; I was yelling more than I was singing—"One monkey don't stop the show! One monkey don't stop the show!" I retrieved from the shed the gas can I usually used for the lawn mower, emptied it in the pit, soaked those fucking seagulls, and then tossed a match. Poof! Just like that, those embarrass-me-even-in-my-sleep paintings were ablaze.

And for some reason, I said right out loud, "So, what do you think of that, Murmur?"

Charleston Rowena Mudd

I had to do it.

The day after I went to Salty's, I woke up in Murmur Lee's bed and knew I couldn't take it anymore. So I got up, peed, washed my face, brushed my teeth, fixed some coffee, put her beloved Allman Brothers on the stereo, went down to the garage, and found five empty boxes and a stack of newspapers. It was a start.

I marched myself back upstairs, stood in the middle of the room, and said, "I'm sorry, sweetie, but I've got to do this."

I swiped at my tears as I began purging the house of Murmur. I began with the photos of Blossom. I removed all but one—it was of her and her mother; they were all dressed up and obviously going somewhere. I packed up all but one of the cobalt vases. I hadn't yet sent the books off to the church or the Zora Neale Hurston collection to Lincolnville—they would have to wait. But I boxed Murmur Lee's clothes. And I did it quickly, refusing to allow myself to linger there in the denim and cotton and linen and silk memories.

When I was done, I sat on the couch and stared at the ocean and wondered how much longer I could go on missing her this much.

Dr. Zachary Klein

I accompanied Murmur Lee's body to the morgue. Silly, I know. But I just couldn't let her take that ride alone. Then I went home, poured myself a tall bourbon, and stood on my back porch, unable to go down to the dock, not wanting to get that close to the place Murmur Lee took up the ghost.

The bourbon went down hot and smooth, but it did nothing for the grief. I wished there was a pill I could take. Pharmacology hasn't come very far, I thought, when it doesn't offer one damn thing that cures grief.

I hadn't been with a woman since Katrina died. My hand, as they say, had become my best friend. So I went inside, walked to my study, logged on, and Googled adult chat rooms. Up came something called AdultFriendFinder.com. That's what I needed. An adult friend. I went to the site, and while my blood pressure rose a hair because my old, expired moral compass was spinning out of control, I filled out all the proper fields. Gave myself the screen name Stallion—now, that made me laugh—and started exploring. I entered a chat room whose description indicated it was a no-holds-barred party place. They weren't kidding.

BIG DICK 1: I'm looking for some ass to fuck.

PUSSY LICKER: Anybody up for a three-way? Let me shove deep in some bitch's mouth, way down her cunt throat.

FUCKSOGOOD: Hey, do me. I got wet, wet pussy and the titest asshole Big Dick1 ever seen. I'll make you cum till u scream.

BIG DICK 1: Bring it on, Fucksogood. Show me that tight asshole.

FUCKSOGOOD: Ok, Big Dick. Here it is. Way up in yur face. Lik it while yur there. Oops! Sorri, I go. My baby is cryin.

Oh my God. I zipped the cursor across the screen, trying to find the button that would log me out. What had I done? I looked at the message on the screen: *Come back soon, Stallion.* I turned off my computer, pissed that I was getting hard, and headed for the kitchen, where I poured another bourbon. I had to cancel my membership. I could never log on again except to cancel. No. I had to log on and find Fucksogood and tell her that she shouldn't let men talk to her that way, that she shouldn't put herself out there as if she was nothing but meat, that her baby needed a mother who respected herself. Out of habit and mental weakness, I stupidly thought that I would tell

Murmur Lee what I'd done and that she'd get a big laugh out of it. No, you stupid fuck, she's dead.

And then I sank to the floor, bottle in hand. I stayed like that, on the floor, drinking, memories of both Katrina and Murmur Lee keeping me there. I held the bottle to the light. The bourbon looked as though it were lit from within. Liquid amber. "You are terminal, my man," I said to the air, and then I took another swig.

Edith Piaf

A party. *Oui!* We must have a party.

I hadn't yet opened my eyes to the leaden dawn, and already I was preparing to declaw February's nor'easter winds by throwing a soiree.

Eyes still closed, I reached for my moisturizing cream on the nightstand. At two hundred dollars a bottle, this stuff was not to be smeared on as if it were dime-store Oil of Olay. According to the package, the emollient base contained pulverized oyster shells, pearls, kelp, sea urchin, seaweed. I felt like a walking sushi bar each time I slathered it on. But the truth is, *la crème* works. And given my aging skin (oh, how I hated to admit that) and the harsh winds, I'd have plastered on cow manure if I'd had to.

I uncapped the jar, dipped two fingers in, patted the cream on my face, began massaging it in, and thought things over. Darling Charlee was back. We'd survived an entire month frozen in grief over Mur. And now it was time to drink.

Together. There had been no gathering in the aftermath of Mur's death. Our grief was private. Unseen, unspoken. No hugs. No shared memories. No witnessing of one another's tears. Only absence. And silence. Except for the wind. That was unrelenting. New Year's Day is when it began: a raging gale straight off the Atlantic. Its howling—incessant and consuming—filled the silence, bloated it, ate it, regurgitated it. One day, I drove to Hastings just to get away from the sound. *Oui,* it is safe to say that all of us on Iris Haven were beginning to feel battered by an invisible but fully engaged force. I won't say the wind was the enemy. *Non!* But surely it was weakening our collective resolve to plunge forward in the face of tragedy.

I lay there in my four-poster, feeling the cream seep into my thirsty skin, gently rubbing the crow's-feet that framed my eyes, and I thought, *Oui, oui, oui:* A party is the only cure, the only possible remedy for our malaise.

With a surprising amount of vigor, given that I'd been awake but a few brief moments, I popped out of bed, reached for my journal, and penned an invitation.

> *Let us try to lift the cold and fog.*
> *Let us use what power we have*
> *to toss the wind back to sea.*
> *Let us gather at my house*
> *for a White Party.*
> *La Soirée Blanche.*
> *Oui!*
> *White in the middle*
> *of winter.*
> *Our own Florida*
> *snowstorm.*
> *We will*

laugh and cry,
eat and drink,
and celebrate Murmur Lee.
Even our undies
will be pure and virginal.
For a few hours,
winter won't have a
chance.

That's right, I composed my invitation in the form of a mediocre poem. Voltaire I'm not, but I doubt he could sing. And what fun this party would be! Everyone in white and all white food: deviled eggs filled not with spicy yolks but a horseradish whipped-cream sauce (ah, the gas that would produce!), white cheeses, white asparagus, white chocolate, white grits, white bread, white fish fillets of some sort, white radishes, silken white vichyssoise, and, of course, martinis. What a hoot! With everyone spun in a monochromatic white palette, surely our pain would begin to lift.

The house resembled a snow palace. I strung white icicle Christmas lights from all the eaves and across the length of my porch. Beach sand anchored white candles in mason jars that I staggered all along my outdoor stairs. I sprayed snow-in-a-can on my windows. I banished anything of color from my living and dining rooms. If I couldn't live without it for the evening (such as the dining table), I covered it in white. I wrapped my turntable in white marabou. White roses, white lilies, white mums, white plastic cutlery (no choice, I had to), white plates, white linens. I placed bottles of Wite-Out here and yonder and stuffed them with single white carnations. If this had been a formal dinner, I would have used the Wite-Out for place cards. Each name would have been written in white fluid on white paper, so everyone would have had to guess where to sit. But this couldn't be a formal affair. Mur wouldn't want it that way.

As for my own decor, I went to the wig shop in Lincoln-ville and bought a towering white wig for the grand price of only twenty-five dollars. An hour before my guests were to arrive, I donned the tower of nylon hair. I slipped into a gorgeous set of white silk brocade pajamas with matching slippers. I painted my nails a glossy, pearly white. Likewise my lips. Pale powder and ivory foundation upon my face. White eyeliner on lids and brows. Miles of white marabou about my neck and shoulders.

Yes, it's true, I looked like a snowy owl in drag.

But I was beautiful.

Dr. Zachary Klein

I went to Edith's all-white party dressed in a rabbit costume. Ordered it off of the Net. A company out of Chicago, the Costume Shop. They had everything—turkeys, monsters, Ronald Reagan, even gorillas. The gorilla was my favorite, but they didn't have it in white. Anyway, the rabbit suit cost me $125. The round puffball tail bouncing on my ass really set it off. I decided I should rent it for a week longer so I could wear it to work. Me in the potato fields, dressed like a giant rabbit. That should cure something.

It was nearly nine o'clock by the time I made it over to Edith's. I walked down the path, sad as hell, my rabbit ears being blown sideways by the ever-present nor'easter gale. Here I was, going to a party that was supposed to celebrate Murmur Lee. But most of the women I loved were dead. What, tell me, what was there to celebrate?

But I don't like for people to know my business. So I hopped inside the house—as usual, I was the last to arrive—and wiggled

my ass, and everyone had a hearty laugh at my expense. Then
there were my props—a person needs props; a person can hide
behind a decent set of props: a giant bag of marshmallows—it
was the only white food I could think of—and a white plastic
lawn chair I'd purloined from a trash pile outside a double-wide
on my way home from Elkton. In lieu of carrots—all rabbits
have to arrive with carrots—I carried a bouquet of parsnips.
I ceremoniously settled myself into the chair, pretended to
chew on a parsnip, and then—I had to say it—asked, "What's
up, Doc?"

Everyone groaned, so I jumped up and tore open the
marshmallow bag and ran about the room, tossing the sugary
white pillows into the air.

"Stop, Zachary, you absolutely must stop!" Edith said,
hugging me and pinching my ass.

"You're stunning," I told her, and patted her three-story-
high white wig with my rabbit paw. "You look sort of like Au-
drey Hepburn with white hair."

She leaned into me, her fake boobs pressing into my fur.
"You are insane, my friend." Her eyes sparkled with what I believe was the threat of tears. "Thank you for being here."

"Of course I'm here. I wouldn't have missed it," I said,
scanning the room. "Where's the booze?"

"Right here, darling." Edith floated over to the table and
poured a clear fluid into a stemmed glass. "Every little rabbit
needs a good stiff bolt of vodka now and again. All that fucking they do! Vodka is their secret!" Edith crinkled her nose
with all the charm of a coed in love and smiled her grand-
hostess smile. She touched my furry arm. "I have to go mingle
now, darling." She and her giant hair and her silk jammies and
her thirty-foot-long boa floated away. And there I stood.
Alone. My true self, existentially and otherwise. Alone.

I surveyed the room. In the corner, sulking, stood the mean little Lucinda in a torn white T-shirt and bleached-out jeans. Her hair was cropped as short as I've ever seen it and was the color of vanilla pudding. She'd powdered herself in white. Where does one find stone white powder? I don't know, but she'd done it. Even her pudding hair was dusted with white grains. She was surrounded by people from Salty's, but she wasn't joining them in their raucous discussion. She just stood there glowering.

Hazel had her back turned to Lucinda and she was putting her finger on Silas's chest, as if to bring home a point. I thought that was not a good idea, poking the forever-angry and muscle-bound Silas. It's not something I would have done. My professional services might be needed tonight, I thought. Absolutely. There she was, giving him shit about something, her double-D breasts squeezed into a shell three sizes too small, a mammarian tidal wave.

And then, my, my, my, there was Charlee. Charlee in a white mohair sweater and white slacks and a simple strand of white pearls. Charlee, with her strawberry blond curls and fair skin. Charlee, whom I hadn't seen in a coon's age, except for one brief visit shortly after she got back into town, when I advised her on the cremation procedures for Murmur Lee. Charlee, who'd run off to Harvard and had returned in the despairing light of her friend's death. Charlee was a lot prettier than my memory had allowed. I stood there sipping my martini, and a foreign urge to kick myself for being dressed like a 180-pound rabbit flashed through what I hoped would soon be my sodden brain.

Me and women: a deadly combination. Me and Katrina. Look who's gone. Me and Murmur Lee—although pursuit and consummation were never in the cards—but anyway, look who's gone. Testosterone, though, is a mighty drug. And some-times a man really does need to experience a level of intimacy that his own hand or a sad foray into AdultFriendFinder.com can't provide. And Charlee sure was pretty, standing there by a pot of soup, playing with those pearls, speaking to the kid who mops the floors at Salty's.

I hopped on over. In my most gallant fashion, I pulled off my rabbit head.

She laughed, pressed her palm against her lips, and then said in her honey-soaked drawl, "Dr. Z, you are amazing!"

I kissed her cheek. She seemed not to object. I told myself I was a motherfucker. To be interested was to betray Katrina. No, my dead wife did not care. But I did. I bear guilt like cit-rus trees bear fruit.

"It's good to see you, Charlee. You look gorgeous."

"And you!" She tossed out her arms as if to embrace the whole package. "You look," she paused—"well, like a giant white rabbit."

"You are so smart." I touched the tip of her nose with my paw. Edith floated by and said, "Bottoms up!"

"Goodness, Edith, you're going to have us all rip-roaring drunk," Charlee said, but she dutifully downed the rest of her martini, as did I, and we accepted the fresh ones Edith placed in our fists.

"*Pour vous.*"

"*Merci,*" I said, responding like a gentlemanly rabbit. "Edith, tell me, something is different about your house. What's go-ing on?"

"You don't know?" Charlee asked, her green eyes widening.

"*La musique!*" Edith said. "I've retired Ms. Piaf for the evening. In keeping with our theme, we are listening to the *White Album.*"

"Ha! Good. You think of everything, Edith." I spied a slight burn under her pale pancake makeup. I felt the vodka ripple down my brain stem. "Did you invite Speare?"

Edith tossed back her head. Her wig dangerously shifted to the right. She looked like George Washington with a bouffant. "I did. I felt I had to."

"What's wrong with inviting Speare?" Charlee asked. "Everyone treats the poor man as if he's a pariah."

I felt my jaw clench, and the bad boy in me suddenly wanted to drink all the vodka in the house. Even worse, I wanted to fuck. Why was my anger attached to sex? I needed counseling.

"Look," Edith said, "call me a pushover. Fine. But I feel sorry for him. I really do think he loved our Mur. And, like you say, Charlee, none of us is exactly behaving kindly toward him. It wouldn't surprise me at all if he didn't show." She looked over my shoulder, rested her fingers lightly upon her arched neck, sighed as if life was just too mean, and said, "*Excusez-moi.* I have to go entertain."

Charlee came in close, sweetly, like she was about to share a delicious secret, and said, "Really, Z, why does everyone— except for the magnanimous Edith—hate the guy?"

I looked beyond her. Nothing could be gained from this conversation. I caught Lucinda's eye and nodded at her. She was still glued to the corner, and this time it was she, not Hazel, who was giving Silas hell. She nodded back, not missing a beat in whatever it was she was saying. "Let's change the subject, Charlee. How about something to eat?"

"Sure, Z," she said, but I could tell by the scowl threatening to creep across her pretty little nose that she would revisit the subject of the entirely dislikable Mr. Speare.

With my rabbit head tucked under my arm and my hand

against the small of her back, we made our way over to the
buffet, where I slathered a piece of white bread with Brie.
Charlee reached for a radish and said, "So, Z, I'm finished
with men. That's it. God and men. I'm done with both
of them!"

"Oh, don't say that. You're too wonderful and too pretty to
give up that easily."

She smiled. She had a big smile. It moved planets, that
smile. I sipped my drink. So did she.

"Really, Charlee, how are you? Where've you been? Are you
settling in okay? Are you glad to be back? Can I do anything
for you?" I shot all five questions.

She pulled on one of her strawberry curls. The tendril
clung to her finger. She said she was doing fine, considering. I
noticed that her green eyes were flecked with gold, and I tossed
my rabbit head onto the couch.

"Let me freshen up that drink." I reached for her glass. Our
hands touched. It felt good.

"No, really, my drink is . . ."

Too late. I had it firmly in hand and topped off before she
could stop me.

She giggled and said, "Oh Lord, I'm going to get into
trouble tonight."

"Charlee, my dear, I certainly hope so. What do you say?
Let's go outside and get some fresh air. The gale wind be
damned."

She was amused. I could tell by the way she cocked her
head and squirreled her lips into a curvy line that wasn't quite
a smile. She looked around the room and then her gaze settled
on me. "Yes," she said, all perky, "let's go."

Something had happened. I was on automatic male. I

guided Charlee through the room, bantering about how if Edith wasn't careful, her wig would collide with a candle and she'd go up in flames. But I wasn't really thinking about Edith at all. I couldn't get my mind off Charlee's cleavage and the smattering of freckles on the sweet rise of her left breast.

Charleston Rowena Mudd

Well, good God Almighty!" I squealed, dry martini in hand, when a giant white rabbit—I mean a human being dressed like a rabbit—hopped into the blizzard otherwise known as Edith's White Party.

I was working on my second cocktail of the evening—I admit that I was downing them a tad fast—when the little hopper showed up and started throwing marshmallows everywhere. Lucinda caught two of them in midair and stuffed her cheeks with them.

"Whaddya think?" she mumbled. "Do I look like an albino chipmunk?"

"Please don't do that," I said. "It freaks me out." I nodded toward the rabbit. "Who is that?"

"Who the fuck do you think it is? Fucking Dr. Z." She spit the marshmallows into a napkin. "Gross. Why did I do that?" She wadded up the spit-slick deflated things and tossed them on a side table.

"That's disgusting," I said, and walked away.

I bumped into Croley. If I had been a normal woman—you know, had married, birthed babies, that sort of thing—I would have tapped Croley to be my daughter's husband. "Did you flunk your chemistry test, or what?" I asked.

He grabbed his heart as if wounded. "Where is your confidence in me? I got a *B!*"

"That's fabulous. Congratulations. You're not drinking. Why?"

"I have a date tonight." He looked at his watch. It always surprised me that he wore a watch. It seemed such an adult thing to do, and he struck me as such a blond sun-streaked surfer child. "In fact"—he searched the crowd as if scoping out his path—"I gotta go soon."

"Ah," I said, and saluted him with my drink as he drifted away. But I wasn't alone for long, because right as I was about to lose sight of Croley, my elbow was grabbed by a certain rabbit, who no longer sported a furry little head. Dr. Z pecked me on the cheek.

"Charlee, my God, it's good so see you," he said. Then, in a hyperfit, he Gatling-gunned about twenty questions, and for some reason—perhaps my sheer brilliance—I found myself foundering in the sudden recognition of his loss. Two women—one a lover, the other a friend—ripped from his orbit by what? God? Chance?

I hugged him tightly, the white fur tickling my mouth. "We have so much to talk about, Zachary. It's been way too long. That brief visit in January simply won't do."

Seemingly at ease in his ridiculous costume, he said, "I agree."

I pulled back and diverted my eyes because I felt that telltale electrical current zip between us—you know, the split-second sexual-awakening jolt that gets us in deep, swamp-muck trouble? I was in no mood to get stuck in the quagmire of animal lust. Sex for the sake of sex was out of the question. Fuck Ahmed, I thought. Fuck him for jilting me and leaving me in such a mess. I would not, on any day a sane person could name, on any planet, in any universe, be attracted to Zachary Klein. It was not going to happen. No way. I silently lectured myself on that point at I stood there biting my lip, thinking, I never realized how darkly handsome Zachary is.

So I don't know why in heaven's name I said, "That sounds delightful" when he asked, "How about I freshen up these martinis and we go on the porch and get caught up under the stars?"

All I know is that I pulled on my blue overcoat—didn't I stick out like an indigo dot in all the white—and we wandered outside and gazed up at the night, and I said that the wind was blowing so hard, it seemed to me that it might rearrange the constellations. And then I managed to make out the Big Dipper, which pleased me no end (my ability to identify constellations ranks right up there with my ability to have a successful relationship), and I told Zachary how sorry I had been to hear about Katrina's death and that I hadn't been a good friend (that is so true—I never even sent a card; I was so wrapped up in my new life at Cambridge, I lost all threads of active compassion for the people at home). He rubbed my shoulder with that rabbit-fur hand of his, which aroused a faint tingling in my nether regions, I'm sorry to say, and then he gazed out at the black sea and offered absolution in the way of some prattle about how he always knew I was thinking only the best for him and Katrina.

And then, in the same breath, he whispered, "I don't think it was an accident."

I didn't get it at first. I thought we were talking about Katrina. How could cancer be an accident? Or, of course it was an accident. No one intentionally gets cancer. "Z, what are you talking about?"

"Tsk, tsk, tsk!" Edith floated onto the porch, bearing exactly what we did not need: more martinis. "Shame on you both for being so serious. For leaving the party. Here. Have another, you lushes, you!" She set the glasses on the rail, adjusted her wig with a firm tug, and then took our empties. She shot us a knowing look, the kind of glance that says, *You don't fool me. I get the sexual drift.* As she spun in her white satin shoes—ever the lady—she said over her shoulder, "Don't be too long, darlings. You're starting to bore me."

Z pulled at the neck of his rabbit suit. "This thing is hot."

"It's really, um, fetching," I said.

"Hey, this is a great costume. And this shop I found online, it's . . ."

He started to detail the many different types of costumes one could order off the Internet. I put my hand on his. "Wait, wait, wait. Back up. I want to know what wasn't an accident."

"Oh. We're back to that." His hypermode swung into a low glower. He took a very healthy swig.

"That bad, eh?"

He nodded and wiped his mouth on the back of his rabbit arm. He put both hands on the rail and pressed down. "Murmur Lee. It was no accident."

I stared at him really hard. He kept his dark-eyed gaze aimed at the ocean. I sipped my martini. Then I gulped it. The vodka tasted like ice and fire and poison.

"I know," I said.

"How did you know?"

"It's an ovary thing—like a gut feeling. Sometimes things just don't set right."

"Why didn't you say something?"

"Whoa!" The vodka helped spark my instant anger. "You're the physician. You were the one who first ruled it an accident. And the autopsy bore you out. And now suddenly you're saying it wasn't an accident and asking why I didn't say something. Well, this pisses me off six ways from Sunday!"

"Oh, calm down, Charlee. You've always been too easy to make mad. You've got to understand: Determining foul play or suicide in cases of drowning is close to impossible through an autopsy alone. She didn't have any bruising consistent with a struggle."

Oh Christ, that was too much information. I didn't want to hear this after all. Why had I said anything? I wanted to go back inside and get very, very drunk. I turned away, but the big rabbit reached for me, spun me back around, and held me by my shoulders.

"Listen, Charlee. The cops said it wasn't a crime scene. And you and I both know Murmur Lee would never kill herself. Fuck! Accident. I had to say it was an accident!" Zachary let go of me and slammed the rail with his rabbit hand.

I emptied my glass, one long shot right down my throat. I was raging angry and didn't know why, so I yelled, "Fuck you, Z. This totally sucks. I mean it just sucks." I started crying.

"Don't start with the tears. You think I don't know it sucks?" He downed the rest of his drink, and as he did, a Volvo pulled up to the house.

"Who the hell is that?"

Z tossed his glass into the sand. "It's the motherfucker. That's who it is." He marched off the porch, his rabbit tail bouncing, mumbling that he was glad he was drunk.

Billy Speare got out of the car and headed toward us.

"Don't, Z! You ain't big enough!" Vodka, fear, and anger had allowed my redneck soul to emerge.

But Z either didn't hear me or didn't care to oblige. Billy Speare paused. He stood in the walkway, his face a mask of confusion as he watched a man in a rabbit suit barrel toward him.

"I've wanted to do this for a long time," announced the good doctor, slurring his words.

Billy looked at the rabbit, then up at me, blinking, totally ignorant as to what was about to happen.

"You no-good son of a bitch," Z growled. He circled his rabbit arm and then—bam!—hauled off and sucker punched Speare. Yes, bam! I heard it. I heard the cartilage snap. I heard the nose break. I watched Speare go ass-down into the dunes.

"Don't get up on my account, motherfucker!" Z screamed over the sprawled body of Speare, who was groaning and holding his nose and moaning something akin to "You stupid asshole, you broke my fucking nose!"

There I was, suddenly sober, the wind tangling my hair and stinging my eyes as I watched a man in a rabbit suit rub his hand as he waddled off into the night.

"Z, get your ass back up here," I screamed. He waved me off, rounded the corner of Edith's drive, and was out of sight.

For some sick reason, I began to laugh. Insanely. Why was I delighted by this violent and odd turn the evening had taken? "Are you okay?" I hollered, and then laughed some more.

He didn't respond. Nor did he get up. Shit, maybe he's dead, I thought. So I staggered inside, vodka rumbling through my veins, even though I felt sober as ice.

"Hey, everybody, listen up!" I clanked a spoon on the side of the martini pitcher. Faces turned toward me. Fuzzy. All of them.

"Don't make us play no fucking game," Silas yelled.

"This is serious, Silas. We've got one down. Let's go!"

In a gangly rush, we emptied into the yard, led by Edith, whose long strides and haunted, drawn face betrayed her other life, the masculine one, which haunted her soft edges. As I rushed toward Billy Speare, who was still on the ground, holding his nose and cursing, I realized we were lost, all of us, the whole damn bunch of us.

Murmur Lee Harp

I am a bullet shooting through what seems to be a thick wall of light. All around me my life—or at least the memories of that life—shatter into ash, sand, pollen, dust, leaving me to ruminate on the lessons I've learned since dying.

My mother was raped.

I was the seed of that rape.

I was not my father's daughter.

I was not a product of love and longing.

I was not a wanted child.

I was the manifestation of torture.

My husband never loved me.

My husband's abandonment of our child was a cowardly act by a man who refused to feel pain.

My husband's refusal to participate in the pain of Blossom's death does not mean that he did not love her. He did.

I fell for Billy Speare out of loneliness. And because I feared loneliness more than I feared pine rattlers, I ignored what I knew to be true: A man is not worth your time, your devotion, your effort if he doesn't love his mother.

Billy Speare was not as good a man as I deserved.

Oster Harp should have never named his island in honor of a goddess who played nanny to the souls of dead women.

I was a lousy dream interpreter.

In death, life's puzzles are beginning to make sense.

No wonder women drop like flies on Iris Haven.

No wonder my mother loved me so fearfully.

No wonder my father remained forever on the other side of the room, watching me with the cautious gaze of a distant uncle.

No wonder my mother disappeared into the rosary.

No wonder she turned golden at the possibility that I was not a bastard product of violence, but holy.

No wonder I never had a successful relationship with a man: I had no role models.

No wonder I lost my ability to breathe when Blossom died.

No wonder I fell for Billy Speare: I needed, wanted, craved a life partner.

These are not forgivenesses.

These are not excuses.

These are not absolutions.

These are not damnations.

All I'm saying is, as I hurtle through this vast ocean of light—understanding what had been mysteries to me in life but clueless as to what is happening in death—there is, at least at this very moment, no wonder.

Lucinda Smith

I'm knocking back my fourth martini—Mennonites are Olympic fucking drinkers; that's one of our best kept secrets—when I hear Charlee yell, "Hey, we've got one down!"

Being an artist and a yoga instructor, I am more observant than most. Thirty minutes before Charlee's call to arms, I watched her sashay out of Edith's house with Z, who was dressed like a giant fucking white rabbit and following her like—well, what else do rabbits do? I looked up at the ceiling and batted the flour out of my eyes (I had powdered myself in self-rising, head to toe, a Mennon-fucking-ite in whiteface for Edith's albino party) and thought about how sad it was that Z had nowhere to place his Murmur love, so as soon as he set eyes on Charlee, he transferred it to her. What a loser.

Anyway, fast-forward: Charlee is yelling "we've got one down" and, of course, we all think it's the white rabbit, because whom else is she out there with. We stumble like some giant,

spastic, drunken amoeba into the cold night, martinis held just
so in an effort not to spill a single drop of what is essentially—
at this point in the night—gasoline. Edith is waving her boa as
if she's fucking Isadora Duncan. Charlee breaks away from the
amoeba pack, running as if she's some fucking angel of mercy,
and throws herself over someone who is writhing on the
ground and sputtering truly disgusting obscenities. The white
rabbit is nowhere to be seen. And then I, before anyone else except for Charlee, realize who the asshole on the ground is.

"Why, you motherfucker!" I scream. (It's the vodka fumes
that make me do it. Being a Mennonite, I am nearly always in
control of my anger. But not this time. Four vodka martinis
have set me free.) I run down the steps, push Charlee out of
the way, and start wailing on Billy Speare. These hands of
mine, artist's hands, which I protect even though they aren't
producing anything other than fucking seagull paintings, sting
and crack as I punch the fucker over and over about his face,
his chest, anywhere I can make contact.

Charlee screams, "Stop! You're gonna kill him!" People—I
don't know who and I don't know how many—pull me off of
him. Blood—the bastard's blood—mixes with the Dixie Lily,
forming dark beads in a shotgun scatter across my skin.

"Goddamned motherfucker!" I scream. I kick him, but
they have pulled me too far away for it to do any good.

"Oh my God, you poor man!" Edith flutters over Billy as
people help him up. "Take him to Dr. Z's at once. He must be
treated immediately. Oh dear, oh dear."

Charlee shoots Edith a cockeyed look, as if she, absurdly,
is going to break into laughter. "No, not Z's," she says.

Billy pushes everyone away. "Leave me the fuck alone, you
stupid sons a bitches." He stumbles toward the road.

"No! You can't leave in this condition!" Edith warbles.

"Let him go. He'll be fine. It's just a broken schnoz."
Charlee puts her arm around Edith and pats the old hag's back.

"At least take your car!" Edith yells.

"He'll be okay. He's probably just going down to the beach
for a minute. Let's go back inside." What the fuck is Charlee
Mudd doing, acting as if she is running this joke of a party.

"Jesus, Lucinda, you broke his fucking nose!" Silas stares at
me, his expression hard. "Goddamned." I can't figure if he is
congratulating or scolding me.

"No she didn't." Charlee lets go of Edith. "Dr. Z broke his
nose." She tosses back her hair as if she is the queen of fucking Sheba and brushes past us. The screen door bangs behind her.

"Fuck it," I say, "I'm going home."

"*Oh, mais oui! Terrible! Terrible!*" Edith dabs her eyes with the
tail of her boa. I don't think she is acting. She seems genuinely
fucked-up.

"Enough with the fucking bad French!" I yell as I walk
down the drive. I hit the road and don't look back. Not once.
Not even when a gale smothers me with the pitiful sound of
Edith sobbing.

*M*e? I didn't cry until I was in the shower and the room was
so steamed up that even my cat wouldn't have been able
to detect my tears. And I discovered something: water and
flour don't mix unless you take a whisk to them. So I had to
scrub the shit off of me, the blood, too. I went through five
wash rags, thanks to the clinging dough I'd inadvertently
created.

Once I was clean, I just stood there, letting the water pickle me, damning myself for losing control. What the fuck had I been thinking? How could I have raised a fist to anyone, even if it was that jerk Speare? My hands were sore. I held them up to the hot water, turned them palm up, palm down, palm up, palm down.

"Dear fucking Jesus, please forgive me," I whispered. "Please don't let me do that again." Maybe it was the vodka, just the vodka. I'm not really an asshole, but the liquor altered my center. It won't ever happen again, never, never, never.

I stepped out of the shower and grabbed a towel. Just as I was about to run it through my hair, Lucinda Williams's voice drifted into the thick wet air. She was accusing someone of stealing her joy, and she wanted it back. This was fucking interesting. I hadn't stopped to turn on the stereo when I got home; I had headed straight for the bathroom. I wrapped the towel tightly around me and tiptoed down the hall and into my living room. Why was God testing me? Just because I asked for forgiveness in the fucking shower didn't mean he immediately had to challenge the sincerity of my request by putting a freaking weirdo robber/rapist/murderer in my house so that I'd be forced to stand passively by—be the good pacifist, be the good pacifist—while the guy did who knew what to me.

"What the fuck are you doing here?"

Silas stood at my bookcase, riffling through the CDs. He turned around. "Well, hello to you, too. I just came by to make sure you were okay." Dressed in a white tee and jeans, he looked like an orderly from a fucking insane asylum.

I secured my towel and stared at the floor. "Thanks."

"Let's take a look at those hands of yours," he said. He walked over to me. He had this funny look in his eyes. It was as if he was trying to be kind. It creeped me out.

"That's okay. They're fine, really."

He took my small painter's hands in his big rough ones. "No, they're not. You need to ice them."

"Hey, I'm perfectly capable of taking care of myself," I said as he sauntered into my kitchen.

"Yeah, Lucy, that's why you lost it tonight."

"Fucker," I muttered, and sat down on the couch. He came back in with two Buds and a kitchen towel full of ice. He pressed the compress on my hands and I winced.

"Why'd you do it?"

"Do what?"

"You know." He cracked open a beer and handed it to me.

"Because I fucking wanted to." I shot him a you-are-dumb-as-shit glare.

"You've got one helluva mouth on you, girlie." He sipped his beer, really dainty like, which was ludicrous, since he was such a big fat fucking redneck.

"I don't like him," I said.

"Really. Well, you sure as hell fooled all of us."

I looked at Silas straight on, this time without too much attitude. I felt myself slipping into a momentary bout of earnestness. Fuck! "I mean it. I really don't like him."

"Well, he ain't my favorite candidate of all time, either. But I just ignore him. No reason to beat on him."

Since when did you become Mother fucking Teresa? I thought it but, to my credit, kept the insult to myself. I gritted my teeth and adjusted the compress. "Yes, there is. Yes, there fucking is." And then things went from horrible to an all-out suck, because I started to cry. In front of him. I don't cry in front of anyone.

But there I was, bawling my head off. And there was Silas—all of Silas—brushing away my tears and smoothing my hair and saying things like "Ah, come on now, things ain't

that bad." And somehow—I don't know what came over me—
we started kissing and tugging at each other's clothes (wasn't
difficult, as all I had on was a towel), and we were close to doing, you know, IT. I hadn't done IT in six years. That and pork.
And I really wasn't into cocks. It was nothing personal. I just
couldn't do it.

Oh yeah, right. I'm such an asshole. I couldn't do it. That's
why I said, "No, this way," and I guided his head down there,
to my place—you know, down there to my business, where I
don't let any fucking person go. Jesus. And as he did his thing,
my mind wandered; it just took to a truth I had been all
worked up over to avoid. In my mind's eye, in my fucked-up
soul, it wasn't Silas going down on me. But Murmur, Murmur,
Murmur. Murmur was doing me.

Yes, I know that Murmur's door didn't swing that way.
And, hell, I don't know if I have a door that swings at all. But
I do know I always wanted to touch her. And to be swallowed
by her crazy-ass laughter.

So when I said, "Baby, slow down. Yeah, like that," I was
speaking to my friend Murmur, whom I miss so, so much.

How fucked-up is that?

Charleston Rowena Mudd

Endings. Are they forms of betrayal? You know, hopes dashed by the indecipherable subtext that pump-pumppumps against the gooey walls of intrepid hearts? Or are they the inevitable last gasps churned out by the failings of fallible minds?

I had a friend in Cambridge, a fellow grad student, who didn't breathe oxygen. She inhaled and exhaled platitudes: Endings are simply new beginnings. Endings are opportunities to begin a new chapter, a fresh page. Endings are the world reborn!

I wanted to choke her.

But back to my point: Let's talk about the pain. Let's talk about how Murmur's end left us adrift in sorrow so thick that even walking across the room took calculated effort. Let's talk about the color of our fear—morning, noon, and night—when we tried to go forward honorably, honestly, even though our hearts had been ripped apart by the passing of our friend.

Let's talk about endings that are so awesome, you fear that to-morrow just might happen.

Let's talk about Edith's party, her little gathering, which was designed to dispel winter and grief.

This is what we know. White. Drunk. Violent. Dr. Z busts Billy Speare's nose. Then Lucinda beats the downed man with her bare hands. Z storms off. Billy storms off. Lucinda storms off. Silas disappears. Edith cries. The party is over. Way over. I stick around, both to try to calm Edith and to help her clean up. Piaf is back on the hi-fi; I take her perpetual spin as a sign that maybe normalcy is settling back in.

"Edith, it's okay. People actually had a good time," I said as I dried a white plate.

"Oh please!" She clawed at the snowy marabou boa that draped her neck and back. "I want this thing off!" Her face twisted and scrunched, and she wrestled the feathery drape as if it were a constrictor that had decided to squeeze. She threw it on the floor. I think her intent was to spike it, but since it was weightless, it drifted noiselessly and landed in a soft pile— resembling a sleeping cat—about her feet. She tried to march forward but became tangled and nearly fell over. I offered her my arm, which she slapped away. She kicked at the boa, eerily mimicking how Lucinda had kicked Speare. Finally free, she collapsed into her sheet-draped wing-back chair.

"It was a disaster!" She grabbed her wig with both hands and shimmied it right off her head like a cork. She looked bald, thanks to the flesh-colored skullcap, which matted down her real hair. "I know about violence. I know what it is to kill a man. You look in his eyes. You see his soul right before you snuff it out. When I left the Corps, that was it. No more violence!" She picked at her silk sleeve. "I hate it when my creed is broken."

I rubbed my fingertips over my eyelids, which were gritty with salt. She was right. This was terrible. Shit. I looked at her. For the first time in our ten-year friendship, I think I really looked at her. Not at the drag queen. Not at the sex change. Not at the profoundly weird person she was. I looked past all that. And you know what I saw? I saw the marine. I saw the tough little jaw. In her countenance—even after God only knows how many martinis and fisticuffs—I saw the steely glint of a survivor and the resigned yet stubborn humility of a loyal soldier who gets the job done. I saw a person who believes in honor but who realizes there are no absolutes—that honor and loyalty and morality are slippery slopes that must be defined and redefined hour by hour, always keeping in mind this eternal and quarrelsome question: Who gets hurt this time? And I saw in her pained eyes, the desire to be free of all that. I pulled over the piano stool and sat. I took her hand in mine.

"How many people did you kill back then? Tell me."

She breathed in. I do believe she stole my oxygen. "That is off-limits, Charlee. It is not to be spoken of. Ever."

"So . . . you saw their souls?"

"I own their souls. And they mine."

I appreciated the present tense. Her fingers danced across the raised edge of her lips even as her jaw tensed. Edith Piaf, this Edith Piaf, the one who had so thoroughly reinvented herself, the one who had put hundreds of thousands of miles between her current self and the nineteen-year-old kid from Palatka, the kid who had hunkered down—him and his penis—in a blood-soaked Vietnamese jungle and who—for the love of God and country and duty—had sniped the souls of fellow warriors, was one hell of a woman.

"You don't think God blames you, do you?" I asked this selfishly, an exercise in exploring my own salvation.

Edith pulled herself straight, like a ribbon unwinding. "I don't think he cares. I think our lives aren't all that important to him."

I felt a tear, the moisture of it, travel across the summit of my cheekbone and then meander toward my ear.

"What about Murmur?"

She pulled at the bobby pins that held the skullcap in place. She ate more air, filled herself up, and then said, "That's why we need to be kind to Mr. Speare. We don't know what happened out there on the river. But if he did have anything to do with her death, we have to forgive him." She curled her fingers under the elastic rim. "Because, like I said"—she got a real good grip—"God doesn't care"—she rolled the cap off of her skull and tossed the second skin—"so we have to."

I leaned over and hugged her. "Thank you, Edith." I held her as tightly as I could. "Thank you." I pulled away. In her disheveled state, she looked both insane and royal. "I'm going to go see Z now."

Edith nodded, as if that was all there was left to do. She stood and walked into her kitchen. I saw her—there at her sink—reach for a sponge and begin furiously to scrape away at a glob of mashed potato. "That's good. Because he must be in pain. The poor man has lost a wife and a flame."

I rose to my feet. The vodka had depressed my normal tendency to talk loudly. So I said steadily, in nearly a whisper, "What do you mean, 'a flame'?"

Edith tossed aside the sponge and pulled off an eyelash. "I

mean Zachary had a thing for Mur. It was so obvious. Everyone knew." She tugged at the remaining lash. "Honestly,
Charlee, if you had come home more often, you'd know these
things. Now for God's sake, please go see Zachary."

The last vision I had of Edith that night was her standing
in her kitchen, tugging at the eyelash, wincing.

I knocked on the front door, the back door, the door to the
screen porch. Nothing. But I knew he was in there. I felt it
tooth and bone. And I knew he was damning himself over losing control and two women. So I decided to assert my Yankee
self and walk on in. The front was locked up tight, but the
back was wide open. I stepped inside the dark kitchen and
caught my breath. The place reeked of rotting vegetables. I felt
the wall for a light switch, but to no avail. I took a step forward and something crunched beneath my feet.

"Z? You in here?"

I shut my eyes for a five count, then reopened them. Slowly,
the darkness became penetrable, and as it did, I said, "Good
God." The place was a mess. The floor was strewn with crack-
ers, cereal, chips. The counters and kitchen table were stacked
madly with dirty dishes, beer cans, shoes, orphan socks, magazines, opened and unopened mail. Pots and pans blossoming
with mold teetered in hazardous heaps. If there were a decora-
tive style to describe Z's approach to interior design, it would
be Clutter and Crap and Chaos. I decided to try to move on,
see if the living room was in any better shape, and as I did, I
felt something soft implode beneath my foot. A putrid gelati-
nous tomato. "Damn it all to hell!" I started toward the sink
in order to wash my shoe but was afraid to touch the faucets.

I wandered in the shadows and ink into the bathroom. There, I flipped on the light.

Oh my. Evidently, Z wasn't in the habit of washing his underwear or even tossing it in a hamper. And don't even remove the hair from a drain, I thought. No, no, no! Just let it pile up until you have a lovely little pube nest. Gross! But the crowning glory of the bathroom was the mushroom forest. Believe it. A colony of 'shrooms circled around the base of his toilet. The tomato goo, I decided, was the least of my worries. I backed away from the toilet, thinking, Dear Jesus, I have entered hell, a place named Depression Made Visible.

"Dr. Z, where are you?" I yelled as I exited the bathroom. To my surprise, he answered.

"I'm back here. Charlee, is that you?"

"Where is 'back here'?" I tried to follow his voice, which seemed to emanate from some faraway combustible garbage heap.

"In the study! Just follow the bread crumbs. Ha!"

Actually, there was a trail. A twisty, hug-the-right-wall trail of chips, popcorn, dirty clothes, baseball caps, more unopened mail, abandoned bottles of water and colas, and balled-up stinky socks led me to a closed door, which I pushed open. "Ah, there you are."

Curled on a small couch, he was lying under a blanket, watching *Rambo.* The study, oddly enough, was fairly clean. The minimal clutter, mainly munchies, were concentrated in a pile on a glass-topped coffee table.

"Hey!" he said, "What brings you over here?" He threw off the blanket. Dressed in a South Park T-shirt and baggy running shorts, he looked like the Z I remembered from high school.

He stood and hugged me. Even though he was simply

being polite, the intimacy zapped me. "I just thought I ought to check on you. That was pretty wild back there."

"Ah, that was nothing. Here, sit, sit." He whipped the blanket off the couch, and a magazine went flying. He scurried to get it before I could see what it was. I moved toward the couch, and as I did, I spied the rabbit suit. It was splayed out on the floor by the French doors—pretty as you please—just as if it were a giant pelt.

"Well, you did break a man's nose."

"No, I broke one particular man's nose. Nothing could make me happier. Want something to drink? Beer? Wine? Water? Hey, I've got a great bottle of Chianti one of my patients gave me. Isn't this a great movie? Have you ever seen it? Of course you've seen it. Everybody has seen it." Z bobbed around as he spoke, making contact with nearly every piece of furniture in the room and refreshing his computer screen twice. I wished I had some Adderall—he needed to be medicated. I wished he'd sit down and confess his sins. I wished I knew why I was here. No, that's not true. I knew exactly what had brought me over. I sat on the couch, reached for a pillow, and hugged it close. Yo-Yo Man made another pass wall to wall.

"I want to talk about Murmur."

He stopped bouncing. He pegged his gaze to his desk. "I don't."

"Please come over here. Sit down and talk to me. Please."

He dropped his head back, that black shock of hair shuddered, and he stumbled over as if he'd been shot. "Oh God, Charlee. It's been a very long day." He flopped down beside me.

"I want to know why you hate Billy Speare."

"Why do you want to know that?"

"Because it means something."

"Yeah? Like what?" He reached for the remote control and

pressed mute. He watched as Rambo kicked down the door to a hut belonging to some poor, frightened Vietnamese peasants.

"I don't know. If I knew, I wouldn't be sitting here grilling you."

"Charlee"—he touched the tip of my nose—"that makes absolutely no sense."

"You were in love with Murmur, weren't you?"

Heavy sigh. He rubbed his face. He wanted to disappear. I just knew it.

"Z?"

"What do you want me to say? Yes. No. Maybe. All of the above. I mean, she took care of Katrina during the bad time. She took care of her when I couldn't, and I'm a doctor. And her husband. A piss-poor one."

"You're not answering my question."

He dug under the couch, and I swear to God, the man pulled out that bottle of Chianti. He studied the label. "Maybe because your question isn't fair, Charlee. Maybe it doesn't deserve a response." He placed the bottle on the coffee table, very carefully, as if he thought it were made of fragile glass. "Maybe it's like asking Clinton if he had an affair. The question is more outrageous than what it seeks to know."

My, my. I despise it when I'm wrong and end up so thoroughly and clearly called on it. I picked at a hair on the pillow. It was coarse and red. I thought, Dog. But I knew Z didn't have a dog. And then I thought, Celibate. "So have you gone out or anything? Dated anyone since Katrina passed?"

"You want some wine?"

"No!"

He reached for the remote and spun it on the table.

"Talk to me, Z." I leaned over and took his hand. The remote clattered to the floor.

"If I tell you, will you drop it? And then can we go on and talk about something else, like the color of your underwear? Did you really wear white underwear tonight, like you were supposed to? Because I didn't."

I dug my nails into his hand. "Z!"

"Okay, okay!" He slipped his hand out of mine and rubbed it. "No. I don't date. I work. That's what I do. And occasionally, I hang out with Murmur Lee and Lucinda and Edith. I mean, I used to hang out with Murmur Lee. You know. Not anymore. And I work."

"Why don't you date? You're cute. You're funny. You're smart. And why don't you get a housekeeper?"

"I went into an adult chat room recently. It made me want to vomit. And I went back on a couple of nights later and found this girl on there who lets anyone cyberfuck her, and she has a kid. I told her to stop. I told her she needed to clean up her life."

"What did she say?"

"She told me to go fuck myself. And I did!" He laughed at his own bad joke, then leaned down, grabbed the remote, hit the mute. Automatic-weapon fire from Rambo's gun popped all about.

"Give me that damn thing," I said. I took it from him and turned off the TV.

"I don't want to do this, Charlee! Now, let's talk about your pretty white underwear."

"No! Tell me why you won't date."

"Because, Charlee, I can't. I can't forget her. I can't stop loving her. I can't betray her. I just can't. Okay?"

And then I knew for sure. He was in love with both women. Murmur and Katrina. It had to be. He'd fallen in love with Murmur while his wife suffered. It was easier to love a living, breathing friend than your dying wife. And way less painful. But now Murmur was gone, too. And the only one left was me. That was it. That's why I'd had to come over and ask him annoying questions. I leaned over and kissed him. He kissed me back. I liked it. A lot. I don't think my forward behavior or his response could be blamed solely on the martinis. I pressed my forehead against his.

"Oh fuck, Zachary, life is so damned hard."

"I know, Charlee. Now tell me, what color is your underwear?" He kissed my cheek.

"Cornflower blue."

He moved my hair aside and kissed my neck.

"Lace. Very pretty lace."

"So you rebelled against Edith's edict, too."

And then there was no chance to respond, not with words anyway, because we locked lips and stayed that way. Ours were tender, soft, aching kisses. For a while—until I gave up thinking—I was aware that we were not only kissing but also honoring the painful endings we had endured for so long: Katrina and Murmur and, for me, Ahmed.

There was nothing bad about this. Nothing at all. Not when our kisses moved from tender to urgent. Not when we pressed our bodies together, allowing ourselves to feel the physical and the unknown. Not when I whispered, "Please, lie down with me. Please. Oh, Z. Please." Not when we grew naked and vulnerable, surprising ourselves with the prayers we poured over each other's bodies—prayers composed of touch and taste and sight, everything swathed in a primal sweetness of shadow and light, both of us searching with tongues, fingers, each of us propelled by an urgency that was by turns tender and insistent, both of us gasping over the beauty of skin, of taut nipples and slick hollows. No, nothing wrong.

We were this way with each other until dawn.

At first light, we pulled on our clothes and Z made us coffee, and then we ventured outside, penetrated the foggy morning, held hands all the way down to his dock, which snagged its way into the moss green waters of the Iris Haven River. We were laughing and playful. I was wholly unashamed for sleeping with this man. There would be no acts of contrition over this union. We sat at the end of the dock and snuggled against the cold. The breeze lifted Edith Piaf's sorrowful voice from that hi-fi in the white house three doors and innumerable dunes down. That's just the way it was in Iris Haven. Surrounded by the brick and mortar of Cambridge, I had forgotten. But here I was—having returned just a few weeks back—and already I had grown accustomed to the nearly constant sound of Piaf swirling on the wind, finding her way to our idle and busy hearts through open doors and wildly flung windows.

I touched three fingertips to Z's face. "You are really quite wonderful, you know. You must be kinder to yourself."

He pulled me close, kissed my forehead. "We will try." He kissed me again, this time on the tip of my nose. Z seemed very fond of noses. And then we grew quiet and gazed at the river and listened to the plaintive cry of gulls as they rose into the shrouded sky in search of a new day.

"I saw them."

"What?"

"I saw them. Murmur Lee and Speare."

"That night?"

Z nodded yes. I looked at him, scared as to what might come next. He looked stricken, like a man who had just recognized he was breathing in death's ripe scent. "I'm a Jew, Charlee, but I'm getting ready to make my first confession."

I had the oddest sensation that an ancient bone—broken for so long—was on the verge of being mended. "There are no sins here, Z. Not a single one."

"Look here. I saw two boats come up. It was late, past midnight. I heard laughter, and I knew who it was. And that was crazy-making. He was in his skiff and she in hers, and then I saw him offer her his hand and she got aboard. He was the cause of her laughter, see. He was playing music for her. He was holding her, kissing her, God knows what else."

"Stop it!" Unlike last night, I didn't want to hear another word. "Please, Z."

He shook his head, and I noticed a knot rise in the center of his temple. "No, I have to do this."

"You aren't supposed to confess unless you know what it is you're saying. Unless you're really, really sorry."

"Bingo. One and two."

I put my hands in my jacket pocket. Suddenly, I was very cold. And this world composed of fog and crying birds and Edith spinning round and round no longer seemed safe.

"So I come out here just to make myself nuts. I decide I want to see everything. I want it to hurt, so that my rage will snap to bits whatever else I'm feeling. I can see that they're dancing and close to fucking. Mist is blowing in off the ocean. I'm having a helluva time seeing clearly, but I can still make out their forms. And then Speare does something insane."

Oh God. A recognition swelled in my gut. I knew this.

Whatever Z was about to say, I already knew it. I could not put it into words, I couldn't recite it or offer it or sing it, but I sure as hell could taste it. The bile was rising. I heard myself say, flat, hard, "What, what does he do?"

"He changes the music."

"He changes the music?"

"Yeah, yeah, to something religious. It's the damnedest thing. And they start arguing, and she puts her hands to her ears and he reaches for her. They're physical. He isn't hitting her; it isn't like that. And then the mist grows heavier. No, not mist. It's fog. It rolls in and I can't see. But I hear him calling her name. He's screaming, 'Murmur Lee!' and you know, sound does funny things in the fog. It gets thick and slow. Nothing makes sense in the fog. But I hear him screaming and throwing stuff, and then all is quiet. And I hear an outboard kick in, and I'm sure it's Murmur Lee. She's taking off; she has had enough of Speare. And I'm glad about it, see? Really, really glad. I mumble something, like "Stupid son of a bitch," and then I go back up to the house and lie down, happy that Speare made Murmur Lee angry. Happy that their night has been ruined. And I sleep. I goddamned sleep through the night."

"Oh, Z, I'm so sorry." I touched his hair. I needed to lay my hands on him, just a brief contact, to try to ease him, and maybe to ease myself. It was the music. Jesus, Mary, and Joseph, the music. "It wasn't your fault. You are not to blame. Do you hear me? What you are is full of grace."

He turned away from the shrouded river. He grabbed my face, the sides. "It wasn't her boat. It was his. He took off, not Murmur Lee. And I slept through the night while she was out there drowning. I could have saved her, Charlee. But I didn't do shit. For the second time in my life, I didn't do shit."

At that moment, I made myself really small. I don't know

how I did it; I just did. I crawled into Z's lap and rested there like a little bird, burrowing into his chest, willing the fog and silence and Piaf to take away our pain, to undo Murmur's altogether-unnecessary ending. I wanted us to stay like that for a long time. I wanted communion, transfiguration, forgiveness, grace. I wanted God to care more than he did. Z kissed the top of my head and whispered my name.

"Oh, baby, baby, you are not to blame," I said. And even while I sat there nestled in Z's arms, I plotted. Sometime soon—probably that very afternoon—I would go in search of Speare. And I would goddamned well force a reckoning.

Billy Speare

orget my nose. It was my manhood that was busted. How did I descend into victimhood, sucker punched by some jerk dressed in a rabbit suit?

Simple. The assault was a curve in the downward spiral I'd been trying to believe was not happening. The kick given *Sex*'s book sales, thanks to the *Times* review? Over. Kaput. Preejaculate. That's the name of that spurt. And forget my agent taking my calls. Once the sales plummeted and it became obvious that the only reviewer in the good ol' US of A who liked my work was Laughton, both my agent and editor suddenly seemed to be out of the office twenty-four/seven.

So there I was, the morning after, pulled up to the kitchen table, my head back, an ice pack held to the snapped cartilage that was my nose—coffee was brewing. Turkey'd been poured and sipped, five Advil had already been popped—when there was a knock at my door.

"Ah, Christ," I mumbled, and considered ignoring it, but

for some malarkey reason I decided to behave like a good citizen. And you know, I think the pussy in me thought it might be the white rabbit, come to apologize. I set down the ice pack and walked over to the door, which technically was off of the living room, but in this tin can, trying to behave as if the kitchen, dining room, and living room weren't all jammed into the same rectangle was an exercise in delusional thinking. I cracked open the door. "Yeah?"

"Mr. Speare?"

I eyeballed her. I mean really. I think my right eyeball was the only thing visible. One bloodshot, droopy-lidded eyeball. She was a kid, maybe eighteen, dressed in skintight jeans that barely made it past her bikini line, a midriff stretch blouse the color of wild onions, a pink faux-fur cotton-candy jacket, lots of chains, pierced eyebrow, nose, tongue—Christ, what else?—tattoos (snakes, Celtic symbols, a spiderweb radiating out of her navel), purple lipstick, Cleopatra eyes. She stood in the dirt, one booted foot on my bottom step, *Sex* in hand.

"Who's asking?"

"I am," she answered indignantly, as if that was a sufficient answer.

My eyeball was growing fatigued, so I cracked open the door far enough for both eyeballs to be visible. She made a face, like she'd just swallowed cat puke. "Jesus, what happened to you?"

It took a few seconds for the reason behind her revulsion to register, and I should have known better, but I went ahead and answered. "I got punched by a rabbit."

She shook her head and stared out toward the river. "I knew you'd be fucked-up."

"What kind of talk is that?" I opened the door all the way, scratched my ass 'cause I felt like it.

"Are you going to let me in?" She looked at me as if she were sizing up whether to give a bum a buck. "Or what?" She had the bitter countenance of a woman twice her age, someone who'd been through more divorces and selfish men than any one soul had a right to.

I met her disapproving gaze, stayed that way for a good long minute, trying to figure out how to get her off my case, and then I felt something. It was as if the earth had begun a descent into a horrible place. Not hell. It was worse than hell. The rumble started in my chest and then split off, winding its way down into the netherworld of my lower intestines and up into the white hills of my cerebral cortex. I think I was in the throes of what country musicians call "a breaking heart."

She was a junior at Duke, majoring in English lit, and her name was Ariela. Her mom, divorced from Ariela's father for three years, had moved to Anastasia Island in the scatterboned aftermath of her marriage. Ariela had stayed in Swainsboro, Georgia, with her dad to finish out her senior year. I'd been to Swainsboro. It's about as far from Western civilization (read that: ambition) as a town can get. And now she was at Duke. You had to admire a kid with all that moxie, even if the little bitch was a smart-ass with a foul mouth.

And she was breaking my heart, because sometimes the past shows up on your doorstep in the form of an eighteen-year-old punk kid.

Little Ariela van den Berg, admirer of my work and perhaps a child genius, claimed she had hunted me down by making discreet inquiries at every beach bar from Avenue A to Devil's Elbow. She also claimed to have medical training.

"Wow," she said as she tossed my book on the couch and removed her cotton-candy jacket, "it's a good thing I came over. That cauliflower of a nose needs to be set."

"No. No doctors. I detest them. Especially now."

She wafted by, waving away my words as if they were shredded bits of early, bad drafts. She went straight to the cabinet above my stove and opened it. "Everyone keeps their liquor above their stoves. Why is that?" She pulled down my very expensive bottle of Patrón. "Hey! Good stuff. There's nothing worse than cheap tequila."

"Well, just freaking help yourself," I said, taking note of the peace sign tattooed on the knobby stob of vertebra number one. For a brief moment, I thought I should pull on my jeans, then decided against it. She was the one who had invited herself in. She could damn well put up with me as I was. I started to take my place at the kitchen table.

"No, no! Don't sit!" She reached into the sink, pulled out a dirty juice glass, rinsed it, and filled it to the rim with Patrón.

"Before drinking another person's liquor, it is polite to ask for permission first." I pulled out the chair and sat grandly. I was a king in my shitcan trailer. The ice pack had begun to melt, and the puddle it created looked like a blister. I wrung it out over the linoleum floor and delicately returned it to my swollen, cracked beak.

"Two summers ago, I interned with the EMS in Swainsboro." She removed the ice pack and closely inspected my schnoz. "That's got to be set. I can do it. I don't blame you about doctors. They creep me out. Here. Drink this." She shoved the juice glass of tequila at me. I didn't have any idea where this was going, but I knew if I didn't drink, it would mean that she had won. I couldn't let that happen, even though the result of my manliness was that I was about to have a tequila back for my Wild Turkey. Thinking about it now, I can see how some people would say that mixing bourbon and tequila was a recipe for disaster. Or at least a bloody wing-dinger of a hang-around.

"Drink," she said, and I did. "Want some lemon? You got any?"

"Nah, I don't want no fucking Yuppie lemon."

"Now who's got the mouth on them, Mr. Literary Genius?" She pulled out a chair, spun it backward, and straddled it as if she were the new James Dean. She tugged on the silver hoop in her brow, and that made me wince.

"Why do you want me to drink this?"

"Trust me. Just do it." She leaned back and shot me the kind of look that lawyers do when they're about to reveal the dollars and cents of their required retainer. "I like your book."

I sucked down more of the agave juice. "Thank you, ma'am."

"You're welcome."

"Is it the only one of mine you've read?"

"Well, yeah!" She rolled her eyes.

I carefully considered the clear fluid. Why can't people be nice? "Just thought I'd ask." This kid's attitude was in severe need of an overhaul. Who the fuck raised her? I tossed back the last of the tequila. I let it settle, sort of like a cherry bomb. I had gas, but I couldn't let her know, so I tried to let it out real slow, soft like, with no noise. I wasn't sure how successful I was being, because the liquor was starting to impair my worldview.

She made the cat-puke face again. "Why are you such a mess?"

"I don't know. Maybe for the same reasons you are."

"Hey!" She jumped up, slammed her hands on her hips. She was going to make some perfectly fine young man miserable one day. "I am not a mess. And neither is my mother." She screamed those words right before bursting into tears.

"Oh fucking Christ! What? What now?" Like I needed an eighteen-year-old crying female in my life.

"Nothing!" Her face trembled as she searched for control. "Nothing nothing nothing!" She attacked her tears with tiny fists.

I farted.

That's all she needed. Her Cleopatra eyes hooded. She was an ancient female, having suckled on the breast of that feminine virtue called Gotcha! She crossed her arms in front of her—not a protective gesture, more like the queenly repose of a superior being. "Case closed."

I farted again. It just happened. Ariela started laughing. She had a beautiful laugh. It sounded like youth and hope, fine-tuned by sadness. "I'm really sorry," I said, and then I started laughing. Surprised the hell out of myself. I was laughing. And it made my nose pound.

"Come on," she said, "I think the tequila has done its job."

"What? *What?*"

"Get up and go to the bathroom."

"Now, see here."

She executed yet another perfect eye roll. "Not for *that!* I'm going to set your nose."

Now there was a sobering idea. "You're serious, aren't you?"

"Of course I'm serious."

I grabbed the bottle of Patrón and took a swig.

"You can look like Eddie Munster the rest of your life.

Or"—she flipped back her hair—"you can let me help you."
She talked slowly, as if I were drunk, retarded, and four. Then
she turned on her booted little heel and started walking the
five steps to the bathroom.

"Bring the bottle with you," she said on step three.

Murmur Lee Harp

The light cracks open and I am free. I tumble and spin. The sky swirls. I hear myself sing, "Tra la la la la!" and suddenly I am back where all of this began: the Iris Haven River. The water splashes and I see myself in each droplet, reflected a thousand times, each reflection a different world. Oh, I was wrong about there being no wonder!

My exile to that strange void has changed me. I am strong. Righteous. You knew I would be. In the wind's fury, I saw the past. I witnessed Oster Harp stroll the beach as his wife lay dying, and my violent conception, which catapulted my mother into a paralysis kept whole by prayer, and my daughter's ecstatic tumble into the arms of a father whose inability to love selflessly made him cruel. I saw myself exact the truth from Billy Speare and then stubbornly—almost pathologically—ignore it. Yes, I saw my life, my wonderful, wonderful life. How could I regret those days? They were precious. Rare. Finite. You've got to love it all, even the sorrow and violence and pain, because—believe me—being alive is a temporary privilege granted by a fickle universe.

The current draws me away from land—perhaps far from the people who have gone before me—deep into the heart of the river. As I'm pulled through the water, ribbonlike, I wonder if the fish can see me or if I remain a nimble spirit.

Edith Piaf

I should never have gone to sleep the night of the White Party, because after our encounter with *un peu de violence*, the nightmare was unavoidable.

The Vietnamese-Laotian border. My name was Jim MacHenry. Yes, they called me Mac.

I fit the profile perfectly. A loner who, paradoxically, understood more than most the importance of being a team player. In fact, the loner in me made Jimmy Mac all that more of a player. A soldier's soldier. I knew without a doubt what I had been put on this planet to do: annihilate the enemy one at a time. Pure. Basic. Divine. The chaos that accompanies *When in doubt, empty the magazine* does not exist for the sniper. We are pure, calculated, controlled death. Click. Click. Click. *One shot one kill. One shot one kill.* That's the creed. It's what I lived by.

And I was good. Don't get me wrong. I was no Carlos Hathcock with ninety-three confirmed kills. But I did my job. My daddy taught me to shoot nearly before I could walk. Perhaps he knew he'd spawned a sissy and was determined to drum any such proclivity right out of me. Handling a rifle was, to me, like drinking cream.

Yes, sir! Gunnery Sgt. James MacHenry was one fine marksman. I brought down children and men and women. I did it because it was my job. I did it because if I didn't, my fellow marines would die. I did it because I was following orders. I did it because I knew how to look through the crosshairs and become one with my prey.

I breathed when they breathed. I blinked with they blinked. Our heartbeats were indistinguishable. I was the rising moon to my enemy's setting sun. *Oui.* It was a very Zen process.

There are an eternal number of dead moments—spaces where nothing exists—every day in every life. That was where I lived. I took my shot between the breath, between the opening and closing of the eye, between one heartbeat and the next. Right then, in that moment, in the in-between, I pressed the butterfly trigger.

Death was already present. I simply made it permanent.

And I never want to dwell there again. But the nightmare, like the sniper, is a hunter. *C'est vrai.* It stalks me. Patient, disciplined, focused. The night of the White Party, it stalked and took me down.

After my guests left, I cleaned my home, put away all the silly flourishes. I wanted to face the next day with a clear slate. And I feared sleep. So I went so far as to wash down my kitchen walls. I admit that I spilled a few tears. I could not get the visage of Billy Speare sprawled and bleeding out of my mind. Nor could I block out the replay of Lucinda attacking him. This is why I feared sleep. *Cela se comprend.* But finally, slumber insisted that I come her way.

They were all there, waiting for me, a gallery of my kills.

Faces, arms, legs, torsos blown to bits. Intestines and brains and white bones blossoming from jagged holes of exploded flesh. The enemy told me their names and shared pedestrian details about their loved ones. They showed me dog-eared ghostly images of sons and daughters and wives. One of them shoved a photograph of his family at me, said, *Here, take it, it's yours.*

I tried to wake up, to escape the knowledge of what a two-and-a-half-inch 700-grain bullet does to a body. *Impossible.*

When I finally did manage to rise out of the nightmare, I no longer knew who I was. I lay there in a misty dawn light and ran my hand across my chest—a chest profoundly different from the one I'd lived with for sixty-two years. I realized that besides two firm breasts and a pussy, all I'd ever really wanted in my life was intimacy. So how did I go so wrong? I had been a good son. A good citizen. A good soldier. How was I to know what the killing would do to me? Sex change or not, what truly had altered me—what had played jacks with my soul—was Nam. The war, not the sex confusion, was the reason I'd never found love.

Indeed. In that misty morning light, I realized that my emergence into womanhood had helped heal—to the greatest extent possible—Gunnery Sgt. Jimmy Mac. As a result of the sex change, I'd grown strong, honest. I'd said to the world, "This is who I am. Deal with it."

Lying there, I fondled myself. I felt my breasts. I pinched my mauve nipples—original to my soul, I might add—and they grew hard and wild. I slid my hand down to that place where once there had been a penis, nearly overwhelmed by the sad acknowledgment that I have never belonged. When I was a man, none of the accoutrements of being a male made sense. My cock in my hand. The sexual imperative to stick it in somewhere. The only ogling I did at breasts was out of envy. I wanted Jackie O hair and a nice fuchsia Chanel suit. But once I was transformed into the woman I'd always wanted to be, I still fell short of the mark. I wasn't a woman in the biblical or DNA sense, as Dr. Z loved to point out. I was a transsexual. Which means confusion. My sexual identity was confusing to others. So despite having attained what I'd always wanted—a womanly body complete with curves and hidden wet places—true intimacy of spirit and soul still eluded me.

I touched myself between my legs, and the skin memory—that which resides in the hand—performed what can only be called a tactile cartwheel. Nerves tumbled end over end at the surprise (or was it loss?) of finding only softness where a cock had once nestled and curled and sometimes awakened, plump and strange. I wrapped my arms around myself—an attempt to bring me back to my center—and decided that the White Party had been my laughable attempt to belong, to be accepted by an outside source, all of which had vanished when Mur died, since she was the only person who had provided me with those charms.

How wonderful it would be, I thought, for someone to love me, to put their arms around me, hold me close, brush their lips across my cheek, whisper through my thinning hair, "I adore you, Edith." I would like for a man who knows what to do with his penis to move it in and out of my new special place.

"I'm so sick of the vibrator," I said to the room. "Sick, sick, sick." And I thought for a moment about the blow jobs I'd received when I still had my male appendage. Truly, that's the only thing I missed about being a man. Ah, *mon ami*, blow jobs! From a male point of view, there's nothing better. And it's a sad fact of the world that there simply are not enough of them being given. I swear, we would fight fewer wars if men were blown more often. Daily if possible. No, it could not be that simple, I thought as I pulled my comforter close to my chin, that the true problem with humankind is that few of us get blown often enough. I was delusional.

And disgusting, thinking about sex and loss and intimacy and death. I decided that every person I'd ever killed was with me always, asking me why. I said aloud, firmly, "I don't know," and my longing for my friend Mur grew bright red. It pulsed.

"Damn it, Mur. I need you. Right now." I needed her furious laughter, her good sense, her pink openness.

But no, there would be no resurrections, no softening of loss, no easing of my devout aloneness or guilt.

I stared up at the ceiling and wondered how I could be alone if I were surrounded by the people whose lives I'd taken. I flipped back my covers, sat up, slipped my feet into my satin flats, pulled on my bathrobe, wandered into my living room, and set the needle in the vinyl groove. *"Des yeux qui font . . ."*

There would always be Edith, I supposed.

I opened my front door, to discover that we were socked in by a fine white fog. I stepped out onto the porch and into the mist. Anything could happen in the fog, I thought, absolutely anything. So I closed my eyes and conjured a new me. I was Edith, the real Edith, a solitary figure centered in a pool of light. *Un très beau visage, tragique et triomphant.* The audience, hundreds of souls, stretched out before me like starlight. They were captivated, impatiently waiting, praying for me to begin. *"Vive l' oiseau chanteuse,"* they cried.

I squared my shoulders and looked skyward—*la couleur blanche de ciel*—and began. Enveloped in light and fog, I became a woman with perfect pitch. But more than that—better than that—pain and joy and hope dotted the whirling dervish of my voice. I moved my people to tears. I reminded them, for a few moments, how exquisite life is. I made them feel as if anything—any sort of love—was possible.

And as my words disappeared into the fantastic veil of this deep fog, as my voice traveled over all of Iris Haven—that thin strip of sand and palmetto—I fooled myself into believing that not only was I not alone; I was loved.

Billy Speare

So I was sitting on my couch, head back, ice pack lightly resting on my newly set and bandaged nose. Ariela "Doogie Howser" van den Berg sat cross-legged in the green crushed-velour club chair opposite me, chattering away, glowing over the fact that she had successfully caused me to yowl in pain and that the pain had forced from me tears, yes, sharp-edged diamond droplets of devout physical anguish. She also kept filling my glass with Patrón, sweetly explaining that as far as she could tell, it was the most effective painkiller I owned and that she was drug-free and had never been drunk a day in her life and planned to keep it that way.

And then, after deciding that the only way to cope with her schoolgirl monologue was to pretend it was Muzak, and just as I was about to drift into sweet, blessed unconsciousness, she said, "I think that what we need to do once you look human

again is introduce you to my mom. She needs a husband."
Ariela propped her feet on my coffee table. "I need a dad." She
smiled brilliantly at me as I lifted my head and looked past my
giant nose. "And you're it."

"Ha!"

"What? How can you say no? You haven't even met her yet."

I took off the ice pack, winced, reached for the Patrón.
"*Exactement*, Doogie Howser! I haven't met her yet. So how
could I say yes?"

Ariela sat there, blinking madly, twisting the ends of the
chair cushion in her pale little fists. I think this deranged child
was serious. She wanted me to be her dad.

"Look, kid, I'm not the catch you think I am. And besides,
about your mom, I'm not in, on, or even underneath the market womanwise."

Her Cleopatras snapped with surprise. "Get out! You're
gay? But all that straight sex in your book. *Hot* straight sex.
What did you do? Make it up?"

I know a few rules. Can even follow them most of the time.
Rule number twenty-six: Don't laugh in the immediate aftermath of having had your nose set if said appendage has been
set without the numbing aid of an anesthetic. But this kid
cracked me up. I laughed a long, hard, genuine laugh, all the
while moaning, "Oh God, it hurts."

"Don't laugh at me," she said indignantly, rising to her feet.

"I'm not laughing at you," I said, trying to catch my breath.
"I'm laughing because of course I'm not gay and I'm not in the
market for women because my girlfriend just died. And I'm
really not prepared to take on the role of being anyone's father,
seeing how I royally fucked up that duty with my own kid. She
won't even speak to me."

Ariela walked over to the table, rummaged through her purse, pulled out a cell phone, and punched in a number.

"Hey! Don't you dare call your mother."

"Fuck you, Mr. No Dick. I'm calling for a pizza. We've got to eat. Figuring out why you're such an asshole—God, you laughed about your girlfriend dying—is going to take us the rest of the day."

"Oh, great."

"Yeah," she said into the phone, "I'll hold, but not for long." She rotated the phone away from her ear. "I hate being on hold. So, give me the four one one. The girlfriend. Are you all broken-up? Did you know each other long? Was it murder, or some ghastly disease?"

"Yes. No. Accident. And I don't want to talk about it."

"You have to—yeah, I want a large veggie with extra cheese, light on the anchovies. . . . What's your address?"

It went on like this for a few minutes. Her interrogating me and ordering pizza simultaneously, me giving her nothing, but all the while feeling slightly amused at her bulldoggedness.

She clicked off the phone, tossed it in her purse, and said, "You know what? You don't act all broken-up."

Bang, bang, bang, there was a knock at the door.

"Shit, that was fast," she said. "You got any dough?" She clomped the three steps to the door and flung it open, not bothering to see who in the hell it was before exposing herself. She looked her poor next victim up and down. "Who are you?"

"Well, aren't we Miss Manners. Billy, you in there?" A woman who looked vaguely familiar—I guess I'd seen her at Salty's—stuck her head in.

"Oh, he's here all right. What's left of him. Come on in."

Clearly, I was not in control. I stood up, wobbled, I'm afraid, and stuck out my hand. "Billy Speare." Yeah, that was her. Seen her at Salty's. She was a handsome woman. What the hell is she doing here? I wondered.

We shook. She had a firm grip, maybe too firm. "I'm Charlee Mudd," she said, tossing back her blond hair, narrowing those startling green eyes. "I'm sure Murmur told you all about me."

I looked at my wanna-be daughter, whose arms were crossed in front of her. She wore the bemused look of a woman who sensed a grand game was about to begin and only she—of all the people in the world—knew the outcome. I looked at Charlee Mudd. I thought, I could fuck her, but I sure would never like her.

"Have a seat. Can I get you anything to drink? Yeah, I think she did mention you."

"She yours?" Charlee Mudd asked, nodding her head at Ariela.

"Yep. That's dear old dad," Ariela chimed in, as speedy as only an eighteen-year-old can be. "Who's Murmur? Your dead girlfriend?" she asked ever so delicately.

"Goodness. You are really something," Charlee Mudd said to Ariela, a definite note of awe creeping into her voice.

"Why, thank you. It's difficult, you know, standing out as a real person when you've got such a famous dad."

"Ah," Charlee Mudd said, "I suppose it would be. I love your tattoos. They really are gorgeous," she added, cocking her head this way and that to get a better look. "Do you have a name?" She spun her gaze back on to me. "Does your daughter have a name?"

"Ariela," we both said in unison.

"Pretty."

"Thank you. My parents named me after a great-great-aunt who was Vladimir Nabokov's ghostwriter and lover. She wrote every word that came out of his mouth."

Oh God, Ariela, that made no sense. Any daughter of mine would know better than to say something that stupid.

"Really? That's fascinating," Charlee Mudd said. She and Ariela's eyes met, and I am certain that some sort of feminine secret communication flew between them. It was two against one. Two strangers were standing in my tin can, strangers with ovaries—and they had experienced an undercover mind meld right in front of me, and I didn't really know what either of them wanted. I mean, Ariela had said she desired a father. But how come of all the writers in all the world she'd chosen me? Just because of my brilliance? I didn't think so. And who the hell knew what this so-called friend of Murmur's wanted. I took a fresh swig of Patrón. I was getting over this warm little scene. And fast.

"How's your nose?"

"Just fine. How's yours?"

"Dad! That was sooooo rude!"

"Listen, Ms. Mudd, I've had a rough eighteen hours. Can I just ask flat out what you're doing here?" That was good. I had scored an offensive shot. I was back in the game.

Ariela zipped over to the fridge, pulled out two soft drinks, and handed one to our guest. "Here, Charlee, have a Coke."

"Thank you." She popped the top, hesitated, and then said, "Ariela, do you mind if your father and I talk in private?"

"Actually, I do," she said.

"My gosh, you're confident for someone so young." She turned to me. "This conversation really needs to take place in private."

I indicated the green velour. "You heard my daughter. She stays." I wasn't happy with the tone that had crept into my voice. But I didn't like her being there. I didn't like her appropriation of Murmur Lee. I hated busybody cunts. "You've got five minutes," I said as I slid the Patrón bottle to the center of the table. "So shoot."

And good old Ariela said, "Bang, bang. You're both dead."

Murmur Lee Harp

Time doesn't really exist where I'm at, so I'm not sure how long I sojourned with the fish. All I know is that a speedboat zipped by, kicking up a mighty wake, which propelled me onto the shore. I am happy about this. I missed the strange happenings on land and I have high hopes that I won't be the only spirit here. Where are the Harps and Katrina and my baby girl? That's what I want to know.

On land, I am once more at the mercy of the wind, but this time it ferries me to amazing places, setting me among the keeled scales of an indigo snake, the deep twilight pads of a bobcat's paw, the gossamer curve of a dragonfly wing, the sky white feathers of a restless gull. I am sand, fine grains that whip through your fingers and disappear into unknown worlds. Rock, shell, crystal. Blossom, leaf, bark. Earth, fire, water. When the wind blows, I fly, all swirl and dust and chaos. When the sky rains, I become an ocean tippling in the cupped petals of a morning glory. I am the smooth, silent movement of a hungry snake. I am the eyes of eagles and meerkats. I am the pant—the hot grassy breath—of a fox at rest. I am a clutch of skink eggs and the gopher who eats them. I am metamorphosis. Maggot and butterfly. Birth and death. Pain and glory. Bone and water.

Coquina. Yes, today I am coquina, and I am learning that all of this—the wind, the surf, the moon's faint glow, the sighs of fading stars—is plainsong.

I can hear it now.

Charleston Rowena Mudd

The fog had lifted and my resolve was strong. I pulled into the oyster-shell drive at the trailer camp, feeling somewhat like an avenging angel. The midmorning light glinted, laserlike, off Speare's little abode, momentarily blinding me. I killed the motor, shaded my eyes, hunched down in my seat, and scoped out the place. His curtains were drawn tight. His red pickup truck faced the road. A rusting boat trailer was hitched to it. A metal drum that looked like it was used for burning trash sat in the center of the sticker-burr lawn. Half a dozen empty beer cans littered the yard. A picnic table that had seen better days appeared lonely under the shade of moss-gnarled oaks. I counted: twelve other trailers, all of them nicer than Speare's. Dear God, for being an allegedly famous author, he surely lived in a dump. You'd think pride alone would have forced him into a double-wide.

I angled the rearview mirror and took a look. I was a tad shiny. I rummaged through my purse, found my compact, and powdered. Confidence arises from the damnedest places. Then I took a deep breath—I was both dreading and hungry for this little encounter with Speare. I told myself, Remember Murmur Lee. Do this for Murmur Lee. I stuffed my purse beneath my seat, got out of the truck, and softly closed the door, well aware that the element of surprise is always handy in manners of war, love, and settling scores.

Just in case he was peeking out the curtains, I walked with large strides, keeping my face steady, stern. He had to know from the outset that I was not a trifle. I knocked firmly, three ominous raps. In no time, the door swung open, and there stood an absolutely darling, edgy girl—she couldn't have been a day over twenty—who looked at me with curious disgust.

"Who are you?" she asked.

I admit that her stance, attitude, and mere presence threatened to knock me off my game. But I couldn't allow her to best me. And since I didn't know if she was friend or foe, I had to play it tough. Otherwise, she'd have me for lunch, dinner, and a midnight snack. I looked at her, unsmiling. "I'm here to see Billy Speare."

"He doesn't live here." She looked me up and down, a smirk marring her pretty face.

"Well then, who's that?" I pointed over her shoulder.

She rolled her eyes. "Come on in."

I stepped inside. There he sat, at his dirty kitchen table, looking battered and drunk, a ridiculous white bandage on his nose. I offered him my hand. "I'm Charlee Mudd. Murmur Lee probably mentioned me to you."

He shrugged. Obviously, he couldn't have given a rat's ass. "Yeah, I think she may have said something."

Cretin. What on God's green earth had Murmur ever seen in him? I remembered getting a letter from her, saying that he

was a "really nice man." Lord, I thought as I stood in his humble liquor-reeking anchovy tin, this couldn't possibly be the
same guy. But I knew it was. Yes, I did. As smart as Murmur
had been, she was always a Class A idiot when it came to men.

And what about this young girl? She bounced on one foot
and said something about her "famous dad." So, she was
Speare's daughter. Murmur had never mentioned him having
kids. She began hopping from one foot to the other. Poor
child.

"May I speak to you in private?" I asked Speare.

"No!" the two of them blurted in unison. And then,
plainly using the girl as a shield, betraying the fact that he
knew mine wasn't a friendly visit, he said, "Ariela, you stick by
me. Okay?"

"Sure, Pops. How's the nose? Feeling any better?"

They were quite the duo. I tossed back my hair and calmly
clasped my hands in case they wanted to do something stupid
on their own, like tremble or slap the bastard.

Poise. I needed quiet, abundant, black-and-blue poise. I
needed to know when to say, "Hey, tell me what happened."
Did I need to make him my friend? Did I need to speak so
softly that he'd think I was weak-minded, thus forcing him into
a mistake? Did I need to pretend to be a ditsy belle to keep him
off-kilter until I pulled the metaphorical trigger? I didn't know.
Despite my resolve to get the job done, I was clueless as to the
methodology.

He shot me a cocky, insincere smile. He was a sad sack, sitting there with his busted nose, an ice pack, and a bottle of
tequila. And all of it in front of his daughter. He told me to
sit down and get to the point, that he didn't have much time. I
tried shooting Murmur a message. *Sister, what in the hell do I
do now?*

Call me crazy, but the stale air in the trailer brightened. I looked at Speare and his daughter to see if they had noticed. They seemed oblivious. Could it be? Could Murmur's spirit be watching all this? Why the hell not? Maybe she was the shadow over there, by that hideous kerosene heater. Or was that her, the ring of light streaming in the front window? And who had opened that curtain? It had been closed when I walked in. Maybe she was settling amid the cobwebs in the corners of the low, dank ceiling. Or maybe I was unstable. But then I heard her voice in my head. This is what she said: *Posture.*

Oh! Right. Of course. Posture. It's what her mother had always preached. "Girls, you will get most anything you want out of life if you carry yourselves well. Next to performing your duties to the church, good posture is the key to happiness." Back went the shoulders. Tummy in. Spine straight. Head high. "Actually, it's turning out to be a beautiful day. Why don't we step outside?" I heard these words come out of my mouth and wondered who in the hell was pulling my string. How engaged in all of this was Murmur?

Billy Speare leaned forward, ready to speak, I could feel a smart-ass comment coming on, but his daughter said, "Oh, yes! Let's! Come on, Dad. It'll be good for you!"

He shrugged and held the bottle up to the dusky light.

"Do you need to lean on my arm? To steady you?" I asked, summoning the manners of the queen of England.

He waved me away and stood on crow legs. He wore shorts and a robe and he hung on to that tequila bottle as if it contained the essence of everlasting life. Poor child, to have a father like this, I thought as the daughter swept past both of us, tumbled into the day, and yelled, "It's gorgeous out here!"

So that's what we did. Speare and I sat at the picnic table under the oaks, facing the river. His daughter, who claimed to be in college but behaved as if she were barely out of junior high, danced to imaginary music near the river's edge. I shouted to her, "I have a boom box in my trunk; it's got batteries in it—in case you'd like some music."

She stopped dead still, her left hip frozen in mid-mambo. Her eyes widened and a delighted grin threatened to break out. But Speare snarled, "No! No music!" The girl stuck out her tongue at her father. "Dad won't let me listen to music. Will you, Father?" And then she did a cartwheel. And then another. I had to stop watching because she was making me motion-sick. She was a very strange child. But this music thing: Sure as Judas's tongue, she gave me my entry.

Billy drank right out of the bottle.

"Do you miss her?"

"Who?"

"Murmur." You stupid son of a bitch.

He wiped his mouth on the sleeve of his filthy cotton robe. "Of course I do. I'm heartbroken."

"Daddy's heartbroken, heartbroken, truly, truly heartbroken." She cupped her mouth with her hands and hollered to the river, "Daddy is heartbroken!"

"Fuck it, Ariela, go inside. Forget what I said about sticking by me. You're driving me nuts."

"Well, yes, sir!" Ariela said, and she pranced past us like a wounded, slightly dangerous waif. "Wait until I tell Mommy!"

I watched her disappear into the trailer. Speare said, "Listen, Ms. Charlee Mudd, I'm in pain, I haven't had any sleep, and my out-of-control daughter is visiting. If you've got something to say, say it. Or else I'm going to have to ask you to leave."

And right then, as if on cue from Murmur, a gust of wind rattled the trees. Brown and lifeless oak leaves rained down upon us. A seagull—all white and angel-like except for those shining black eyes, which revealed an über soul—swooped out of the arms of the sudden breeze and landed but a few feet away. It pecked the oyster-shell dirt before cocking its head and studying us. A wild blast of music—Gregorian chant—issued forth from the trailer. Dear Jesus! I jumped and Speare jumped, but the bird just kept staring. My sense of place and time and urgency became liquid. The bird lifted its head skyward and screeched. The awful sound seemed to last minutes, but surely not. I heard myself whisper, "Please, no," because it was the cry animals make when they spy death, when they see it right there in the reeds.

Speare leapt to his feet and screamed, "Goddamn you! I told you no music!"

The daughter's laughter swirled amid the falling leaves even as she taunted her father, yelling, "God, these tunes suck."

Speare collapsed back onto the bench. "Goddamn it!" With each syllable, he pounded the table. His hair fell into his bloodshot eyes and the top left edge of his bandage curled. I felt I knew what the expression "end times" really meant.

Then it got worse. Speare began to weep. His body heaved. The swollen strains of chant swallowed the wind. And as the white gull, still screeching, rose on unsullied wings into the oak, the man, the mortal, the fuckhead confessed.

I wondered if God and all his angels were listening. Did they bend their heads closer to earth? Did their celestial eyes open wider in pain or compassion as one of their sons, a child of God, spilled his sins into the light and shadow of that awesome day? Did Murmur hear it? Did his words splatter onto her invisible skin like acid rain?

There I sat, grim but my posture good, thanks to Murmur's directive, hoping the entire population of heaven could hear the pitiful son of a bitch say, "I didn't mean to kill her. I really, really fucking didn't mean to kill her. Oh Goddamn me. Fuck me. I really didn't mean it."

"Turn off the boom box!" I screamed.

But the little girl did not oblige. In fact, she turned up the volume, and the ancient chant grew fuller in the swift wind. Weeping, Billy Speare dropped to his knees and repeated over and over, as if stricken with autism, "I didn't mean to kill her! I didn't mean to kill her."

And still the music raged.

*B*illy Speare had no idea that Murmur had suffered from the rarest form of epilepsy—musicogenic. That is, until I told him that day under the oaks while the white bird squawked and the sacred chants pounded and as his confessions pooled all about like wet ash.

Before that, I was the only one who knew. Anybody else who'd had a clue was dead.

I don't know why Murmur had kept it a secret. Secrets kill. Look at what this one had done. Maybe that had been her problem: Pride.

Hell, no, forget that. If we didn't have pride, we'd all go around scratching our asses in public.

Men, that had been her problem. Just like all the rest of us womb-bearers. Men, even when they aren't trying, fuck us up.

No, no, no! They only fuck us up because we are prone to being fucked-up. Men aren't the problem. We're the problem. We're all our own individual humongous problem.

I mean, look at Speare. There he sat, sniveling and scared, not truly listening to me when I said, "Understand something.

Musicogenic epileptics almost always have above-average musical aesthetic appreciation. You were never going to stump her. And how could you know that Murmur responded to plainsong the way other epileptics respond to strobe lights?"

"But I didn't mean to kill her! She started jerking and shit. I tried to calm her down. Nothing worked."

I set my hands flat on the table. I didn't want to let anger ruin my chances of knowing everything, of hearing very, very clearly. "Billy Speare, tell me the truth: Did she trip or did you help her? Did you do something that made her fall?"

His face crinkled up like a squalling child's. He pawed at his tears and wailed, "No, no. I didn't push her. I would have never done that. Never. She fell. The woman fell. There was nothing I could do."

"Why didn't you go in the water after her?"

That was the question. I nailed him. In a flat second, he quit crying. His face steadied. He gingerly touched the no-longer-very-clean bandage. His quiet delivery ran counterpoint to the chaotic air. "The water was dark. The current was swift. I looked and looked. I called her name. I was a little drunk. I was also confused. The woman had just had some sort of fit. If I had gone in after her, I'd be dead, too. Hypothermia kills in seconds."

I sat on my hands so I wouldn't hit him. Seconds, my ass. Motherfucker. I wanted to scratch out his eyes. I wanted to smash what was left of his nose. I wanted, as they say, to shit down his throat. I leaned in real close and almost whispered, "You disgust me," but the music suddenly ended, and in that unexpected vacuum of sound, I lost my voice.

Speare hugged the tequila bottle and said, as if this truly made sense, "I knew she was dead. There was nothing I could do."

In the leaf shade, the white bird watched, and I wondered what was moral. What was vengeful? What was just? Where did compassion and forgiveness and settling the score fall? Was this the real Speare? Was the demon truly revealed? I thought about Murmur and what she had brought to this earth—her generosity, her chestnut laugh, her humor, her desire to see the best in people, her insistence on making green things grow—and the old age she'd never see. I thought about Z and Lucinda and Edith and the crew down at Salty's, how her passing had torn through them with the effectiveness of shrapnel. And then I thought about the asshole demon sitting in front of me. Arrogant, brilliant, narcissistic, cowardly.

"Ms. Mudd," he said, "this has been really nice. But I'm going inside now. Our conversation is over."

"No. Not yet."

To my surprise, the fool stayed put.

And me, I stared into the day and mulled things over. What should happen to Billy Speare? What would be a just punishment for an unintentional murderer whose selfishness was so bloated, it smelled evil?

A trial would be an exercise in public humiliation. A conviction might end his career. But more than likely, legal proceedings would make him famous. And what would he be charged with? Involuntary manslaughter? What good would that do? A few years behind bars, with him being interviewed by TV and print tabloids every week, even as he penned his next book?

Did the people who loved Murmur need that brand of retribution? What effect would a trial and all the dirt and all the maneuvering have on Z, Lucinda, Edith, me, and all the rest? Would we love Murmur any more? Would we hurt any less? If her loved ones knew the truth—that her death had been a cruel and careless accident, that God hadn't called her home for any special reason, that he hadn't called her at all, that it had been one gigantic fuckup—would that make us feel better? And what about Z? Poor Z. If he knew that what he had seen through the gauze of fog was a medical emergency, not a lovers' quarrel, he would not be able to go on.

I reached over and took the bottle from Speare. I drew my own healthy swig. "Okay. Let's talk. Let's finish this."

He shot me a squint-eyed glance. "What are you gonna do?"

"I don't know, Speare. I'm still thinking on it."

He was snotty, red-patched. He looked out at the river.

"What's your real name?"

He jerked around, glaring. I didn't flinch. I wanted an answer.

"Joe."

"Joe what?"

"Waddlesberg."

Now that was amusing. William Speare—what an egomaniac! "Well, Joe Waddlesberg, Murmur was sweet on you. That's unfortunate, but it's the truth." I looked up at that bird—the Murmur bird—and wondered what the hell I should do.

The wind gusted and the bird didn't budge. After two more draws on the bottle, after slipping over the pulse points of my own life—one in which I'd sabotaged my own success at every turn; what a dumb ass to leave Harvard because some pretty man I fell in love with had lied to me about the very foundation of our relationship—I started toward something. An idea. I had to think really hard about it. But the spark felt right. This was it, the flash that started me thinking: I'm tried of hating.

Oh my God. The breeze lifted my hair off my shoulders

and I thought it again: I'm tired of hating. I'm tired of hating. I looked at Billy Joe Waddlesberg Speare, that sad sack excuse of a human, and said, "Give me your hand."

"What?" He looked at me as if I'd just said, Take off your pants.

I hit each word hard and slow: "Give me your hand."

"Christ," he grumbled, but he did it.

"Listen to me. I'm tired of hating. I'm tired of hating me. I'm tired of hating you. I'm tired of hating God. I'm tired of hating that son of a bitch asshole I was engaged to. And I'm tired of being scared." It was those last six words that almost pushed me to sudden tears, but I was saved from that embarrassment, because another blast of music from the trailer sobered me up: "You're . . . the kinda girl who looks better naked." Speare squeezed my hand. He stared at me as if I were the one who'd just confessed. Jesus, Mary, and Joseph, I was losing my bearings. Again. I looked up at the tree. The Murmur bird remained quiet. It preened amid a fluttering of Spanish moss. I thought I might run to the truck and blaze away. Forget about a reckoning, I needed out of here. And right then, a single white feather curled its way from the bird to me.

I gritted my teeth. In my head I said, I'm sorry my parents died when I was not yet twenty. I love them. I'm sorry Murmur's mom was a religious nutcase and her father acted distant. I love them. I'm sorry Murmur's husband was a mean asshole. I don't love him, but I sorta forgive him. I'm sorry I fell in love with a man who was already married, even though there was no way for me to know he was married. I love him. I'm sorry that Dr. Z has experienced so much pain—the loss of two great women. I love him. I'm sorry that Edith has never experienced romance. I'm sorry that she understands the responsibility of having snuffed out lives, that she knows anything at all about the Zen of murder. I love her. I'm sorry that Lucinda is fucked-up from top to bottom. I hope she can discover a way to be kinder to herself. I love her. I'm sorry that I have turned all of my disappointments in life into acts of self-loathing. I will try to begin to love myself. I'm sorry that Billy Joe Waddlesberg Speare is a narcissistic jerk. I'm sorry he ever met Murmur. I'm sorry that he is partially responsible for her death. I will try to love him, in the way of compassion. I am sorry for that little girl in the trailer, that she is lost and hurting and obviously in need of comfort. I do love her. I am sorry that Murmur is dead. I miss her. I am sorry that nothing I can do will bring her back. But I am grateful for having known her. She fed me. I love her.

I finished this rosary of words and then I looked at Billy Speare and said with the conviction usually reserved for people of faith, "Listen to me. No one can absolve you. And there is no criminal justice brouhaha that will make up for your failings as a human being. So I'm not going to tell anybody what I know. But you have to do this. You have to send your daughter on home, because you are a lousy excuse for a caretaker and she doesn't need to know about what has gone on between us today. That's the first thing. Here's the second. Listen to me, Billy Speare. This is important. Once she's gone, you pack your shit and you get out. Never show your face here again. Never. Don't let this place, this land and water that Murmur loved, be stained by your shadow. Not one more day. Don't hurt us any more than you already have."

He stared at me. The demon Speare receded and the cowardly little boy returned. His lips trembled. His eyes shifted. He looked insane, him and that shaking face and that precarious white bandage.

I leaned in close. I whispered, "I mean it, Speare. Hell hath no fury like a Harvard-educated redneck woman who's just been jilted and who knows how to handle a knife and all the places to bury a body."

He looked over my head. I was scaring him to death. I could tell by the way his lips looked chalky. He stood up. I stood up. "Go on," I said. "I'll be back in the morning to make sure you've cleared out."

He opened his mouth to speak. I felt certain he was going to say he was sorry. I could not allow it.

"Don't you fucking dare."

He nodded. And he turned. And he made his way back into that trailer. He left his bottle behind. I emptied it on the ground and then tossed it. The thing went flying, end over end, zipping through the moss and landing with a low thud at the base of a palm.

I heard a car pull up behind me. A horn honked. I spun around. A kid with sun-bleached hair yelled, "Hey, did you order a pizza?"

"No. Try that trailer. I think they're the only ones home." The kid huffed, as if actually getting out of his Celica and walking ten feet required too much effort. I ambled by and got in my car. I was shaking, but I finally managed to get the key in the ignition. The boy pounded on Speare's door, pizza box in hand. I didn't wait to see who answered. I slid into reverse, and then I noticed the Murmur bird. It tried its wings three times—Caw! Caw! Caw!—and then ascended, snowy and clean, from its bough in the oaks and flew on silent wings, westward, over the river and beyond, to where the ancient oak hammock hugged the shore. I have no idea why, but I sat there and watched that bird grow smaller and smaller in the egg blue sky—the pizza boy watched, too—and once it was gone, I whispered, "Oh, my dear, dear Murmur Lee, God bless you."

Murmur Lee Harp

At first light, the bird awoke. From its perch among the jade green leaves, it watched the world. Mist rose from the river. Clouds hung low, nearly touching the crown of the canopy. Dragonflies stitched the air and skimmers sliced the river's rippling surface. Wind ruffled the bird's white feathers. It felt good. The creature was, I believe, happy to be alive.

Its cry tripped across the canopy and then the bird rose—as simple as smoke—into the fresh sky. It flew east, across the river, toward the ocean, and settled in a mossy oak grove it had favored the day before. When Billy Speare trundled out to his truck and sped away—towing his trailered boat behind him—the bird followed. It cruised the thermals whenever possible, but mainly it flew hard, keeping watch on Billy's red truck and white boat, tracking them north on A1A, resting on an electric wire when Billy stopped at the Sunset Grill for breakfast. A half hour later, the bird followed him across Anastasia Island and the Bridge of Lions into town. It flew past the Castillo de San

Marcos and Ripley's Believe It or Not museum and the park where Charlee's parents had taken her as a child to ride the carousel on Saturday mornings and then west and out of town. The bird did not stop shadowing Billy until the red truck eased onto I-95 and headed north. That was good enough.

The bird spiraled once, twice, and then flew in the direction it had come from. It did not give in to hunger or thirst or fatigue. It did not stop flying until it arrived at an old house in need of a new roof on a street named Aviles. Parked in front of the house was a '92 Dodge pickup with a FOR SALE sign taped to the windshield. The bird careened through a cross-hatching of maple branches and landed on a brick patio that was buckled, thanks to the root system of a nearby giant magnolia. A tall, gaunt man in rumpled gray pajamas shuffled out of the house and headed down the walkway to the street. His thinning hair was matted against his skull, leading me to believe he had not bathed in several days. A rough cough welled inside him. He paused, bent over, hacked. He straightened up and spit into the privet hedge. His veins crawled big and fat beneath pallid skin and his eyes were lightless. He unlatched the iron gate, reached into the newspaper box, and then, with his arms dangling at his sides, as if the short trip from the house to the street had been too trying, trudged back inside, coughing all the way.

I had not seen Erik Nathanson in over five years. He was not a well man, nor any longer a handsome one. Cruelty had taken its toll.

The bird continued on, beating its wings against the humid air, which had grown much warmer since first light. Despite its hollow bones and lithe body, the bird began to struggle on this journey south to Iris Haven. Its wing strokes became uneven and a sudden head wind threatened to knock it off course. On the outskirts of St. Augustine Beach, the bird floated to the earth and briefly sipped water that had collected in a pothole, thanks to a realty company's ill-aimed sprinkler. But there was little time for rest, so again the bird rose up and cut a labored path through the sky. *

We flew against an unrelenting wind, and with each wing stroke, the sun grew stronger, hotter. Still, we did not stop. When we arrived at the inlet and Iris Haven, they were already gathered at the shore in front of my house. Charlee, Edith, Lucinda, Z, Hazel, Silas, Paul Hiers, Croley, and that young girl—tattooed all to hell and back—who was not, I knew, Billy Speare's daughter. The bird circled high and wide, squawking a long, forlorn cry. No one noticed. Nor did they give so much as a glance in the bird's direction when it landed nearly face-down in the soft wet sand. At the south end of the beach, a young couple lolled in the sun. Their dog barked and chased the incessant tide.

My friends pulled themselves into a ragtag half circle. They listened, weeping, as Edith sang a mournful ballad in words none of us understood. But when Edith sang Piaf, the words didn't matter. She spilled her pain and grief into every note. I listened with my soul wide open and I began to grieve—really grieve—for this world I'd lost. When Edith rang out the last piercing note, Charlee went down the line with my favorite reed basket, which held cut flowers from my garden. Each person took a small floral bundle and then, one by one, offered a prayer or a wish or a loving thought and then tossed the flowers in the surf. Even the tattooed girl spoke. She said, "I didn't know this Murmur Lee, but I wish I had. It sounds like she really rocked, and it totally sucks that she's dead."

"Murmur Lee sat down in the back of Salty's with me and talked about *The Catcher in the Rye*," Croley said as he batted back tears. "I'll never forget that conversation as long as I live." And then he broke up and couldn't go on. Silas slapped a ham-bone arm around his shoulders.

As I listened to my friends say such sweet things, I wished I could join them in their tears. But fleshless spirits cannot cry. So all I could do was listen and watch and wish things were different.

When they were done, Charlee pulled from her skirt pocket a small glass jar. She said, "Well, everybody, I think it's time. We know that Murmur Lee loved this place—her family place—and that she loved each one of us. We're not losing her by spreading her ashes. Maybe we are somehow getting closer to her. I don't know. But I do believe she will remain with us, and not just in our memories. I mean, we're talking about Murmur. With any luck, she's going to haunt us the rest of our days. Zachary, will you read from the spell book while we spread the ashes?"

"Certainly," he said. She handed him my notebook, in which I jotted down all my cures, curses, and recipes. He opened it to a bookmarked page.

" 'A Cure for the Blues,' " he read. Charlee unscrewed the lid—they had me and all my talismans in a jelly jar, for goodness sakes—held it at arm's length, and slowly tapped the ashes.

Z read in a firm, clear voice, his thick black hair on end in the wind: " 'Find a fern with new growth. Cut the young curled tendril with a knife that has been dipped in lemon water. Place the tendril against your heart. Tape it if you have to. And say these words: I am a gift to the universe. I am loved unconditionally by at least one person on this earth (say their name). No matter this current sorrow, my heart's ease will be the knowledge that, just like the ancient ferns, I am always emerging, growing.' "

As he read, the wind caught me—that old me—and there I went, my bones and tissues and ligaments and skin, blown to smithereens across the earth's four corners.

And then my friends gave me a wonderful gift. They sang "Amazing Grace." In some ways, it was a have-to-sing tune. This was an ash-spreading service, after all. But still, the gesture moved me. Dr. Z held Charlee's hand and got every word right. Lucinda slipped her arm around Silas's waist and rested her head on his shoulder. Edith dabbed at her tears with a silk scarf, closed her eyes, threw back her head, and whispered the song. Hazel hung on to Silas and Paul Hiers as if she might faint. Croley and the girl looked at each other amid all that sadness, and I was fairly certain that before the next sunrise those two would have sex.

When the song was finished, they hugged and cried some more and then made their way up to my house. As I watched them go, my sadness grew. I would miss the warmth of their living friendship. I would miss the soft press of lips on my cheek and the dewy promise of a lover's breath against my neck. I would miss skin.

Even after they were gone, I stayed focused on the house, knowing that my friends would mourn into the night. They would watch the sun stumble across the sky and the moon pull itself from the sea. They would stare at the breaking waves, hoping that their pain would soon grow small and manageable, like an origami bird they could carry in their pockets. But, too, there would be laughter. They would share old stories, mostly at my expense, and that's when the pain would begin to sprout pretty little paper wings.

The bird, the white one who had—at its own peril—carried me north and back again, remained on the beach all afternoon. We were alone except for the suntanned couple and their barking dog. In need of nourishment but too weak to fly, the bird stayed in the sand, fully aware that it was dying. In the salt wind and hot sun, its downy feathers became brittle and stiff. Its heart slowed as its breathing ran shallow. The world became blurred and dangerous, so the bird shut its eyes. Unlike me, it longed for death. I suddenly felt a great well of compassion. This creature deserved its rest. I didn't care that in the past—in life—I had cursed the universe for not heeding my prayers. I tried again anyway: *Please take this bird. Do not let it suffer one moment longer.* I had barely mulled over the irony that I was praying for death, not life, when the sand began to shake and an awful uproar jangled the air. The dog was upon us. He tore into the bird, snapping its quilled feathers and puncturing the thin skin of its neck. The bird struggled. Even though it wanted to die, it still struggled. Its gut-sundered, panicked cry filled me and I was afraid. The dog ripped apart sinew and muscle and crushed the bird's bones in its strong jaws. With one immense snapping blow, the dog cleaved open the bird's chest and revealed to the hard sun its beating heart. When the bird's breastbone snapped in two, I was released into the air. It was then that I knew my prayer had been answered and that the bird was dead. Still, the dog attacked. But I was free.

The wind swept me into the dunes. I tumbled, end over end, through nettles and oats, eventually coming to rest betwixt the heart-shaped leaves of a railroad vine. That is where I stayed.

As the evening grew long and still and the dew settled, another change took shape. I felt myself becoming root and stem, seed and soil. And that is when—finally! finally!—I knew where they were. Orchid Harp. Oster Harp. Iris Harp. Blossom Harp. Katrina Klein. They had become the beginnings of life long ago. And that is where I was headed: I would become a speck of energy pulsing inside the taproot of this vine. There was no choice. It's what the world demanded: death and birth—the process of becoming—bonded forever in a single eternal heartbeat.

I knew that come morning, my human consciousness would be no more. All the privileged gifts of humanity: no more. Voice, sorrow, guilt, grief, joy: no more. So I did the only thing a blithe spirit could: I hunkered down among the tender leaves and listened to the surf song. And I watched the moon slowly arc across the sky. And the constellations spill into the sea. And the shooting stars pierce the night's infinite dome. I pushed with all my might, opening my spirit's eye wider and wider, celebrating what would be my final truth: I loved this world.

1. On the frontispiece is a quote from John Berger: "There is never a single approach to something remembered." What does that mean, in terms of this novel? Why do you think Connie May Fowler chose that quote? Discuss Fowler's use of multiple narrators and multiple perspectives, and especially Murmur Lee as narrator after death.

2. Aside from the first-person narration of the characters themselves, Fowler also intersperses written ephemera—diary entries, a shopping list, a note passed during childhood. What purpose do these scraps serve to the progression of the story and our understanding of Murmur Lee?

3. Murmur Lee describes herself on page 12 as "the lover to many men, a good friend to a well-chosen few, a daughter who'd been secretly wild but openly obedient, a mother who'd never stopped viciously mourning the loss of her only child, a woman who despite some tough breaks and lapses in judgment had made her own way in this world." Is this an accurate description? Compare it to the "lessons I've learned since dying," on pages 217 and 218. How has Murmur Lee's perspective on herself changed?

4. Birds appear over and over throughout the novel, from a swan feather on the first page to a seagull on the last. Why? What do the various bird images mean to you?

5. Murmur Lee is a witch, and her status is presented very matter-of-factly throughout the book. Why do you think she began to practice witchcraft? Did it have anything to do with her religious upbringing? Do you believe in the power of spells?

6. Discuss Murmur Lee's experience with childhood religious visions. As she says on page 97: "How astounding to be the focus of my mother's ecstatic passion, how bone-breaking delicious to be the object of her approval!" How much of Murmur Lee's seizure do you attribute to medical causes and how much to the desire to please her mother? What effect did they have on her as an adult, aside from the obvious one?

7. Charlee Mudd left the South behind, hoping to transform herself into a Northerner. Was she successful? In what ways did she fail? And what about the novel itself—would you consider it a "Southern" novel?

8. The circumstances of Murmur Lee's death are questioned and discussed throughout the novel, and the truth is revealed only at the end. Does that make this a mystery? How does the novel fit into the conventions of classic mystery writing, and how does it break them?

9. According to Murmur Lee, her great-great-grandfather named their island Iris Haven after the Greek goddess of the rainbow, but without realizing that Iris also "had one hell of a job: She received the souls of dying women." Murmur Lee asks, "Did his ignorant foray into the world of nomenclature curse this place? Is that why we keep dying out here, again and again, so young?" (page 44). What do you think of Murmur Lee's assessment of the situation? Is it possible for a name to curse a place like that?

10. Murmur Lee didn't know that she was the product of a rape until after her own death. In what ways did it affect her while she was still living?

11. Compare and contrast Zachary's behavior while Katrina was dying with Erik's during Blossom's illness. Do you see a parallel? Does Murmur Lee's compassion for Zachary result from her own experience with Erik?

12. On page 160 Charlee wonders about Murmur Lee's will: "Did she know her time was up? Had she made a decision—watery

and vague, but a decision nonetheless—that she'd best set her affairs in order? How does a healthy thirty-five-year-old woman come by that sort of precognition?" How would you answer those questions? Does the existence of a relatively young woman's will indicate a subconscious readiness to die?

13. After Murmur Lee has sex with Billy for the first time, she asks him if he loves his mother; he replies that he was happy when she died. Murmur Lee is tremendously upset by his response, recognizing an old pattern of hers. What is the significance of this? If Murmur Lee hadn't died do you believe she and Billy would have ended up together? Why, or why not?

14. Discuss the characters of Lucinda Smith, Edith Piaf, and Ariela van den Berg. What purpose(s) do they serve in the novel?

15. Why does Zachary punch Billy?

16. Throughout the novel there are countless references to ghosts and wind. After death, in fact, Murmur Lee is surrounded by gusts and flows. What do you think this means? What do you think happens to us after death?

17. What does the title mean? What *is* the problem with Murmur Lee?

For free supplementary materials including information on book groups, suggestions for further reading, chances to win books, phone-in author appearances, and much more, e-mail Broadway-Reads@RandomHouse.com.

© Deborah Feingold

ABOUT THE AUTHOR

Connie May Fowler is an essayist, screenwriter, memoirist, and novelist. Her novels include *Remembering Blue* and *Before Women Had Wings*, which received the Southern Book Critics Circle Award and was made into an Emmy-winning *Oprah Winfrey Presents* movie for television. She founded the Connie May Fowler Women with Wings Foundation, a nonprofit organization dedicated to aiding women and children in need. She is the Irving Bacheller Professor of Creative Writing at Rollins College in Winter Park, Florida.